The Reconciliation

Center Point
Large Print

Also by Susan Lantz Simpson and available from Center Point Large Print:

The Mending
The Promise

**This Large Print Book carries the
Seal of Approval of N.A.V.H.**

The Reconciliation

Susan Lantz Simpson

CENTER POINT LARGE PRINT
THORNDIKE, MAINE

This Center Point Large Print edition
is published in the year 2019 by arrangement with
Kensington Publishing Corp. Publishing.

The text of this Large Print edition is unabridged.
In other aspects, this book may vary
from the original edition.
Printed in the United States of America
on permanent paper.
Set in 16-point Times New Roman type.

ISBN: 978-1-64358-333-4

The Library of Congress has cataloged this record
under Library of Congress Control Number: 2019943643

The Reconciliation

*For all the people who
have walked with me
on my faith journey.*

God bless you!

Acknowledgments

Thank you to my family and friends for your continuous love and support.

Thank you to my daughters, Rachel and Holly, for believing in me and dreaming along with me.

(Rachel, you patiently listened to my ideas and ramblings, and Holly, I couldn't have done any of the tech work without your skills!)

Thank you to my mother, who encouraged me from the time I was able to write. I know you are rejoicing in heaven.

Thank you to Mennonite friends, Greta Martin and Ida Gehman, for all your information.

Thank you to my wonderful agent, Julie Gwinn, for believing in me from the beginning and for all your tireless work.

Thank you to John Scognamiglio, editor in chief, and the entire staff at Kensington Publishing for all your efforts in turning my dream into reality.

Thank you most of all to God, giver of dreams and abilities and bestower of all blessings.

$\mathcal{P}$rologue

"Hey, Isaac," Atlee Stauffer called as he closed the door of the Clover Dale Dairy behind him. He took long strides to catch up with Isaac Hostetler. He and Isaac had completed their workday and headed out into a blustery January wind. Darkness would creep in early on this cloudy winter day, so both young men hurried to hitch up and get home to do their outside chores before daylight entirely vanished.

"*Jah*?" Isaac slowed his pace a tad but didn't stop. It seemed to Atlee that Isaac generally tried to steer clear of him. He probably felt embarrassed after the mess he'd made of things with Atlee's sister, Malinda. It was pretty hard to blend into the background, though, in a small community and hard to avoid each other when they worked at the same place.

"Are you going to the singing on Sunday? I hear the visitors from Oakland may postpone their trip home. There might be some new acquaintances to make." Atlee gave Isaac's arm a playful punch.

Isaac pulled his jacket tighter around his neck as if trying to keep the brutal wind from flying down to numb his torso. He hadn't been to singing in a long while. Atlee sincerely doubted this coming Sunday would be any different—even if there

11

were some pretty girls in the load visiting from another community—but he thought he'd inquire anyway. Isaac gave a noncommittal shrug.

"You aren't still pining away for Becky, are you?"

"Good ol' Atlee. You can't let a subject die a natural death," Isaac muttered not quite under his breath.

Atlee knew the fiasco with Becky had been ever so much worse than the failed relationship with Malinda, but it was time for Isaac to get over that and move on. That was Atlee's humble opinion, anyway.

"*Nee.*" Isaac rubbed a gloved hand across his eyes. "Hooking up with Becky was a mistake from the very beginning. I was too much of a *dummchen* to realize that."

"Don't be so hard on yourself. You weren't the only fellow to fall prey to Becky's charms. Besides, we all make mistakes."

"Some of us make more than others. I was stupid enough to think she really cared. Was I ever wrong! I threw away anything Malinda and I had, but I guess that wasn't right, either. Maybe I'll never get it right."

"You will. That's what *rumspringa* is for—to learn and find out what we want, ain't so?"

"I guess, but you haven't fallen flat on your face twice."

Atlee chuckled. "Who knows what blunders I'll

make? Think about Sunday." Atlee clapped Isaac on the back and hurried to hitch his own horse.

Atlee barely clucked to the horse to get him moving. The poor animal was as anxious as Atlee to get home and out of the cold. Atlee glanced at the heavy gray sky in front of him as they trotted away from the dairy. If it didn't snow tonight, it was missing a *gut* chance. One thing you could always count on about Southern Maryland weather was that you couldn't count on Southern Maryland weather. In a matter of a few short hours the weather could go from sunny to stormy. Some years they had snowfall after snowfall, and some years they didn't even have a trace of snow.

They'd had a mere dusting at Christmas this year, just enough snow to cover the grass and coat the tree limbs like cream cheese frosting on Mamm's carrot cake. At mid-January, they weren't out of the woods by any means. They still had plenty of time for snow. Some years, winter seemed to last until almost May.

Atlee rubbed first one hand and then the other on his pant leg to create some warmth. He must have left his gloves at home that morning. He'd have to remember to search for them. Frostbite or cracked and bleeding fingers were no fun, that was for sure and for certain.

Atlee's stomach rumbled louder than the clip-clopping of the horse's hooves. He hoped Mamm or Malinda had cooked a big pot of beef vegetable soup or chicken noodle soup. He could almost feel the hot broth sliding down his throat. Maybe his younger *bruders*, Ray and Roman, would have finished helping Daed with the chores by now.

He still missed Sam. Older by two years, Sam had married Emma Swarey in November. He would probably be a *daed* before too long. Atlee's only sister, Malinda, two years younger, already had a beau. She'd gotten over Isaac in record time. Now she and Sam's best *freind*, Timothy Brenneman, were courting. That was all hush-hush, of course, as was the Amish way, but everyone expected Timothy and Malinda to end up married. That was probably a big part of the reason Atlee held no grudge against Isaac. If his little *schweschder* had been weeping and moping about, forgiving Isaac for hurting her would have been a lot harder.

Maybe Atlee should heed the advice he had offered Isaac earlier. Maybe he should check out the visitors at Sunday's singing. He hadn't felt ready to settle down before, but those settling-down feelings had been stirring more and more of late.

He shook the reins to get the horse moving a little faster. "*Kumm* on, Star. We're almost home." Star—what a name for this big, sleek beast. Too bad Daed had let Malinda name him. Even if he did have that tiny white star-shaped spot above his eyes, he deserved a more powerful name.

Catching the lights of an approaching vehicle in his side mirror, he slowed Star and tried to scoot horse and buggy over as far as he could toward the edge of the country road that had no shoulder to drive on. Most *Englischers* who regularly traveled this road looked out for buggies and patiently waited to pass them. Every once in a while, though, someone unfamiliar with the area or someone in a big hurry made travel downright scary. Since he was able to see around the curve up ahead, he leaned out of the buggy to signal the driver that it was safe to pass him.

Slowly the van drove up beside him. Before Atlee pulled his head back into the buggy, he returned the driver's wave and locked eyes with the passenger in the back seat. Becky? Of course it was Becky. No one else had hair the color of honey dripping from a hot, flaky biscuit and eyes a brighter green than his own. Had she returned home to stay? He smiled and waved again, but she dropped her eyes and withdrew into the shadows of the van.

"Brrr!" Atlee shivered as he closed up the buggy. He didn't know what was frostier—the air or Becky Zook's attitude. The girl in the van did not act like the flirty, flighty girl of a few months ago. He wondered what had happened to subdue that carefree spirit sort of akin to his own. Atlee shrugged and urged Star on again. No doubt, any news about Becky would trickle down the grapevine soon enough.

Gut. It looked like his *bruders* were finishing up the chores. He should be able to get away with simply parking the buggy and caring for the horse.

"Great timing!" Roman, his sixteen-year-old *bruder*, called as he exited the barn with thirteen-year-old Ray on his heels. "You managed to show up right when we're finished."

Atlee shrugged. "It couldn't be helped. I had to work a little later."

"Sure you did." Ray tried to scowl but ended up grinning.

Atlee thought Ray was the sibling most like himself. Both of them loved to tease and laugh. "I'll have you know I did not stop off any place but raced right home." Atlee feigned hurt at Ray's remark. "Where's Daed?"

"Still in the barn. He told us to go on inside and wash up," Ray replied. "I'll beat you, Roman."

Atlee chuckled at his *bruders'* playful shoving as they sped toward the house. He had half a notion to run, too. The wind's bite had intensified, and with the increasing clouds, full darkness was almost upon them. Atlee finished up at the same time as his *daed*, so the two walked to the house together. "I've got to find my gloves." Atlee blew on his hands.

"I probably have an extra pair somewhere."

"*Danki.* I'll search for mine and let you know."

They clomped up the back steps. Warmth and delicious smells enveloped Atlee the moment he crossed the threshold. "Smells like"—Atlee paused to sniff deeply—"beef stew?"

Daed sniffed the air. "I believe you're right."

"Great. I'm starving and freezing!"

"Then we'd better hurry."

"Hey, my gloves!" Atlee lifted his heavy, dark gray gloves off the kitchen counter.

"You must have dropped them in your haste this morning," Malinda said. "I found them near the door. I even sewed up the little hole on the right thumb."

"*Danki*. What would I do without you? Tell me that's beef stew I smell."

"It is."

"I knew it." Atlee scooted past Malinda and took his place at the big oak table.

After the silent prayer, a plate piled high with thick slices of golden corn bread was passed around. For a few moments only the clinking of stainless steel spoons against blue ceramic bowls and slurping sounds broke the silence. Then the chattering and laughing began. The Stauffer house was generally not a quiet one. Atlee kept his strange encounter with Becky to himself. What in the world had been going on in her life?

Shadows felt safe. Maryland felt safe. At least she hoped it would be safe. It had to be safer than New York had turned out to be. Rebecca leaned forward only enough to see black-and-white cows happily chewing their cuds in the wide open field. A windmill spun in the breeze at the next farm. Across the road a pickup truck and a sports car sat in an *Englischer*'s driveway. That's the way it was in Southern Maryland. The Amish and *Englisch* lived peacefully side by side with fields of corn or soybeans or hay in between them. Nothing like what she had seen in the city. Had it been only a little more than six hours ago that she had woven her way among throngs of pedestrians trying to get to the bus station without being followed?

Rebecca was beyond tired. Even her eyelashes and toenails were weary. She pulled back into the shadows again and leaned her head against the window, just like she had done on the bus. The vibration rocked her, and the van's engine sang her a lullaby. She didn't have much farther to go, but she was powerless to keep her heavy eyes from closing. Scenes from New York played out in her mind. Would she be forever tormented by her horrible experiences, her frightening memories, and finally, her mad dash to escape the city?

Chapter One

Rebecca Zook hunkered down on the wide, dark green bus seat. If she could make herself invisible, she surely would. How her life had become such a mess in such a short time was almost beyond her comprehension. Could she even begin to right all the wrongs and mend all the fences she'd most likely broken beyond repair?

What was the saying—misery loves company? Not true as far as Rebecca was concerned. If she could, she'd crawl under the big bus seat or throw a blanket over her head. She did not want to have to make polite conversation with anyone. She leaned her head against the ice-cold window and truly hoped no one plunked down on the seat beside her. She supposed she could always feign sleep, but closing her eyes brought all those horrible memories dancing and leaping to the forefront of her mind.

Rebecca struggled to calm her racing heart and ragged breathing after her sprint to the bus. She wished the driver would start the engine so she could leave this too loud, too crowded, too scary city behind. Since she had been one of the first to board, the doors probably wouldn't close any time soon. Would she spend the rest of her life looking over her shoulder or waiting for hands to reach out from the shadows to drag her back to a life she wanted no part of?

She had only wanted to see the city, to experience something besides caring for a home and a garden and animals. She had wanted to see what else was in this vast world the Lord Gott had created. She had ended up seeing and experiencing a whole lot more than she had bargained for.

Rebecca shivered, and not just from the cold. The stiff wind had practically stolen her breath away on her jaunt from the café to the bus station. She had had to hold on to her hat with one hand to keep it from flying away while juggling her bag with the other. She must have made a comical sight, if anyone rushing about had even noticed her.

"*Nee*! *Nee*! Leave me alone!" She ran until her breath came in hiccups and gasps and her legs ached from the extreme effort they put forth. She couldn't let those three horrible men catch her. They thought she belonged to them since Vinny's death. She couldn't stop. Her body screamed at her, but she had to keep running. Faster!

Rebecca jerked upright. A dream. She'd dozed off with her head against the window for only a few minutes, but that had been long enough for the nightmare to take control. She patted her chest, hoping to coax her heart into returning to a more normal rhythm. Her life had been so ruled by fear lately she couldn't even escape it in a quick catnap. Since none of the passengers who had trickled onto the bus were staring in her direction, she must not have cried out, even though the dream had been frighteningly real. When her heart had settled down a bit, she raised her hand to rub her moist eyes. If only she could rub away her memories as easily as she rubbed away the sleep and tears.

She lowered the big canvas bag she'd been balancing on her lap to the floor and wedged it between her feet. Where were the rest of the passengers and the bus driver? She wanted to leave New York behind forever. Sure, she'd been thrilled to visit the big city. She'd been amazed by the tall buildings, the Statue of Liberty, Broadway, the fancy stores, and all the other attractions. After all, she'd left her rural home in pursuit of adventure and happiness. She'd found the first all right, but definitely not the last.

Things had gone along okay at first. She'd found a job in a café—the only one she could get with an eighth-grade education. It wasn't a high-paying job, but the owner rented her a small room for a pretty reasonable price. She had enough money to buy a few secondhand clothes from the thrift store and a little food to keep in the cupboard for snacks. The coffee shop provided a uniform for her and free meals while on the clock, so that saved her some money. She certainly didn't live in luxury, but she wasn't used to luxury anyway. If Vinny had never started hanging around the shop, life might have continued to be okay. But "okay" wasn't really "happy," was it?

Rebecca sighed and swiped again at a stray tear. If she hadn't been so naive, she wouldn't have fallen prey to Vinny's charms. Oh, he was a smooth talker, that one, and handsome, too. He charmed her right off her feet. She quickly fell madly in love with him and believed he loved her, too. Pshaw! Who knew what love was?

She clenched her teeth and her fists. It had been her own stupidity! It was her fault she had gotten mixed up with Vinny and his so-called *freinden*. When he convinced her to marry him after they'd barely known each other a few weeks, Rebecca was ecstatic. She thought he was sincere and caring. She couldn't have been more wrong.

Rebecca had thought Vinny would be so pleased when she told him she suspected a *boppli* was on the way. Weren't all men happy about such things? Not Vinny. He insisted she get rid of "the problem." When she refused, he said he had no use for her. He said they weren't really even married. It had all been a sham, and the marriage license was a fake. He'd laughed at her—a harsh, scornful sound that still echoed in her brain.

She'd run out of the tiny apartment they shared and wandered the crowded city sidewalks for hours. She'd hoped Vinny would run after her and tell her he loved her and wanted their *boppli*.

Rebecca put a fist to her mouth and bit a knuckle. She couldn't break into sobs again. The bus was beginning to fill with passengers who would gawk at a bawling woman. Hadn't she shed enough tears? Still, a stray tear trickled down her cheek. She shook her head slightly, but that last scene wouldn't dislodge from her memory. When she had returned to the apartment to gather her few belongings after her wandering, she'd found Vinny's glassy-eyed pals standing over him. He was sprawled on the floor, unmoving. Dead. Overdose, they said.

She stuffed what she could into the big canvas bag and fled. She could still hear the voices of those creepy guys calling out to her. "Come back, baby. You're ours now. We'll take care of you." Their words were followed by raucous laughter that haunted her dreams. She ran as fast as she could and prayed they were too drugged to be able to chase after her. She glanced over her shoulder every few minutes anyway as she ran to the apartment of one of the other waitresses, where she holed up for a few days until she could make a plan.

Now here she was alone, scared, unmarried, and pregnant. She'd not likely be welcomed home with open arms, and she couldn't really blame Mamm and Daed if they didn't want her back.

A gnawing in her gut brought to Rebecca's attention how little she had eaten lately. The nausea of the past few weeks had rendered practically every food unpalatable. Crackers had become her favorite companion. She'd been so sick she thought she was dying. When she gathered some courage, she visited a free clinic. The kind doctor offered to give her some medication for the nausea and told Rebecca she was about three months along. Rebecca declined the pills but did take the doctor's advice about natural remedies for nausea.

Her stomach growled again. She should have eaten something earlier. When her stomach got this empty, the nausea was even worse. She had thought someone was following her when she left the other girl's apartment so she didn't stop in the café for breakfast. Instead, she ran toward the bus station.

Rebecca couldn't suppress the sigh that escaped as a shuddering gasp. Vinny had lied about so many things. He swore he didn't use drugs. He gave no indication that their marriage vows were phony. He said he loved her. Sure! He had never cared for her at all. He had just used her. He figured a naive country girl would be too stupid to know the difference.

She may be naive about the ways of the *Englisch* world, but she was not stupid. She was . . . she was . . . she was pitiful, that's what she was. Shame burned her soul and warmed her cheeks. She never, ever would have moved in with Vinny if she hadn't truly believed they were married. She may have been a flirt back home, but she'd never . . .

Ach! It was too shameful to think about. Somehow she had to get her life together. Somehow she had to provide for a little one who would depend solely on her. That's what she should ponder on her long bus ride.

Her stomach rumbled louder. Cookies! The woman at the little store she'd dashed into to inquire about the bus station had given her a small bag of cookies. Rebecca leaned down to fish around in her canvas bag. That little paper sack must have wormed its way to the bottom. *Jah*, there it was in a bottom corner. She lifted the paper bag out and opened the top. Heavenly smells wafted out. Chocolate. Ginger. Cinnamon. They mingled, but in a pleasant way. She'd try a gingersnap. The clinic doctor had said ginger was supposed to help soothe tummy troubles. She broke off a chunk of the gingersnap inside the bag to avoid leaving a trail of crumbs on the bus floor and popped it into her mouth. It wasn't quite as *gut* as her *mamm*'s gingersnaps, but it was tasty. And her stomach accepted it.

At last a wiry man with a thin, graying mustache climbed into the driver's seat and pulled the handle to close the door. The bus was only partially filled with passengers, and to Rebecca's relief, the seat beside her remained empty. She nibbled a few more bites of the cookie before settling back in the seat.

Rebecca squeezed her eyes shut, not one bit interested in the scenery outside her window. She wanted to forget the city and everything that happened here. Her body craved sleep. As long as no one boarded the bus at another stop and plunked down beside her, she would sleep until she got close to home.

Home? Did she have one of those? Maybe she should stay on the bus until the end of the line, wherever that happened to be. She wanted to see her parents and her community. She'd missed them more than she had dreamed she would. But would they want to see her? Would they take her back? If they didn't, she supposed she could hop on the next bus out of Maryland and head farther south or west or whichever direction the bus headed. Rebecca leaned her head against the window, hoping its coolness would ease her pounding headache and the vibration would lull her to sleep.

Chapter Two

Rebecca's head thumped against the window when the bus braked hard, rousing her from her drowsy, woozy state. More passengers clambered aboard. She had a feeling she would no longer have the seat to herself. She scooted over as far as she could get and kept her bag lodged between her feet. She hoped she didn't end up with a chatty seatmate. Maybe if she pulled out a book to read, the person would take the hint and leave her in peace—whatever that was. Rebecca bent forward to paw through her bag for the paperback novel one of the other waitresses had given her.

"Hello, dearie. Mind if I share your seat?"

Rebecca jerked upward, dizziness causing the face before her to swirl. She blinked hard to bring the wrinkly face of the tiny, elderly woman into focus. "*Nee*, uh, no, of course not." Rebecca took in the thick, gray hair gathered into a neat bun, the clear, twinkling blue eyes, and the sweetest smile ever. This must be peace. Rebecca attempted a wobbly smile of her own.

"Are you all right, dearie?"

"*Jah*, uh, yes." Even after living and working among the *Englisch*, Pennsylvania Dutch words were the first ones out of her mouth.

"You look a bit pale. Beautiful, but pale." The woman took up less than half of the bus seat. She, too, stowed a canvas bag between her feet, which barely reached the floor. "I'm Vivian Holbrook, but everyone calls me Viv." She reached out a tiny hand toward Rebecca.

Rebecca shook the small, warm hand, careful not to squeeze too hard. "I'm Rebecca."

"Pleased to meet you, Rebecca. I've been visiting my son and his family in Princeton and will be glad to reach my home in Delaware. My son always tries to get me to fly or take the train, and I always tell him the bus is fine with me. It isn't that long of a ride. Where are you headed?"

"Um, Maryland."

"Lovely state. I've visited there many times."

Rebecca nodded. It really was a nice place. She should never have left it six months ago. Six months? It seemed a lifetime. In six short months, she'd managed to completely ruin her life.

Viv reached for a big ball of yarn with a half-finished project attached and knitting needles protruding like chopsticks from the bowl of fried rice Rebecca'd had at a Chinese restaurant. Then she wiggled twice and smiled. "There. I think I'm settled now. Have you ever visited Delaware, dear?"

"N-no."

"It's really quite nice, too. I live in Bethany Beach, so I can look at the ocean or walk along the beach whenever I want. I love the salty smell of the ocean."

"That must be nice." Vinny had taken her to the ocean once. She'd been mesmerized by the powerful waves crashing to shore and then slithering back out to sea. Such a mighty and awesome force. She could have watched the waves for hours with the sea spray misting her face and the wind whipping her long braid around her. Vinny had even collected shells with her until his cronies had shown up with a cooler full of beer and who knew what else. Then her magical trip had turned into a nightmare. Being the only sober person in a crowd of drunks was no fun. Having to ride in a car driven by an intoxicated person had been absolutely terrifying.

Rebecca gave her head a little shake. Some memories were best kept buried. From the corner of her eye she could see Viv's knitting needles flying. The clackety-clack of the needles somehow soothed her. "What are you making?"

"My oldest granddaughter is expecting her first baby. Imagine! I'm going to be a great-grandmother in a few months! It's a girl. They already found out." Viv paused to flick away a tear. "In my day, we had no idea if our babies were boys or girls. We considered whatever the good Lord gave us a blessing. Oh, I know. Couples are so busy nowadays, with mothers-to-be working and all. They want to have everything all set before the baby arrives. But we thought being surprised was part of the excitement. Don't you think so?"

"Surprises are nice." Rebecca's *boppli* would be a surprise for sure and for certain. Her people felt as Viv did. All *bopplin* were a blessing. She supposed she should start preparing for her little one's arrival. She wished she had paid more attention when her *mamm* so patiently tried to teach her to knit. She always dropped stitches, became frustrated, and shoved the barely begun project into a bag. Watching Viv knit, though, was absolutely fascinating.

"Do you knit, dear?"

"I never could seem to learn. I kept making a tangled mess and giving up."

"It's not so hard. I've taught all my daughters and granddaughters to knit. I have extra yarn and needles if you'd like to try."

"I don't want to interrupt your work."

"It's no problem at all. You know, we knitters are happiest when we can recruit a new knitter. Trust me, knitting is a balm for an anxious mind. I've knitted many a troubled thought or bad mood away."

Then I definitely need to learn. Rebecca almost voiced her thought. "It looks like fun."

Could she learn? Maybe she just wasn't interested before.

"Here, I'll show you." Viv slid forward on the wide bus seat to once again rummage through her bag. She handed Rebecca a ball of soft yellow yarn and a pair of wooden knitting needles.

Rebecca fingered the yarn. Yellow. It could be for a girl or a boy. She picked up the needles and caught her bottom lip between her teeth. She was determined not to get frustrated and give up this time.

Viv scooted back into position with another ball of yarn and pair of needles. "Some people use metal needles," Viv explained. "Some use plastic. I like these wooden ones. It doesn't matter, though, which ones you use. You start by casting on the yarn. I'll show you the easiest way to do that."

"You must have an endless supply of yarn and needles in that bag."

Viv threw back her head and laughed. "It looks that way, doesn't it? I always bring extra along. My youngest granddaughter wanted me to show her some patterns, so I brought an assortment of yarn and needles with me."

Rebecca struggled to make the yarn obey. She chewed her lip as she concentrated. "I feel so clumsy."

"You'll get the hang of it. Relax. If you keep biting your lip, though, you're going to bleed all over the place."

Instantly Rebecca released her lip from its captivity. She didn't want to ruin Viv's lovely yarn. The older woman made her cast on stitches over and over until Rebecca felt she could get the yarn onto the needles in her sleep.

"Now we'll learn the basic knit and purl stitches. And don't worry if the stitches aren't perfectly even. I want you to bond with those knitting needles."

"Bond?"

Viv smiled. "Yes. They are your friends. Get used to the weight of them, the fit between your fingers. Try not to grip too tight—though everyone tends to do that in the beginning—or your hand will cramp. Once you get the hang of how to make the stitches, you'll find the grip that works best for you."

With Viv's close supervision, Rebecca knitted row after row of stitches. "They look a little wobbly."

"Maybe the first few rows, but look how neat the stitches are in the last part you knitted."

Rebecca allowed a little smile. "They did improve, didn't they?" Maybe she could learn to knit after all.

"Now we'll do some purl rows."

Purling felt more awkward. Rebecca's fingers wanted to knit instead. The familiar frustration threatened to surface, but Rebecca tamped it down.

"Take your time. It's different but not really harder."

The bus rumbled along the highway and miles

passed as Rebecca practiced her stitches over and over. Every now and then she paused to glance out the window and to wiggle her fingers. Viv, apparently a seasoned traveler, told Rebecca as much as she could about the towns they passed through. Rebecca prepared to wrap her yarn around the needle to begin another row but first flattened her swatch to examine it. She gave a little cry. "I've dropped a stitch or something."

"Good."

"*Gut?*"

"Now you'll see how easy it is to fix that. There's no need to panic." Viv patted Rebecca's arm before reaching for her bag. She withdrew a crochet hook from a side pocket of the bag. "This is all you have to do. Here, take the hook."

Viv guided Rebecca as she hesitantly inserted the hook and pulled the lost stitch through the rows of knitting and onto the needle. If she'd been at home, this would have been the point when Rebecca would have flung the whole project aside and given up in utter frustration.

"There. You did it. See, it wasn't the end of the world. All knitters drop stitches sometimes. Here, now I want you to fix these." Viv held up her lovely blanket, which showed gaps in the stitching here and there.

Rebecca gasped and dropped her swatch in her lap. "Your blanket! It's ruined. You deliberately ruined your beautiful blanket to teach me?"

Viv chuckled. "Oh my. If only you could see the horrified expression on your face. The blanket isn't ruined at all. You just saw how a mistake could be corrected. All these mistakes can be fixed, too." Viv handed Rebecca her project.

"Do you trust me to fix this?" Rebecca stroked the soft blanket.

"Of course I do. It's like life, you know. We all make mistakes—sometimes big ones." Viv pointed to a big gap in her stitching. "And sometimes teensy ones." She pointed out a tiny flaw. "All mistakes can be forgiven. We repent and move forward, trying hard not to make the same mistake again. But we're human. Inevitably we make another mistake. We can't be perfect no matter how much we may want to be. The Bible says all have sinned, every one of us, even if we don't want to and try hard not to."

Rebecca carefully lifted Viv's blanket and wiggled the crochet hook through the rows of stitching to pull up the dropped stitches. "So all mistakes can be fixed?" She needed a giant crochet hook to fix all the mistakes in her life! If only it could be so easy.

"Yes, dear. All mistakes can be fixed, just like all sins can be forgiven."

Rebecca bit her lip again, letting Viv's words sink in. Even if the Lord Gott forgave her myriad mistakes, would her parents be as forgiving?

"There. Good as new." Viv held up the baby

blanket. "You can't detect any flaws now, can you?"

Rebecca shook her head. For the first time in quite a while, she missed her white *kapp* strings swinging to and fro whenever she tossed her head. "It's as lovely as ever."

Viv smiled a warm, comforting smile, and her eyes smiled along with her lips. "Exactly. Just like we are all washed whiter than snow when we seek God's forgiveness." She patted Rebecca's arm with a wrinkled, spotted hand. "I think you're ready for a real project now. Here's how you can cast off. You're finished practicing."

"I'm not so sure."

"Have faith." Viv patted Rebecca's arm again.

Faith. Had she ever had faith? Rebecca wasn't so sure. She had grown up learning about her family's faith and obeying the rules—until she had hit her running-around time, that is. Could she find that faith, that assurance, that peace Viv possessed?

"Would you like to make a baby blanket, too? That yellow could work for a boy or a girl. And I have another big ball of that yarn, so you should have enough."

"A baby blanket?" Rebecca resisted the urge to rub the soft yarn against her face. She could picture an infant swaddled in the fuzzy, lemon yellow blanket. Her infant. When she looked up, she found Viv staring at her expectantly, knowingly. Had the wise old woman figured out her secret? "A baby blanket would be nice."

"That's what I always think. Someone is always going to have a baby, so when I need a knitting project, I can't go wrong with choosing a baby blanket."

"That makes sense. I'm not sure I can manage such a fancy one as you've got there."

"Well, it just so happens I have a plainer pattern etched in my mind. You'll get the hang of it quickly, I'm sure."

"Plainer"? How much had the woman figured out about her? Maybe she was an angel the Lord Gott had sent to help her. *Nee.* She definitely was not worthy of any angelic visitors. Rebecca returned her focus to Viv, who had again bent to prowl through her bag. Rebecca half feared the little woman would topple off the seat headfirst. She had a hand ready to catch Viv should that scenario play out.

"Here. You'll need this size knitting needles, I think. I made sure that other ball of yarn was down there, too. You're all set. Are you ready to cast on? I'm sure we can get through the entire pattern several times so you feel comfortable with it before we reach my destination."

Rebecca picked up the different sized needles and mentally counted each stitch as she cast on. Following Viv's directions, she began her *boppli*'s first blanket.

"You're doing a great job, Rebecca. Are you comfortable with the pattern now?"

Rebecca finally looked up from the little yellow blanket forming on her knitting needles. She'd been concentrating so hard she hadn't even realized how much time had passed. "I-I think so. I hope I don't forget it."

"Have no fear. I've written it down for you."

"When did you do that?" Rebecca hadn't seen the woman pull out a pen and piece of paper.

Viv laughed. "You were so intent on your stitches you didn't even notice my squirming on the seat. Here. Look at this and see if anything is unclear or confusing. My penmanship is not the greatest."

"It's fine." Rebecca skimmed the pattern quickly. "It makes perfect sense."

Viv began poking her own project back into her bag. "Well, dear . . ."

"*Ach*! It isn't time for you to get off the bus, is it?"

"Yes. We've been in Delaware for some time."

Rebecca bent forward to reach for her own bag. "Let me pay you for the yarn and needles."

"Goodness, no, child." Viv grabbed Rebecca's hand and pulled it away from her bag. "I don't want money."

"You can't go around giving yarn and needles to every stranger you meet." Rebecca tried to reach for her bag again, but Viv's grasp tightened.

37

"Seeing your delight with knitting and your enthusiasm and quickness is payment enough. I think I may have converted another lifelong knitter."

Rebecca smiled. "I believe you have. I should have listened to my mother years ago." *About many other things, too.*

"You weren't ready then. Sometimes our preferences and interests change as we mature."

"Are we almost at your stop?" A sudden panic seized Rebecca. She didn't want her time with the kind, wise woman to end. Maybe she should get off the bus here, too. She could make Delaware her home. She could start over here. Surely Viv knew some place she could stay and work.

"Just a couple more miles."

"I'll miss you." Rebecca's voice came out so soft she didn't think Viv heard her.

"You are a very sweet young lady." Viv patted Rebecca's hand. "Thank you for making my trip home so enjoyable."

"I didn't do anything."

"You were you, dear. That's all you ever need to be."

Tears gathered in Rebecca's eyes. How long had it been since anyone had considered her company enjoyable? She hadn't treated people at home very well before she left, and she hadn't been treated very well in the past few months. This one tiny woman had made a huge difference.

"*Danki*, I mean, thank you for helping me and for being so kind."

"I wish you all the best, dear. It was lovely meeting you. I know your family and all your people will be delighted to welcome you home. You and your little one." With a final gentle squeeze of Rebecca's hand the little woman hopped off the dark green bus seat and bustled down the aisle toward the open doors.

Rebecca, mouth agape, stared after her. Viv knew!

Chapter Three

Viv knew but didn't judge. She didn't condemn. Rebecca swiped at a tear and turned to peer out the window. Her eyes fastened on Viv's back as she left the bus behind. Almost instantly, the tiny woman was swallowed up in the welcoming hugs of a middle-aged man and woman. It must be one of the daughters and sons-in-law Viv had mentioned. Two girls, maybe about ten or twelve years old, hopped about waiting for their turn to hug their returning and obviously revered grandmother.

Oh, to have such a homecoming reception. She imagined her homecoming would be quite different. No doubt she'd be greeted with scowls and frowns rather than smiles and hugs. She expected accusations and bitterness and harsh words instead of heartwarming endearments. Maybe she should get off the bus now, run after Viv, and beg for her assistance. Maybe she should stay on the bus until the end of the line and create a new life wherever she ended up.

Another tear slid silently down Rebecca's cheek. To her surprise, Viv turned to scan the bus windows until she located the one with Rebecca's face pressed to the glass. Viv smiled her big, beautiful smile, nodded once, and gave

Rebecca a thumbs-up sign. Rebecca sniffed. She raised her hand and returned the sign. Viv had faith things would work out for the best. Rebecca would do well to find a little spark of this faith and try to fan it into full flame. She smiled and waved goodbye to her new *freind*, her angel in disguise, as the bus jerked forward.

Rebecca pressed her head against the high back of the bus seat and squeezed her eyes closed. If Viv believed she was a *gut* person, perhaps her family would believe she had changed. There was a slim chance Mamm and Daed would welcome her home, but the rest of the community—well, that could be a totally different story. Would she be able to live as an outcast if it came to that?

She could seek forgiveness, and she would. The people would forgive her because they had to. It was their way. But would they truly accept her back into the fold, or would they simply murmur polite words while keeping their distance? She could imagine Viv saying, *Live one day at a time, dear. Don't borrow tomorrow's trouble.* That's what her dear *grossmammi* would say, too. Rebecca bowed her head and silently poured her heart out to Gott.

She flicked a wayward strand of hair from her face and tried to poke it into the elastic band holding her long hair back in a ponytail. She examined the few inches of the baby blanket she'd begun knitting. A new blanket. A new skill.

A new Rebecca. A scared Rebecca, but a hopeful one.

Rebecca focused on her knitting as the bus rumbled along the highway, hoping the activity would settle the butterflies that stirred with increasing intensity every time she glanced out the window and realized she was another mile closer to home. She fought real fear when she glimpsed a *Welcome to Maryland* sign. Her heart rolled over itself, and her breath caught somewhere between her lungs and her nose. She patted her queasy stomach and thought of the tiny *boppli* riding the waves of nausea. Poor *boppli*. It didn't ask for any of this.

Public transportation could not take her all the way to Southern Maryland. She'd have to find out other options and determine how far she could get on her own before calling an *Englisch* driver to fetch her. Thankfully, the phone number of Sherry Davis, an *Englisch* woman who often drove her Plain neighbors places, was burned into Rebecca's memory. She certainly didn't have enough money to pay a cab to take her all the way to St. Mary's County. Besides, she'd feel safe with a familiar driver. Depending on the reception she got once she reached home, she might have to enlist the driver's services to drive her out of Southern Maryland.

Rebecca gave her head a little shake. She wouldn't think those negative thoughts. She wouldn't panic. Yet. Her heart rate continued to increase, with an occasional erratic beat thrown in, too. Her breathing quickened, and she forced herself to breathe in slowly to a count of four and out slowly to a count of four. She read somewhere that was supposed to help calm a person down. Not true. Well, maybe if the person could stay focused on the breathing it would work. But when the person's mind flitted about like it was skipping on stones across the creek, that relaxation breathing was a joke.

When the bus driver announced the upcoming stop near Baltimore-Washington Airport would be the only stop in Maryland before he continued on toward Northern Virginia, Rebecca folded her little blanket, jabbed the knitting needles into the ball of yarn, and carefully settled it all in the top of her big canvas bag.

She'd have to find out how she could get a little farther south before calling the driver. Should she change clothes now or wait? Despite Vinny's ribbing, she had kept the blue dress and white *kapp* she'd worn when she made her escape from Maryland. Rebecca plunged her hand to the bottom of the bag to ensure the clothes still lodged there.

When the brakes squealed and the big bus rocked to a halt, Rebecca stood and hoisted her bag. She shuffled toward the front of the bus, one hand grabbing each seat as she passed to steady herself. She weaved and wobbled like she'd just stepped into a bobbing rowboat. She hadn't realized how cozy and warm the bus had actually been until a blast of cold air slapped her as she clumped down the bus steps and set foot on Maryland soil.

A huge plane roared overhead so close Rebecca involuntarily ducked. If she strained her eyes a bit, she thought she'd be able to count the passengers on board since the plane flew so low as it approached the runway. Rebecca pulled her gaze from the plane and hurried into the combination convenience store and bus depot. After speaking with the clerk and arranging to board a small shuttle bus to Annapolis, Rebecca figured she'd better place that call to Sherry. Annapolis, even though it was more than an hour from her home, would be the closest she could get. She prayed Sherry would be available on such short notice.

Rebecca wandered to a far corner of the store and pulled a simple little cell phone from a pocket inside her bag. It was only a basic phone, not one of those smartphones she had never figured out how to use. Just the same, she'd have to get rid of the phone once she knew for sure she'd be staying in Clover Dale. She'd hang on to it for the time being, but it would need to be charged soon.

Please let her answer. Please let her be able

to make the trip to Annapolis. Rebecca counted the rings. At five, she feared the thing would go to voice mail. Then what would she do? What would she do if Sherry couldn't make the trip? It would be expensive to get a hotel room in Annapolis for sure and for certain. Her finger hovered over the end button, ready to disconnect, when a voice crackled across the line.

"Hello?"

"H-hello."

"Hello? Is anyone there? I can't hear you."

Rebecca forced herself to talk louder, even if her voice did carry across the store. "Sherry Davis?"

"Speaking."

"Hi, um, this is Rebecca Zook."

"Rebecca? Well, what a surprise. Where are you, honey?"

Rebecca was sure news of her departure had run throughout the Amish grapevine and jumped clear over to the *Englisch* neighbors. She hadn't elicited Sherry's help when she had slipped away for fear Sherry would try to talk her out of leaving the community. Sherry was a *gut freind* to her Amish neighbors and cared about their well-being. Rebecca cleared her throat. "I-I'm going to be in Annapolis soon. W-would, uh, c-could you pick me up? I know it's short notice and—"

"You bet, Rebecca." Sherry jumped in before Rebecca could continue to stumble over her request. "I've got to change my clothes, and I'll be there as soon as I can. You know it will take a good hour to an hour and a half for me to get there, depending on the traffic."

"That's fine. *Danki*, Sherry."

"Oh, honey, I know your folks are going to be so happy to see you."

Rebecca didn't count on that, but since Sherry was a mother herself, Rebecca hoped the woman was right. They made arrangements for meeting before Rebecca ended the call. She dropped the phone back into her bag and made her way across the store to the restroom. According to the big clock over a sign advertising some new soft drink, she had time to change clothes before the shuttle arrived.

Chapter Four

Rebecca twisted her long hair into its familiar bun and pinned the white *kapp* on her head. She needed to pin her dress only a little looser at the waist. Her weeks of nausea had kept her from putting on the expected weight. An Amish girl looked out of the mirror at her before leaving the restroom; a pale, scared-looking girl with big, green eyes. She would have to wear the *Englisch* jacket, though. Since it had been summer when she left home, she hadn't brought any kind of cloak with her.

Rebecca thought about leaving the other *Englisch* clothes behind but stuffed them into the bottom corner of the bag where the Amish clothes had been just in case she should need them again. She dragged in a deep breath and yanked open the door. A very different young woman emerged from the restroom. She hoped the store clerk wouldn't comment on the change.

It was funny how the Amish clothes she couldn't wait to throw aside now felt comfortable and right. Rebecca rushed to the front of the store to see if the shuttle had arrived. She didn't want to miss it, for sure and for certain. She almost grabbed a package of crackers or pretzels or something dry and salty to soothe her upset stomach, but then she would definitely have to face the clerk.

A short, white bus, more like an extra-long van, screeched to a stop just outside the store's front window. Big black letters proclaimed the vehicle was indeed the shuttle. Rebecca hurried to the door and out into the cold. She climbed the steps, handed the driver her ticket, and made sure the shuttle would let her off in the shopping center where the Amish market was located. Sherry was familiar with the place and had told Rebecca to try to get off the shuttle there.

With that settled, Rebecca scooted back to take a middle seat so she would be a little farther from the open door and the cold air blasting inside. She thought about knitting some more, but her fingers were too cold to bend. She briskly rubbed her hands together to get the blood flowing, but she suspected her ragged nerves contributed almost as much to the condition of her hands as the cold air did. She couldn't rub away nervousness. Instead she thrust her hands under her legs, hoping whatever body heat she possessed would thaw them. When the bag she'd set on the floor between her feet began to slide as the bus started moving, she pressed her feet tighter together. *Gut.* No one sat beside her. She wouldn't have to make polite conversation with anyone. She could decide what to say to Sherry Davis, who would probably not allow a silent ride home.

At least Rebecca didn't feel out of place at the Amish market. She altered her plan to wait outside for Sherry when the wind nearly ripped the *kapp* off her head. Now her fear was that Sherry wouldn't arrive before the market closed and she'd be forced to stand in the cold. Heavenly scents wafted in her direction as soon as she pushed through the door. Rebecca wandered around checking out the various offerings. Her stomach growled and her mouth watered. Everything looked so tasty. Most of the cookies in her bag had cracked and crumbled during the long bus ride. She'd eaten the largest crumbs, but the sights and smells in the market stimulated her appetite anew.

On one side, a long glass case held all sorts of cheeses, lunch meats, rolls, breads, and sandwich fixings. Rebecca doubted her stomach could handle a big deli sandwich. Across the way, another display case contained shoofly pie, peach pie, apple pie, chocolate cake, fudgy brownies, oversized snickerdoodles, and oatmeal raisin cookies. An oatmeal cookie might be the best thing for her stomach.

The workers were dressed very much like her, except for the *Englisch* jacket. They nodded and smiled at her as she passed by. If she hadn't been so cold, she might have shrugged out of the jacket so she didn't feel so self-conscious. As it was, she'd have to endure her qualms rather than sacrifice the warmth of the jacket. She hoisted her heavy bag higher and quickly explored the rest of the market. Some of the workers had begun cleaning their work areas, so Rebecca assumed the place would be closing fairly soon. The market reminded her of the dairy back home, though the dairy was much smaller. It, too, sold a variety of cheeses and assorted baked or preserved foods.

When she spun around to return to the entrance to watch for Sherry, she spied a sign for big, soft pretzels. Her stomach let out a loud rumble. The pretzel would be dry and salty and filling. Surely her belligerent stomach wouldn't revolt at that. She moved closer to ask for a pretzel but figured she'd better make sure she had enough money for a pretzel and a drink and still have Sherry's fee, which would be pretty hefty since she had to drive so far. Rebecca set the canvas bag on the floor and began rummaging through it for her wallet when a soft voice made her look up.

"You can have a pretzel."

"What?"

"We'll be closing soon. You can just take a pretzel. No charge."

"I can pay." Did she look that destitute?

"Of course, but we don't save these, so please take one. My treat. I'll grab you a small soda, too. Which kind would you like?"

"Any one will be fine." Rebecca only cared that

the drink was bubbly so it would help the pretzel stay down.

The girl, who was probably about Rebecca's age, smiled as she handed over the soda, a straw, and a small bag with a big pretzel peeking out. "Here you go."

"*Danki*. I appreciate your kindness."

"*Nee* problem. Have a nice evening."

That was doubtful, but Rebecca could always hope. She smiled at the girl and headed for the entrance. Sherry's big green van had just stopped outside the front door of the market. Perfect timing. Rebecca juggled her possessions so she could push the door open with her arm. The assault of an icy wind gust made her hurry across the sidewalk. She climbed into the van carefully to avoid spilling the soda everywhere.

"Rebecca Zook, you're a sight for sore eyes." Sherry turned to offer Rebecca a huge smile. "Do you need help with anything?"

"*Nee*. This is all I have." How sad that all her worldly possessions were shoved inside an over-sized canvas bag. She hadn't taken much with her when she left, and she definitely had little to bring back from New York. "I appreciate your driving all the way here on such short notice."

Sherry glanced over her shoulder before maneuvering the big van out of the parking lot. "It's perfectly all right. My family was scattered hither and yon today, so I left a note and a big pot of chili. They'll be completely happy with that."

"I'm sorry to interrupt your dinner and evening plans."

"I had no plans to interrupt. And I scarfed down a bowl of chili before I left the house. Have you eaten? We can stop some place if you like. It looks like your mother may need to fatten you up a bit." Sherry chuckled.

"I have a big pretzel from the market but haven't eaten it yet." She didn't add that she'd "fatten up" soon enough.

"You can go right ahead and eat it. You can't hurt this old van any."

"*Danki*." Rebecca reached into the paper bag, tore off a piece of the pretzel, and popped it into her mouth. For some reason, hunger made her queasiness worse, so she'd better send something down to her stomach right away.

"Do your folks know you're coming?"

Rebecca swallowed before she could choke on her bite of pretzel. She licked the salt from her lips. "*Nee*, they aren't expecting me. Maybe I should have tried to get a message to them."

"Oh, they will be so surprised and so happy to have you home."

Surprised, yes. Maybe "shocked" would be closer to their reaction. Happy? Well, that was a big question mark. "I hope so."

"Don't you worry, honey. Parents always rejoice when their children return home. No matter where they've been or what they've done or how old they are, they are always beloved children."

Rebecca prayed that would be true for Amish parents, too. She pinched off another bite of her pretzel as Sherry concentrated on merging onto the highway. Once their pace had evened out in the flow of traffic, Rebecca ventured a sip of her soda.

"So where have you been, if you don't mind my asking?"

The gulp of bubbly soda burned Rebecca's nose and caused her eyes to water. "New York."

"Did you see all the sights in the big city?"

"I saw a lot." She'd seen a lot she wished she hadn't seen.

"Are you home to stay?"

"I-I hope so. I-I guess that depends on my *mamm* and *daed*." And the bishop and whoever else had a say in whether she could return to the fold. She hadn't yet been baptized. She had almost taken that step, but had run out of the service, to everyone's surprise and her parents' horror. She supposed she'd have to ask for forgiveness, and she may have to repeat the instructional classes—if she'd be allowed to once they all knew about the *boppli*. How did her life become such a mess? She should have behaved herself, been satisfied with her life, and stayed home! She gulped more soda to push down the huge lump in her throat.

"Well, you mark my words. Everyone will be so glad to have you home. I'm sure your parents have been worried about you."

"I'm sorry to have caused them to worry."

"You know, we parents always worry over our children. My Jenny got a little wild and crazy in college, but she came home and finally settled down. She's teaching first grade now and loving every minute of it. We prayed for her every day she was gone and were overjoyed when she came home. Your parents will be, too."

Rebecca nodded at Sherry's reflection in the rearview mirror. She'd been unable to get that lump down or to talk around it. Sherry fell silent for a few minutes to concentrate on navigating the traffic. Rebecca set her soda in a cup holder and returned the half-eaten pretzel to the bag. A dull ache across her forehead made her close her eyes and lean her head back against the seat. She started to pray but must have dozed off instead. She jerked upright when Sherry spoke.

"Almost home!"

The *Welcome to St. Mary's County* sign appeared right outside her window. How had they traveled all those miles so quickly? Familiar businesses came into view—grocery stores, gas stations, a bank. Then there was the big farmers' market, which, thankfully, was closed now. If it had been open, Rebecca would be squirming every which way in her seat to remain concealed

54

from the buggies full of Amish folks heading home. She wanted her parents to be the first in the community to know she had returned. It wouldn't do for them to hear the news through the grapevine.

Rebecca reached to smooth loose tendrils of hair back into place and straightened the *kapp* that had gotten knocked lopsided as she dozed. She leaned to take a swig of watery soda to moisten her desert-dry throat. She wasn't sure which pounded harder—her heart or her head.

"Do you want to stop anywhere or do you want me to take you straight home?"

"Home, please." Home, she hoped.

Rebecca reached for another sip of soda to calm the waves of nausea as Sherry signaled to turn off the highway. She nearly swallowed the straw when Sherry swung the van out again to avoid a gray buggy. At the precise instant Rebecca glanced up from the cup holder and looked out the window, the smiling young man leaning out of the buggy looked into the van. Atlee Stauffer.

Fun-loving, teasing Atlee. Older than Rebecca by a couple of years, he was one of the few *buwe* who had never succumbed to her silly flirtations. Her face burned. She was so overcome with shame she was unable to return his friendly wave. They'd almost made it home without being seen. What was Atlee doing out here at this exact moment? Rebecca slunk back farther on the seat and pretended she didn't see him. But she did see him. And she knew in her heart Atlee recognized her. Ready or not, now everyone would know she had returned to Southern Maryland.

Chapter Five

In a matter of seconds the big green van left Atlee behind and passed the Clover Dale Library. Sherry drove slower on the side road lined with *Englisch* and Amish homes. She made another right onto Ryland Road. They were almost home. Rebecca's breath came in such short gasps she could hardly exchange oxygen and carbon dioxide. Her hands, which had warmed up nicely thanks to the van's hardworking heater, were now stone-cold. She leaned over to extract her wallet from her bag and with stiff fingers counted out the money to pay Sherry. She still had a little money left, so she wouldn't have to ask her *daed* for anything. Not right away, at least.

The van bumped along the long dirt drive leading to the Zooks' big white two-story farmhouse. Before her four rambunctious older *bruders* had married and moved out, the house had seemed small and crowded. With Rebecca, the youngest, and her parents as the only occupants the past few years, the house seemed much too big. Her oldest *bruder*, Emanuel, had talked about moving back to Maryland from Indiana, where he lived with his wife, Sally, and their *kinner*. Unless he had moved while Rebecca had been away, his talk still had not panned out.

It would be rather nice for her little one to have cousins to play with, though—if she stayed.

"I'm sure it's been a long day for you, but you're home at last." Sherry stopped the van close to the house and turned to look at her passenger.

"You are right about that." Rebecca leaned forward to hand Sherry the payment they had agreed upon. "*Danki*, Sherry. I sure appreciate your help today."

"No problem. Do you need help or, uh, want me to wait around?"

"*Nee*, I should be fine. You go back home to your family."

Sherry chuckled. "Maybe some of them have come home by now. If not, I think I'll take a nice, hot bath in a quiet house."

Rebecca smiled as she slid from the van. "Enjoy your evening."

"Thanks, dear. You, too." Sherry expertly turned the van around and headed toward the main road.

Rebecca stood rooted to the sidewalk. "Enjoy" might not be an appropriate word to describe the evening she had ahead of her. She had been the apple of her *daed*'s eye, but now she might be a rotten apple to be cast away.

In the waning light of day, her eyes roamed the land. The yard offered no bright flowers this time of year, but it had been neatly trimmed before the first frost. The barns and outbuildings had all been closed tight for the night. Evening chores must have been completed by now. Rebecca guessed supper was over, too, unless her parents were still sitting at the big table. It was odd they didn't hear the van and rush out to investigate.

The chill began seeping through her clothes to settle in her bones. She could postpone the inevitable no longer. She straightened her shoulders, dragged in a deep breath of fresh country air tinged with wood smoke, and stepped determinedly toward the front porch.

Before she climbed the first step, the front door creaked open. Both her parents stood in the doorway, silhouetted by the lamplight behind them. Rebecca stopped in her tracks. Her mouth opened but no words came out. All her practiced speeches abandoned her at the sight of them.

Her *daed* stood straight and tall, his hand still grasping the doorknob. His long, curly, dark beard had more gray streaks than she remembered. Her *mamm* clutched her *daed*'s arm with one hand. Her other hand flew to her heart. Rebecca thought her *mamm*, always a thin woman, now looked almost frail. Had she been sick? Her blond hair, once the same honey gold color as Rebecca's, had faded to a much paler shade.

Time froze. How long would they stand staring at one another? Yet Rebecca still could not make either her voice or her legs work.

"Becky?" Sylvia's voice came out in a whisper. "Amos, it's Becky." The sickly-looking woman pushed past her husband and ran across the porch. She flew down the steps and opened her arms wide to embrace her daughter. "*Ach*, Becky! You're home."

Her *mamm*'s tears splashed Rebecca's cheeks as she held Rebecca with a strength that belied her frail appearance. Were they Mamm's tears or Rebecca's? She didn't know when her own tears began cascading down her face to drip from her chin. Sylvia held her and rocked to and fro as if Rebecca were a *boppli*.

"M-Mamm, I-I'm so sorry."

"Hush. You're home. That's all that matters."

Rebecca felt her *daed*'s presence even though she didn't see him approach. "Are you home to stay? You broke your *mamm*'s heart, you know." His voice came out loud, forceful even, but Rebecca detected a tremor underneath the almost harsh words.

"I-I'm sorry, Daed. I-I want to stay. I . . ."

"Shhh." Sylvia pulled back slightly to wipe Rebecca's tears with one trembling hand. "We'll talk in a bit. Let's get you in out of the cold." With an arm wrapped firmly around Rebecca as though afraid she'd vanish into thin air, Sylvia led the way up the steps. "Amos, get Becky's bag." She nodded to the canvas bag Rebecca had dropped at her feet. "Child, your hands are blocks of ice. I can feel how cold they are through my dress. And you don't even have a warm bonnet on your head."

"I didn't have my gloves with me." Rebecca instantly felt silly for making such a comment. Anyone could purchase a pair of gloves anywhere. She didn't need the gloves from home. The black Amish bonnet would have been much harder to find in New York.

Rebecca ventured a quick glance in her *daed*'s direction as soon as they entered the house. He hadn't said he was glad to see her or even touched her. The man who used to bounce her on his knee and toss her high in the air amid giggles and laughter remained stiff and stoic. She had broken his heart, too. Remorse flooded her, and more tears threatened.

Chapter Six

Rebecca let her *mamm* lead her into the living room. "*Kumm* sit near the stove and warm up. I'll get you a cup of tea. Or would you rather have *kaffi*?"

"N-neither, Mamm. I'm fine."

"*Ach*, Becky, let me look at you. I've missed you so much." Sylvia began unfastening Rebecca's coat as if she were a little girl again. "You won't need this coat now."

Rebecca took her mamm's hands in her own to still them. "It's okay, Mamm. I can get this." Rebecca didn't think her condition was obvious yet but didn't want to take the chance her *mamm* would discover her secret. She wanted to be able to explain. Somehow she'd have to find the right words. "A-are my things still here?"

"Of course. Where else would they be? I counted on you to return home. I prayed for it every day."

"*Danki*." Rebecca cast a sideways glance at her *daed*. He still looked like a thunderstorm about to hit. Rebecca pulled her arms from the sleeves of the coat and laid it across her lap, its bulkiness hiding her midsection just in case. With a toe, she sent the old oak rocking chair her *mamm* had most likely just vacated into a gentle to and fro motion. The rhythm gradually soothed her jangled nerves and her queasy stomach. Until her *daed* spoke, that is.

"Where have you been, Dochder, and what have you been doing?"

"The important thing is our *dochder* is home, Amos." Sylvia threw a frown at her husband before fixing her girl with a fresh loving look. "Are you hungry? I have leftover casserole or I can make you a sandwich."

"*Nee*, Mamm. I'm not hungry." Rebecca managed a small smile for her *mamm*. *Please let her still love me and want me to stay after I tell them.* Rebecca gathered the courage to squarely face her *daed*. "I will tell you everything, Daed. I-I need to tell you. Why don't you both sit down?"

Rebecca didn't miss the panic-stricken glance Sylvia shared with Amos before they settled side by side on the sofa. Their wary but expectant faces nearly made Rebecca want to invent a story, a prettier story, but the truth had to be told. She cleared her throat and sucked in a deep breath. *Gott, please help me and help them. Please give them understanding and forgiving hearts.*

"When I left here, I had the notion I wanted to see something different, experience city life and new adventures." Did she ever experience new adventures! City life had turned out to be nothing like her foolish, childish dreams. It hadn't taken too long for her excitement to be snuffed out by reality. If she hadn't been so naive and gullible, she would have faced reality much sooner and probably experienced a lot less heartache.

"Where did you go? What did you do there?"

"Let her tell it her way, Amos." Sylvia patted her husband's arm. Her face had grown paler and her eyes misted with tears.

"New York. I went to New York."

"What do you mean you *thought* you were married? What kind of nonsense is that?" Amos's thundering voice matched his stormy countenance.

"It's the truth, Daed. Honest." Rebecca turned to her *mamm* for support but found Sylvia staring wide-eyed and on the verge of tears. "Wait!" Rebecca pushed herself up from the rocking chair and crossed the room to where her *daed* had plunked her bag down on the floor. She tore through the bag, letting its contents spill onto the hardwood floor. A ball of yellow yarn rolled across the floor. The knitting needles stuck in the second ball made a clacking sound as they hit the floor. "Here it is." Rebecca drew out a folded piece of paper and returned to kneel in front of her parents. She shook the paper open and handed it to her *daed*.

"What's this supposed to be?"

"My so-called marriage license." Rebecca had almost torn the worthless piece of paper

64

into bits when she found out she'd been duped. Now she was glad she'd hung on to it. "Doesn't it look real, Daed? I'd never seen one before, so I assumed this was authentic. We stood before a man who read from a little book and had us say our vows. He signed that paper. It has a seal of the state of New York, or a good copy of one. I-I thought Vinny loved me. Why would I suspect it was a sham?" She drew in a shaky breath. "I guess I was pretty stupid, because I trusted him."

"Hmpf!" Amos's eyes scanned the paper.

"It does look real, ain't so, Amos?" Sylvia had leaned closer to read along with her husband.

"Daed, I know I made a lot of mistakes here. I-I toyed with a lot of fellows' hearts. I-I thought it was fun to flirt. But, Daed, I never, um, went any further than flirting. Never. I didn't really love any of those *buwe*, but even if I did, I would have waited until we were married." Rebecca swiped at a tear that had rolled unbidden down her cheek. Surely her parents would believe her. They didn't think that ill of her, did they?

"What about Isaac Hostetler? You wanted him to leave with you. What were you planning with him?"

"I only wanted him to be my traveling companion so I wouldn't feel so completely alone. I never intended we would, uh, be involved, uh, any other way."

"Isaac sure seemed pretty hurt when you up

and left like you did." Amos's stern expression had not softened one whit.

"I'm sorry for that. I'm sorry for all the hurt I caused. I'm willing to ask forgiveness. I-I want to join the church now." Rebecca sniffed and searched her parents' faces. "If you'll let me stay."

"Where is this Vinny fellow now? Did he just turn you away when he got tired of you or when he learned about the *boppli*?"

Rebecca flinched at her *daed*'s harsh words as if she'd been slapped. "He's dead. I didn't know he and his *freinden* were involved in drugs. They said he died of an overdose. They thought they could keep me with them, but I ran away. I stayed with another waitress until I could sort things out and catch a bus out of New York."

Sylvia gasped. Rebecca wouldn't have thought it possible for her *mamm*'s face to lose any more color. "My poor *boppli*." She reached out both arms to pull Rebecca into a sheltering embrace.

Before she had left home, Rebecca had shied away from her *mamm*'s touch. She was in her *rumspringa* and was too grown up to need her parents' hugs—or so she thought. Now she craved their love. She had grown up enough to realize she needed her parents and loved them.

"Amos, the Lord Gott spared our *dochder*. She could have been forced to stay with those bad people, but she got away and returned to us. She wants to stay and be baptized."

Rebecca could hear her *mamm*'s heart pounding as Sylvia held her tightly. Relief flooded her at her *mamm*'s speech. Mamm wanted her to stay. But what about Daed?

"Do you want to be baptized because you are afraid and have nowhere else to go or are you truly ready to seek forgiveness, commit to our faith, and abide by the Ordnung?"

"I-I'm ready to make the commitment, Daed. I will take classes again if the bishop says I must. I have sought Gott's forgiveness. I-I will kneel and confess before the church if that is what the bishop says I must do."

"You aren't a member yet. She wouldn't have to do that, would she, Amos?"

"I don't know what the bishop will say."

Rebecca felt helpless to control her trembling despite her *mamm* rubbing her back in small circles. Daed had not addressed Rebecca's request to stay. Her hope trickled away.

"And what about the disgrace and shame of having a *boppli* out of wedlock?"

"It isn't like other Amish couples haven't gotten carried away and pushed up their wedding plans," Sylvia countered.

"But those couples got married!"

"I thought I *was* married, Daed." Rebecca wanted to bury her face in her *mamm*'s shoulder forever, but she pulled away to face her *daed*. "I know I will be an embarrassment to you. I'm

67

sorry for that. You can show the bishop and anyone else that paper there." She waved a hand toward the phony marriage license. "Once people know about that, maybe they will withhold judgment and not keep their distance. I-if it becomes too unbearable for you, then I'll leave."

"*Nee!*" Sylvia fairly shouted, causing Rebecca to jump in alarm. "Amos, she cannot leave! She did nothing wrong, not intentionally, anyway. And there's the little one to think about. An innocent infant. Our *dochder*'s *boppli*. Our own flesh and blood."

Amos rubbed a large, calloused hand across his face. "We will visit the bishop tomorrow."

Rebecca nodded. She watched as her *daed*'s face softened. His wrinkled brow smoothed, and little smile lines crinkled around his eyes before the smile reached his lips. Rebecca's hopes soared.

"I've missed you, too, Becky." Amos opened his arms to hug his *fraa* and *dochder*. "You are my only *dochder*. You will always be my little girl. We will help you."

"*Danki*, Daed." Rebecca's tears of relief mingled with tears of joy. Her *mamm*'s tears and even her *daed*'s tears blended with her own.

Sylvia was the first to pull away. "Let's get you settled."

Amos stood and practically lifted Rebecca to her feet. "Did you have any more bags to bring in?"

Rebecca nodded to her overturned canvas bag. "That was all I took time to grab. Besides, I didn't want to bring any *Englisch* things with me."

Sylvia scurried over to retrieve the bag and its spilled contents. "*Ach*, Becky, you took up knitting?" She held up the beginning of the blanket.

"*Jah.* I know you tried to teach me many times, and I was too impatient to learn. A nice older woman sitting next to me on the bus taught me how to start this blanket, but I'll probably need your help later."

Sylvia smiled. "It's lovely. You learned quickly."

"I think all your instructions were stuck in my mind somewhere, so it made Viv's work easier."

"Viv?"

"The woman on the bus. She also talked to me about forgiveness and family and parents' love—all the things you and Daed tried to tell me before. Things I turned a deaf ear to. I guess I finally grew up enough to listen and believe."

Chapter Seven

Atlee peeked into the lunch box Malinda had prepared for him to make sure she'd thrown in some of those lemon cookies she'd recently baked. Chocolate chip cookies and anything else chocolate were usually his favorite treats, but those lemon cookies ran a close second. He rummaged through the box, moving aside two sandwiches and an apple until his fingers found the little plastic bag. He tugged it out and groaned.

"Something wrong, Atlee?" Malinda closed Ray's and Aden's lunch boxes so they could head out to school.

"These are gingersnaps."

"Very *gut*. You got that right."

"Where are those *wunderbaar* lemon cookies?"

"Do you mean the little lemon cookies covered with sugar sprinkles?"

"*Jah*, those would be the ones."

"Well, it looks to me like we had a thief slip in overnight who gobbled up every one of those cookies." Malinda clucked her tongue and wagged her head.

"A crime! What about the chocolate chip?"

"The thief must have moved on to those next.

There were only two left in the cookie jar."

Atlee thrust out his hand. "Hand them over and all will be forgiven."

"I put one in Ray's lunch and the other in Aden's lunch."

"Why? They'll eat anything. They don't care what kind of cookies you give them."

"Atlee, *you* will eat anything. I'm crushed. Don't you like my gingersnaps?"

"Sure, but if there's chocolate around . . ." Atlee reached for one of his younger *bruders'* lunch boxes.

Malinda smacked his hand. "*Nee* you don't, you scoundrel."

"Scoundrel?" Atlee tucked the gingersnaps back into his lunch box and clicked it closed. "If that's the way you want to be, I guess I'll go to work." He poked out his lower lip in an exaggerated pout.

Malinda laughed. "Go on with you, Atlee. You're incorrigible."

Atlee nearly collided with Ray and Aden, who zoomed into the kitchen to grab their lunches. "Enjoy your cookies, *bruders*!" Atlee looked over his shoulder and caught Malinda shaking an index finger at him. He backtracked a few paces and lowered his voice. "Say, Malinda, it didn't bother you that Isaac was at the last singing, did it?"

"Of course not. He has every right to attend."

"*Jah*, but . . ."

"Whatever we had was just a passing interest, nothing more."

"So you won't be mad if I tell you I encouraged him to attend?"

"*Nee*, why should I? I have—"

"I know. You have another interest now."

"Shhh!"

"It's not like nobody notices how your face lights up at the mere mention of Timothy Brenneman's name. It's not like we don't know about his frequent visits."

Malinda poked out her tongue at her older *bruder*.

"That was a mature response."

"And did you give anyone a ride home from the singing?"

"Well, if you had stuck around a little longer, you'd have seen for yourself. But, alas, you must have had other plans."

Malinda swatted Atlee with a rolled-up dish towel. "Aren't you going to be late for work?"

He glanced at the teapot-shaped battery-operated wall clock. "*Nee*. I think I'll be on time." Atlee sauntered toward the door. "By the way, I left the singing entirely by myself—as usual."

"There were some visitors there."

"*Jah*. Nice girls, from what I could tell, but not for me."

"You'll never know if you don't try . . ."

"*Ach*, Malinda, you are so right about the time. I really need to go,"

"Coward!" Malinda chuckled. Maybe she'd bake more cookies today.

After all the dark gray clouds the previous day, only a skim of snow covered the grassy areas. The sun had shoved the clouds aside today to rule the sky. The wind still carried a bite, so the sun had its work cut out for it if it planned to warm things up a bit.

Even though Atlee was glad he'd found his gloves and remembered to wear them, his fingers still ached from the cold by the time he reached the dairy. He unhitched and cared for the horse as quickly as possible so he could get inside. He'd be sure to warm up once he got busy lifting and carrying and whatever else needed doing today. It was strange no one had mentioned the return of Becky Zook. Could it be Malinda and his *mamm* hadn't heard any vibrations from the grapevine? Maybe no one had seen Becky except him. *Ach*, they'd all know soon enough, he guessed. It wasn't his place to tell tales. He whistled as he loped off toward the building and set his mind on having a *gut* day, even if he did have to eat gingersnaps for dessert. Maybe something special would happen this day. Hope was a *gut* motivator.

Chapter Eight

The visit with Bishop Menno Lapp had to be one of the most difficult things Rebecca had ever endured. It took every ounce of her courage to sit still and actually get her voice to cooperate. Bishop Menno stroked his salt-and-pepper beard as he listened to Rebecca's confession but did not utter a single word until she finished her tale with tears streaming down her cheeks. At some point, the bishop's wife, Martha, had slipped into the room and poked several tissues into Rebecca's wringing hands. The bishop, still silent, leaned forward to read the phony marriage license Rebecca had brought to validate her story. Amos sat like a stone behind Rebecca. She wondered if he even blinked or breathed.

Rebecca thought she would scream from the oppressive silence. Would the bishop ever speak, or was this crushing, interminable silence her punishment? When the man cleared his throat, Rebecca stopped shredding one of the tissues in her hands and raised her eyes to meet his.

"It seems you have had quite a learning experience, Rebecca."

That was an understatement. "*Jah.*"

"What do you think about the *Englisch* world and life in the big city?"

"Like everywhere, I suppose, there was *gut* and bad in the city and *gut* and bad in the *Englisch* world. I saw some beautiful and amazing sights and met a few nice people. I also saw evil and met people who believe it's fine to lie, cheat, and prey on others." Rebecca paused to inhale a shaky breath.

"Would you want to return there?"

"*Nee!*" Rebecca barely let the bishop finish his question. "I don't belong there. That life is truly not for me." Rebecca leaned forward and somewhere found the strength to look the man in the eye. "I want to live here. I want to be baptized. This is my home, the only place I want to live. I am so sorry for my past behavior and for hurting people. Really I am. I have prayed and sought the Lord Gott's forgiveness." Rebecca caught her lower lip between her teeth and bit down hard enough to taste blood. She held her breath as she waited for the bishop to speak.

Bishop Menno uncrossed the arms he'd folded over his chest as the pensive look slid from his face. "You have given *gut* answers, Rebecca. I believe what you have told me, and I believe you have learned valuable lessons. You will not be required to kneel and confess before the church since you are not yet a member. 'Almost a member' doesn't count." The bishop's lips quirked above his beard.

Heat flooded Rebecca's face at the memory

of her shameful behavior on her baptismal day. She'd run from the church meeting, leaving a stunned community to stare after her. She wiggled in her chair.

"It's better you didn't make the commitment if you weren't ready."

"I'm ready now."

"I believe you are ready. It won't be easy to raise a *boppli* on your own, but we will all help however we can. We are glad you returned, Rebecca. We will discuss your baptism after you've settled back in."

"I won't change my mind, Bishop Menno. This is what I want. This is where I belong."

With one index finger, Bishop Menno pushed his wire-rimmed glasses higher on his nose. "*Wilkom* home, Rebecca."

Rebecca's pent-up breath whooshed out when arms wrapped around her in a hug. Either Martha Lapp had crept back into the room unnoticed or she'd stayed in the background and listened to the entire exchange. "It's *gut* to have you home, dear."

Rebecca followed her *daed* out to the buggy, her step a bit lighter than when she had entered the bishop's house. Not that it had been at all easy, but the visit had gone better than Rebecca had dared hope. Still, Amos had uttered nothing more than a few polite grunts. Had this whole meeting been so humiliating for him that he'd changed his mind about having her home again?

By the time they reached the end of the bishop's long dirt driveway, Rebecca summoned the courage to look at her *daed*. A single tear slid down his cheek and hid in his bushy beard. "Daed?"

Amos reached over to squeeze Rebecca's hand. "You handled yourself well in there. It looks like my little girl has grown up."

"It's about time, ain't so, Daed?" Her real test would occur on the next church day, when she'd have to face the entire community.

Rebecca couldn't decide if she wanted to rush so she could arrive at the Stauffers' house early to face people as they arrived for the church service or dawdle so she would be late enough to only have time to slip into the service at the last minute. Her original idea to stay in bed with the covers pulled over her head was not really an option, tempting though it was. She had helped Mamm clean the kitchen after their simple Sunday breakfast. Now there was nothing left to do except don her cloak and black bonnet.

She wrung her gloved hands as the horse pulled the buggy along the blacktopped road. What would people say to her? The grapevine had no doubt been buzzing for days. Most of the girls her age always thought she was nothing more than a flirt who wanted to steal their fellows.

The few she'd seen since she'd been home had been polite, but they kept their distance from her. She'd have to face them again today. And she had flirted with many, if not most, of the *buwe*. How embarrassing! How could she make amends? How would she make it through this day? A little headache began to nag at her.

Rebecca's breathing and heart rate increased as the Stauffer farm came into view. Malinda Stauffer had always been nice, but Rebecca's latest conquest before she ran off had been Isaac Hostetler, who had been interested in Malinda before Rebecca had butted in. Rebecca sighed. She wouldn't count on Malinda being cordial. At least Rebecca had never attempted to flirt with the two older Stauffer sons. Sam had married Emma Swarey, and Atlee was—well, he was Atlee.

"Everything will be all right, Becky. You'll see." Sylvia gently squeezed Rebecca's arm and gave her a reassuring smile. "Just smile and be nice." Being nice she could manage. Smiling, though, she was not so sure about.

Chapter Nine

Rebecca climbed from the buggy and surveyed her surroundings. As usual, people gathered in groups until time to enter the church service. Should she join a group of young, unmarried women? That didn't seem quite right. Nor did she seem to fit in with the older, married women. Where did she belong? She pulled her cloak tighter around her.

"Relax, Dochder. You're among *freinden*."

"*Freinden*"? Did she have any of those? "Wait, Mamm. I'll help you." Rebecca grabbed a basket of food Sylvia had brought to share at the common meal. She'd hide out in the kitchen until the last possible moment and then slip into the big cleared-out barn where backless wooden benches would be arranged for the church service. Hopefully, she would be able to sit unnoticed on a back bench.

"Becky, *wilkom* home!"

So much for hiding. "*Danki*, Malinda." If Malinda Stauffer could be pleasant to her, perhaps there was hope. "How have you been?" Poor Malinda had her ups and downs with Crohn's disease but always seemed cheerful. She didn't look as thin or as pale as Rebecca remembered. Maybe her disease was in remission now.

"I've been very well lately. *Danki* for asking. I can take that basket for you, if you like."

Rebecca handed over the basket and backed away to observe from a corner. Other women entered the kitchen with bowls and baskets. They chattered as they arranged food to be served at noon. Those who noticed Rebecca in the shadows nodded or said hello. Most of the girls her own age had gathered outside near the barn and were probably discussing the singing to be held in the evening. She wouldn't be a part of that, either. Maybe she should have gotten off the bus with Viv.

"It's time," someone called. Rebecca watched the women file out the back door. She fought rising panic and nausea. She dragged in some deep breaths. She absolutely could not get sick here in front of everyone.

"Are you all right?" Sylvia touched Rebecca's arm, concern written on her face.

Could she say she was sick and needed to go home? *Nee.* That's what the old Rebecca would do. "I-I think so."

"*Kumm.* Sit with me." Sylvia linked her arm with Rebecca's. "We'll sit in the back in case you need to go out."

Rebecca nodded. She could do this. She *would* do this. After today, things should get easier, shouldn't they?

She sat ramrod straight on the hard wooden

bench and stared dead ahead. She sang with the others as they waited for the ministers to enter. She prayed when she was supposed to pray. She fought to keep her wandering thoughts focused on the long sermons. It had been a while since she'd sat through a three-hour church service. Her back ached and her eyes watered from staring in one spot. She briefly allowed her gaze to dart around the gathering.

A couple of the older men's white-bearded chins had dropped to their chests, and their eyes had drooped in slumber. One snored softly. Women in blue or purple or green dresses held infants or young children on their laps. Their arms and backs must be kinked in pain without any kind of support. Funny, she had never before considered how uncomfortable those young *mudders* might be. She'd be joining their ranks in a few months. Well, she'd be holding an infant in her arms, but she might not actually be accepted as one of them.

Rebecca wiggled ever so slightly, careful not to bump into her *mamm*. At least she was sitting on the end of the row, so only Sylvia would be affected by her movement. For some reason she felt uncomfortable, as though eyes were watching her. She looked at the minister who was speaking, but it wasn't his eyes boring into her. She glanced at the other ministers and the bishop. They were all staring at the speaker. Yet Rebecca couldn't shake the feeling of being watched.

Ever so slowly she ventured a gaze in the direction where the young men sat. All seemed intent on the sermon, or were at least pretending to be. All, that is, except one. Atlee Stauffer's bright green eyes looked right into her own. How long had Atlee been staring at her? No doubt he had recognized her in the van on her way home the other evening. He'd probably enjoyed a laugh or two over her attempt to hide from him.

Now he smiled at her. It wasn't a mean or joking kind of smile; not a smirk at all. She had never known Atlee to be mean, but he did like to joke and pull pranks. A genuine smile curved his lips and crinkled the corners of his eyes. He almost imperceptibly nodded at her before turning his attention to the minister.

What was that all about? She and Atlee had not really been *freinden* previously. They were acquaintances, for sure and for certain, but Atlee had been two grades ahead of her in school. She and Malinda were the same age, but they had never been close *freinden*, either. Rebecca wasn't at all sure she could name a single person who was a close *freind*. And she could certainly use one about now.

Rebecca knelt for the final prayer, then slipped out of the barn. Sylvia trotted to keep up. "Are you all right?"

"I'm fine, Mamm." Rebecca tried to offer a

reassuring smile but knew her attempt fell short. She patted her *mamm*'s arm. "Do you think it would be all right if I help out in the kitchen?" If she could refill serving plates and bowls as needed and clean up in the kitchen, she could avoid serving at the tables and thereby avoid facing the folks gathered around them.

"Of course. I'm so glad you're back, and so is everyone else." Sylvia squeezed Rebecca's hand.

Rebecca nodded but wasn't so sure everyone shared her *mamm*'s sentiments. The warmth of the Stauffers' kitchen came as a relief after the wind had nearly yanked Rebecca's bonnet off her head during the brisk walk from the barn. She stowed her cloak and bonnet and followed on Sylvia's heels to the kitchen. She was going to have to stop hiding behind her *mamm*'s skirt like some shy little girl. Maybe she'd do that another day.

Rebecca busied herself working in the background as much as possible. She wiped up spills, set empty dishes in the sink to be washed in a little while, and set refilled bowls on the table for some of the other girls to carry to the barn, where the men would have converted the church benches into makeshift tables. She felt like an outsider observing the action around her, like a peeping Tom peering in a window.

When the women headed out for their meal, Rebecca shrank farther back into the shadows.

Clusters of women chatted about their families or news from the *Budget*, the Plain newspaper, or an upcoming work frolic. Her *mamm* eventually joined in with her own *freinden*. Only Rebecca was the odd person out, it seemed.

She filled the sink with soapy water and began to tackle the dishes piling up on the counters. As she scrubbed, she gazed out the window at the *kinner* running about despite the frosty breeze.

"Becky, dear, you can leave those for a bit. *Kumm* get a bite to eat." Saloma Stauffer smiled. She had always been kind. "It's so *gut* to have you home."

"*Danki.*"

"You need to eat and leave this mess."

"I'm not really very hungry."

"At least *kumm* sit and have a cup of *kaffi*. Maybe something will tempt your appetite."

Rebecca didn't want to join the others. She didn't want all eyes turning to stare at her. But she didn't want to ignore Saloma's kindness, either. She dried her hands, pulled on her cloak and bonnet, and let Saloma lead her out to the waiting meal. *Help me get through this, Lord Gott.*

Saloma nudged Rebecca to the food table and handed her a plate. "Try to eat something, dear. I know this is a difficult day for you, but we are all your *freinden*. We all care."

Rebecca nodded. The lump in her throat grew

to boulder proportions. Saloma's words were a balm to her injured soul. She had to put some kind of food on her plate, but honestly, nothing at all appealed to her. She chose a few crackers, a cheese slice, and a dollop of coleslaw. Saloma handed her a Styrofoam cup of steaming *kaffi* and led her to a seat.

"Look who I found slaving away in the kitchen. Becky, if you scoot in here next to your *mamm*, I'll sit on your other side."

Rebecca forced herself to look at the other women, who all murmured or nodded a greeting. Obediently she sat next to Sylvia and slid as close to her as possible to give Saloma room. The other women briefly stopped their conversations and watched Rebecca wiggle across the bench. She felt like an animal on display at the zoo and had to suppress the urge to reach up to see if she'd grown another head. When Saloma perched next to her, quiet conversations resumed.

Rebecca had never been a huge fan of *kaffi*, and the brew had become even more of a challenge to stomach lately. Not wanting to offend Saloma, she raised the cup to her lips and pretended to take a sip. Even that proved to be impossible. She quickly set the cup down and picked up a cracker.

"So, Becky, I don't know if your *mamm* told you, but we have a work frolic coming up soon. We're planning to get Lena Troyer's house ship-shape before her new bundle of joy arrives."

"Uh, Mamm hadn't told me." Had Mamm planned to tell her, or was she embarrassed about taking her there? It really didn't matter. She probably wouldn't go anyway.

"We've been so busy I haven't had the chance to catch Becky up on all the latest news," Sylvia said.

"That's understandable. We hope you'll both be there." Saloma speared two pickled beet slices and popped them into her mouth.

"Are you all right?" Sylvia spoke directly into Rebecca's ear.

"I-I hope so." Rebecca nibbled the corner off her cracker. She picked up the plastic fork and raked up a small bite of coleslaw. She'd always loved the shredded cabbage and carrot dish. She prayed her stomach wouldn't revolt, not now in front of so many watchful eyes.

After her third tiny bite of coleslaw, Rebecca had to eat more of the dry cracker to appease her queasy stomach. Would this nausea ever end? She'd heard a few women in the past say they'd been sick for the entire nine months. Surely that wouldn't happen to her. She wasn't sure she could endure that. Suddenly she nudged her *mamm*. "I've got to get up—quick!"

Sylvia slid over as far as she could to give Rebecca room to move. She swiped the paper napkin across her mouth and prepared to stand.

"I-it's okay, Mamm." Rebecca patted her

mamm's arm. "You eat and visit." As gracefully as possible, Rebecca escaped from the table.

When out of view of the doorway, she ran toward the clump of trees behind the barn and promptly lost the little food she had ingested. She leaned her head against the rough bark of a tall, leafless oak tree. She squeezed her eyes tightly closed to hold back the tears burning the insides of her eyelids. She didn't expect returning home to be easy, but she didn't expect to feel so utterly alone, either. And this dreadful nausea did nothing to help. Ever since she was a little girl, she always cried after throwing up. Today was no exception.

"Becky, are you all right?"

"Ahhh!" Rebecca jumped and swiped a hand across her eyes and mouth. She thought she'd escaped unnoticed, but someone had evidently observed her flight. She turned to look up into the bright green eyes looking down on her in concern. "Atlee, you scared me." She patted the spot above her pounding heart. "Wh-what are you doing out here?" Despite the cold, Rebecca's face flamed. She hoped she didn't look like someone who had just lost her lunch.

"I had just *kumm* from the house and saw you run by. Is everything okay?"

"*Jah*, I, uh, needed some air."

"Did someone upset you or treat you unkind?"

Why should Atlee Stauffer care how anyone

treated her? Why did he even bother to check on her at all? "I-I'm not upset. Everyone has been kind." She guessed.

"Are you sick?"

"I-I'm feeling better now." She dragged in a deep breath of the frosty air.

"Do you want to walk for a minute or are you too cold?"

What did he want? Was he playing some kind of joke or game at her expense? Surely not. Atlee had always been a prankster, but she'd never known him to be unkind. "I'm not too cold."

"*Gut.* Sometimes a brisk walk in the cold settles the nerves and clears the mind."

"I suppose so." Rebecca hoped so.

They shuffled along in the opposite direction of the big barn where folks still gathered. Dried brown leaves crunched beneath their feet. Overhead, bare tree limbs scratched the sky. Rebecca tried to relax, but her wariness kept her muscles so tense they were ready to snap. She jumped again when Atlee touched her arm. So much for his theory about a walk settling the nerves. She was as jumpy as a toad.

"Shhh! Look, Becky."

Rebecca's eyes followed where Atlee pointed to a small clearing through a stand of loblolly pines. Three does nibbled at ground-level bushes, their ears twitching to alert them to any sound. "They're beautiful," she whispered. As if on some silent cue, all three deer silently bounded into thicker woods. "You probably wish you had your gun with you."

"*Nee.* Don't tell anyone, but I really don't care for hunting—especially deer. They're such graceful, amazing creatures."

Rebecca's eyes widened in surprise. She never would have guessed Atlee had a soft spot for deer. She had always loved seeing the deer graze in the fields and leap high in the air as they fled from perceived danger. She had once wanted to make a pet of a little spotted fawn, but she assumed all men wanted to hunt them. Atlee was a mystery, for sure and for certain.

She stared after the deer for a few seconds even though they had vanished from sight. When she could no longer contain her curiosity, Rebecca asked the question that had been rattling around in her brain. "Atlee, why are you walking with me?"

"Huh?"

"Why are you out here in the cold walking with me?"

"I saw you run off, and I wanted to make sure you were okay."

"That's all?"

"What else?"

"You weren't thinking that I, um, that I would be, um, well, I don't know for sure what kind of reputation I have, but I am not a bad girl."

Rebecca knew her face must have turned ten shades of red. She was too embarrassed to even glance in Atlee's direction. She spoke again, whisper soft. "I'm not even like I used to be."

Atlee coughed like he was choking on his tongue. "I can assure you, Becky, I have no ulterior motive. As I said, I came to check on you. I don't pay attention to rumors and gossip. I've had my share of criticism with all my pranks over the years. I only thought you might need a *freind*." With a sheepish grin, Atlee peeked at her from beneath the brim of his black Sunday hat. He blew out a breath, ruffling the brown hair hanging on his forehead.

"*Freind?*"

"*Jah.*"

"We were never really *freinden* before."

"You were, uh, too busy and didn't seem to, uh, need other *freinden*." Atlee dropped his gaze to the ground, where his foot swirled the faded and dried leaves.

Rebecca burst out laughing at Atlee's discomfiture and then clapped her hand over her mouth to muffle the sound. "*Ach*, Atlee, I suppose you're right. I was too busy adding to my collection of conquests. It's a wonder you or anyone else in your family even speaks to me after the fiasco with Isaac. I truly have grown up a lot since then."

"Isaac made his own choices. It didn't look like you twisted his arm or anything."

"And Malinda? How does she feel about everything?"

"Malinda is doing fine. She's happier than she's ever been."

"*Gut.* She's a nice girl."

"So what do you think, Becky? Can you use a *freind* or do you want me to get lost? I promise I am not planning any jokes or pranks. I've grown up a bit, too."

"I can definitely use a *freind.*"

Atlee stuck out his right hand to shake as if they had just concluded an important business transaction. After a moment's hesitation, Rebecca placed her hand in Atlee's large, rough one and shook it.

"Since you are my *freind*, Atlee, I don't wish for you to be the subject of any gossip by hanging out with me. To spare your reputation, we'd better head back."

"I'm not at all worried about my reputation, but we can head back if you want. Are you feeling better?"

"Much better."

Chapter Ten

"*Kumm* to the work frolic with me." Sylvia bustled around the kitchen packing a basket with the snickerdoodles, fudge brownies, and lemon bars she had baked to take along.

"I don't know if my help would be appreciated or if my presence would be a *gut* thing." Rebecca still sat at the big oak table, nursing a cup of hot tea. A petrified piece of toast that she'd nibbled the corners from sat in front of her.

"Don't be silly. Of course you would be *wilkom*, and your help would be appreciated."

"I can't say that people have been overjoyed to see me so far, but I really can't blame them." Rebecca held the cup to her lips without taking a sip. The heat of the ceramic cup warmed her cold hands.

"You've only been to church since you've been home. This would be a *gut* opportunity for you to mingle a bit."

"That's just it, Mamm. I'm not sure how to mingle. I don't fit in with either the young women or the older women."

"We all fit in everywhere. You'll see."

"I didn't exactly have *freinden* before, you know."

"Rebecca, you were young and in your *rumspringa*."

"It was only a few months ago, though it seems I've lived a whole lifetime since then."

"You will not be judged by anyone. That is not our place."

"I'm sure I probably made a lot of girls mad at me."

"Those girls have moved on with their lives, too. They will have forgiven you as is our way. We all did silly things when we were young."

"Not you, Mamm!" Rebecca gasped in mock horror.

"I'm sure I did. I'm sure my *mamm* sighed in relief when I grew up and joined the church."

"I know I caused you and Daed a lot of concern and heartache. It's a wonder your hair isn't completely gray. I am so sorry, and I'm so glad you believed me and accepted me back. I will join the church, Mamm. Now I know that is what I want."

"I believe you, dear one. Now, get ready for the frolic. You can put aside your own cares while helping someone else. No one will criticize you, and you might just have fun."

Rebecca shrugged her shoulders, but set her cup down and pushed back from the table. Fun was something she wasn't sure about, but she could help Lena out with something. The poor girl had looked pretty worn out at church on Sunday. She was maybe five years older than Rebecca's nineteen years, but she looked much older. Apparently this new pregnancy on top of caring for two other little ones was taking a toll on Lena's strength, and possibly her health. The diagnosis of her husband's cancer and his untimely death surely added additional stress. Her two little girls were as cute as could be but had been quite rambunctious on Sunday. Since Lena's family had moved to Indiana several years ago, she probably felt pretty alone, and about at wits' end, despite the community's support.

"I'll go with you, Mamm. Lena looks like she could use all the help she can get."

Rebecca slapped a hand to her head to hold her bonnet on as the wind threatened to snatch it off as soon as she stepped out of the gray buggy. A few other buggies already lined the Troyers' driveway. Rebecca reached inside for the basket of baked treats at the same time Sylvia reached for them. "I'll take them, Mamm. It will give me something to do with my hands besides pick my nails."

"Don't be nervous, Becky. You've known these folks all your life."

"*Jah*, but things are different now. I've been fodder for gossip for months, I'm sure. I know people elbowed each other and whispered about me before, but now it's worse. I'm the prodigal."

"You just hold your head up and smile."

"I'll try, Mamm, but I feel so guilty causing you so much shame."

Sylvia grabbed her *dochder*'s arm. "I love you. It took a lot of courage for you to return home. I am not ashamed of you."

"What about when people find out about . . ." Rebecca glanced down at her midsection.

"*Bopplin* are always a blessing. Everyone will rejoice with us."

Outwardly, maybe. Rebecca could imagine the twitterings and whisperings that would occur once her news sizzled along the grapevine. "I hope so, Mamm."

"Let's get inside. This air has a definite bite today."

Rebecca crept into the kitchen to leave her basket. To her dismay, she practically plowed into Malinda Stauffer on her way out. "*Ach*, Malinda! I'm sorry." She reached out a hand but yanked it back for fear Malinda wouldn't want Rebecca to touch her.

"It's okay. I'm glad you came, Becky."

"*Danki*." Malinda seemed sincere, but did she mean the words she spoke? Rebecca sighed softly. She may as well begin to make amends now. "C-could I talk to you?"

"Sure. Just let me set this casserole dish on the table. I'll be right back."

Rebecca tiptoed to a far corner, hopefully out of earshot of other arrivals, and waited for Malinda to return. She tried out several conversations in her head, but all her pretty speeches evaporated at Malinda's approach. Instead, she blurted out unrehearsed words. "I'm so sorry, Malinda, for the trouble I caused between you and Isaac. I hope you can forgive me."

"*Ach*, Becky, there's nothing to forgive." Malinda reached out to squeeze Rebecca's upper arm. "I'll admit I was upset at first when Isaac turned away from me, but everything worked out for the best. We weren't right for each other anyway. So if you want to see him, it won't bother me at all."

"*Nee. Nee.* I-I don't plan to see him—or anyone. It was just ridiculous flirting on my part. I didn't mean to hurt anyone."

"I believe we're all fine and have moved on."

"Are you happy now, Malinda? You seem to have a special glow. Is that due to a special person?"

"I am happy. And there could very well be someone special." Malinda's wide smile gave away feelings the Amish usually kept hidden until an upcoming wedding was announced in church.

"I'm glad. I hope Isaac doesn't bear any grudges, either."

"I don't believe he does. I think he is still trying to figure out what he wants to do. He still works at the dairy with Atlee, but I don't think his heart is in that."

A mysterious little tingle zipped up Rebecca's

spine at the mention of Atlee's name. It must be because he'd been so nice to her after church.

"I really am glad you're back, Becky. I guess I'd better get busy."

"*Jah*. I'll check to see what Lena wants me to do."

Rebecca found Lena Troyer in the living room already looking a little haggard for first thing in the morning. Two tiny girls peeped out from behind her, one on each side. "Hi, Lena." Rebecca infused her words with all the cheerfulness she could muster.

"Hi, Becky. I heard you were back but didn't get to see you on Sunday."

"*Jah*, I saw you Sunday, but you were busy with two beautiful little girls."

Lena chuckled. "You wouldn't believe they are the same two *kinner*, would you? Sunday I had to chase after them everywhere. Today I can't get them to detach themselves from me."

Rebecca laughed. "I'm sure this is strange for them to have so many women descend on their home. Several crews of women are already getting busy. Is there something in particular you'd like me to do, or should I just join one of the groups?"

"Well, I was going to go through baby things and get them all ready since I can't really crawl around and scrub. But these two have suddenly turned shy on me. Would you like to help me?"

"Sure. That would be fine." Rebecca didn't add that helping Lena might just get her away from the strong cleaning smells that were making her sensitive stomach churn. "Maybe we can get the girls to help. Can you big girls help us?" Rebecca reached down to tickle each little girl beneath the chin, eliciting giggles from both. She'd never considered whether she had any talents or skills with *kinner*, but she guessed she'd better be finding out pretty quickly. "How old are the girls now?"

"Mary is four and Eliza is two."

"My! You *are* big girls! I'm sure you can help." Both girls stepped out from behind their *mamm*, grins breaking out on their faces. To Rebecca's amazement, they each took one of the hands she stretched out toward them. Lena's weary sigh of relief was almost palpable. Maybe Rebecca could persuade the obviously exhausted young *mamm* to take a nap later. Lena was so thin, except for her protruding belly. She made Rebecca think of a big, round snowman with stick arms. She must surely be due to have the *boppli* soon.

Rebecca dusted, swept, and wiped down walls in the bedroom while Lena pulled out baby items. She found little chores for the girls to do until they finally could be persuaded to play with some of the older *kinner* who had tagged along with their *mamms*. Even then, the girls would periodically run back into the room to assure themselves their *mamm* was indeed still there.

The two young women had gotten into a rhythm of cleaning, sorting, and rearranging things. They chatted as they worked. Despite the age difference, a comradery developed between them, as if they were members of some secret sisterhood.

With a grunt, Lena dropped to sit on the edge of the bed and gasped for breath. "Whew! I feel like I've been working hard, but everyone else is actually doing all the heavy jobs."

"Why don't you rest a bit, Lena? The *boppli* must be due soon, ain't so?"

"Two weeks, the midwife said, but I have a sneaky feeling it may be sooner. Eliza was a week early. What about you?"

"Huh?"

"Your little one. When is your *boppli* due?"

"What are you talking about?" Unwittingly, Rebecca's eyes shot to her midsection. She couldn't detect any telltale bulge. Had one of her parents already told someone about her? She couldn't fathom that.

Lena laughed and squeezed Rebecca's hand. "*Nee*, Becky. You don't look in the family way. Not there anyway." Lena nodded toward Rebecca's belly.

"Then what are you talking about? How could you possibly . . . ?"

"Your eyes."

"My eyes?" *I have pregnant eyes?* Self-consciously, Rebecca blinked and lowered her gaze. What in the world did her eyes tell Lena?

"Your eyes have a slightly bluish tint beneath them. I've always been able to tell a woman was expecting by that hint of color, since I've always had that sign early on, too."

Rebecca wished she had a mirror. She reached up a hand to rub across her eyes. "So a strange little color—which could be there because I just made a long trip home and am still tired—makes you think I'm expecting?"

"Am I wrong?"

Rebecca couldn't raise her eyes to meet Lena's. Nor could she out-and-out lie. She must truly have turned over a new leaf. The old Rebecca would have laughed and invented some sort of story.

Lena's bony finger raised Rebecca's chin. "Am I wrong?" This time her question was the merest whisper.

Rebecca's vision clouded as she raised her gaze to stare into Lena's big brown eyes, eyes that were almost too large for her small oval face. "*Nee*, you aren't wrong. I am tired, but there is more to it than fatigue." Silent tears overflowed their banks and cascaded down Rebecca's cheeks. Suddenly she felt arms wrapped around her, arms much stronger than they appeared.

"It's okay, Becky. I won't say anything to

anyone. I'm a *gut* secret keeper." She patted Rebecca's back and then rubbed her hands in soothing circles as she gently rocked the younger woman in her arms. "Do you want to talk? I'm a *gut* listener, too."

Rebecca shook her head but then found herself pouring out her story as if her tongue had a mind of its own.

"Oh my, Becky. You've had a horrible time. I am so sorry you had to endure such hardship."

"I should never have run off."

"We've all done things we wished we'd never done. Don't think you're the only one."

"No one will believe me, Lena. They'll all think I'm . . ."

"I believed you."

"I'm amazed you did."

"Why? Becky, you were never a bad person. From what I saw, you liked to flirt and step out with different fellows, but that isn't evil. You're young. Young folks are supposed to have fun and get to know each other before they decide who they will marry."

"Maybe, but I sort of stole other girls' fellows sometimes."

"If the fellow's head could so easily be turned, he must not have been very committed to the girl he'd been seeing. Look at it this way, Becky. You might have saved some couples from making serious mistakes. It was better for them to know they weren't right for each other before marriage, ain't so? You're a lifesaver!"

Rebecca burst out laughing. "You do have a way about you, Lena."

"When do you expect your little one to arrive?"

"I'm not sure. I think in about five months."

"I guess you haven't seen the midwife yet, since you haven't been home long. Or are you planning to go to a doctor?"

"I hadn't really thought that far, but I'd rather see the midwife. I did see a doctor at a clinic right before I left New York because I've been so sick. I thought I had the flu or something. She told me I was expecting. *Ach*, Lena, what am I going to do?"

"You're going to have this *boppli*—a healthy *boppli*—and be just fine."

"I feel like an outcast."

"Has anyone treated you that way?"

"Not really. Not yet anyway. I've seen some folks whispering behind their hands, and a few conversations have abruptly ended when I walked into a room. But they don't know about the *boppli*. People might not want to be around me once they know. They won't want their children around me. Girls my age will probably be advised to stay away from me so they won't end up like me. Honest, Lena, I really believed we were married. I even showed the marriage certificate to the bishop."

"Does anyone else know other than the bishop?"

"My parents, the bishop and his wife, and you."

"Your secret is safe with me, Becky."

Rebecca sniffed and blinked back more pesky tears. "Mamm always says everything works out for *gut*. I'm not sure I see how in my case."

"You have to have faith. I believe you will have a beautiful infant and you'll get married to have your happily ever after, as the *Englisch* stories say."

"I'm not counting on getting married. I can't believe any of the *buwe* around here would be interested in me now. If I can make a *gut* life for my little one, that will be *gut* enough for me."

"*Nee*, that is not *gut* enough. You need a husband, and your *boppli* needs a *daed*."

"I know that's how it's supposed to be, but . . ."

"You may be surprised, Rebecca Zook. Someone you might never even have thought of could be just the man for you."

"Don't hold your breath, Lena."

"Help me up from this bed, and I'll drag out more stuff to sort through."

Rebecca grabbed Lena's hand and tugged until Lena stood. "Does the fatigue and sickness ever go away?"

"Usually. I always felt better in the middle of each pregnancy. I'm tired now because this giant pumpkin doesn't let me roll over to sleep at night." Lena patted her protruding abdomen.

"Are you sure you aren't having twins?"

"Not that I know of. There's supposed to be only one volleyball player rolling around in there. Quick, give me your hand!" Lena placed Rebecca's hand on her round belly. "Did you feel that?"

Rebecca's hand jerked at the movement beneath it. "He kicks you that hard? That must feel awfully strange."

"Strange, but *wunderbaar*. You'll be feeling it before too long."

Rebecca pressed a hand to her practically flat stomach. A feeling of awe at the miracle growing inside of her overcame her so powerfully she feared she would begin weeping uncontrollably. She knew her eyes must have widened to rival the size of the round throw rug on the polished wood floor. Lena's thin arms caught her in a tight embrace. "It truly is a miracle," she whispered into Lena's shoulder.

Chapter Eleven

Rebecca visited Lena daily to help out with chores or to entertain the little girls, giving Lena a chance to rest, even if for only a few minutes. She planned to continue helping Lena after her little one arrived. To Rebecca's surprise, she discovered strong maternal instincts she'd never have guessed she possessed. Lena patiently answered her hundreds of questions about pregnancy and infant care. Rebecca even took Lena's advice and visited the midwife's office in the next small town, only a few miles away.

She'd been hesitant and even a little fearful to visit the midwife. She had expected a crowded, noisy office like the clinic in New York and a work-weary health-care provider trying to keep up with an overwhelming caseload of patients. She'd been pleasantly surprised from the moment she first stepped inside the front door of the converted two-story house.

The waiting room was clean, neat, and quiet. Magazines and brochures filled a standing rack in the corner. Comfortable, cushioned chairs, rather than hard plastic ones, were clumped in several groups around the room. A small play area in the corner boasted a tiny table with four chairs tucked under it for little ones who accompanied their *mamms* to appointments. A basket of puzzles and books sat next to the table.

The receptionist smiled and greeted Rebecca warmly before handing her a clipboard full of forms to be completed. Rebecca perched on the edge of a soft chair to circle or scribble an answer to each question. She had to leave a few blank since she didn't understand what they were asking. An equally pleasant nurse called her to the exam area to check her weight and blood pressure. The gown she handed Rebecca turned out to be much more modest than the flimsy one she'd had to wear at the clinic.

Midwife Laurie Allen looked very young with her face free of makeup and her pale blond hair pulled into a high ponytail. Despite her youthful appearance, she turned out to be very knowledgeable and professional, yet warm and considerate. After a thorough history and examination, she guided Rebecca on a tour of the birthing center in the back part of the house. She handed Rebecca an assortment of pamphlets and brochures to read at her leisure.

Rebecca scheduled a follow-up appointment in four weeks and headed out to her waiting horse and buggy. She'd been thinking how different this experience had been compared to her previous appointment and how homey the birthing center looked when the clip-clop of a horse's hooves pulled her out of her reverie. She had hoped to make this visit without being seen by anyone in the community. She quickly lowered her head, but not before the eyes in the approaching buggy connected with her own.

Fannie Glick. Of all people, it had to be Fannie Glick who witnessed her departure from the midwife's office. The news Rebecca wasn't quite ready to share would now spread like a fire in a dry hayfield on a windy day.

Atlee had found Isaac already eating when he took his noon break at the dairy. He slid onto a chair at the scarred oak table that must have been in someone's shed for a hundred years before finally finding a home in the dairy and opened his lunch box. His mouth watered as he unwrapped one of his thick ham sandwiches.

"It's not my *boppli*!" Isaac burst out, breaking the silence in the room.

Atlee's bite of sandwich lodged in his throat. He coughed and swigged from his water bottle to get the mass moving again. He and Isaac had been busily chomping their lunches in companionable silence until Isaac's outburst nearly caused him to choke to death. "What in the world are you talking about?"

"Rebecca Zook's *boppli*. It isn't mine."

Atlee was glad he hadn't taken another bite of his sandwich. Had Isaac had some crazy dream last night that he was confusing with reality? "Rebecca Zook does not have a *boppli*."

"Not yet."

"You aren't making any sense, Isaac." Atlee dropped his sandwich onto the napkin he'd spread out on the table to give Isaac his full attention.

"Fannie Glick told my *mamm* she saw Rebecca leaving the midwife's office the other day."

"Fannie is a gossip. You know that."

"True, but she doesn't lie."

"I'm sure women go to see the midwife for other, uh, issues. She is a *nurse*-midwife."

"Becky's young and healthy. She wouldn't see the midwife for any other reason. That's what my *mamm* said, anyway."

"We don't know about anyone else's health issues."

"Well, you can ignore the obvious all you want, but for the record, I'm saying the *boppli* isn't mine." Isaac's face turned the color of pickled beets. He brought his fist down on the table so hard Atlee's sandwich danced half off the napkin.

"Calm down, Isaac. There isn't any way anybody could accuse you of anything. Becky was gone for months, so if Becky is in the family way—and that's a big 'if'—you couldn't be blamed, unless you followed her to New York, which we all know you didn't."

Isaac blew out a big sigh and relaxed the shoulders he'd drawn up to his ears. "I guess you're right."

"Of course I am. You're worrying for nothing."

"*Jah.*" Isaac balled up his trash and scooted his chair back with a screech that grated on Atlee's nerves. "My break time is up. See you later."

Atlee nodded. He picked up his sandwich, bit off a small chunk, and chewed absently. Suddenly it didn't taste as *gut.* He dropped it back onto the table and washed the bite down with another gulp of water. Was Fannie Glick spreading unfounded tales, or could Becky have been visiting the midwife for the normal reason women visited the midwife? What had happened to Becky Zook during the months she was away from Maryland?

It was probably none of his business, but he did recently tell Becky he wanted to be her *freind.* He wondered if Malinda or Mamm had heard anything, but how would he tactfully broach that subject? He picked up his sandwich again, looked at it as though it was some foreign object that had dropped from the sky, and stuffed it back into his lunch box. Maybe he'd feel like eating later.

Atlee stayed busy all afternoon, but his mind continually wandered to his conversation with Isaac. Never once did he have the urge to retrieve the sandwich, or even the oatmeal raisin cookies, from his lunch box. Maybe he was coming down with the flu or something. He could always eat, and even if his stomach was full he could never turn down a cookie. He didn't feel feverish or achy or queasy, though, so his lack of appetite remained a mystery to him.

Dusk had spread a gray blanket across the sky by the time Atlee left work. Nightfall put in an early appearance during the winter months. When the horse automatically turned onto the Stauffers' driveway, Atlee whispered a prayer of thanks for such a smart, reliable animal. His safe arrival home had been entirely due to the Lord and his trusty horse, since he hadn't a clue how he'd gotten here. He shook his head to clear the cobwebs from his mind. He couldn't enter the house in such a distracted state. Mamm and Malinda would pick up on it immediately. They both had a knack for reading him like a book.

By the time Atlee had helped his *daed* and *bruders* finish the outside chores, the scarlet streaks of sunset were fading from the sky. Atlee shivered. It sure would feel *gut* to get inside the warm kitchen, but he forced himself to walk beside his *daed* and watched as the younger *buwe* raced each other to the house. He hoped the smells of whatever Mamm had cooked would spark his appetite.

After the silent prayer, Mamm passed a platter of fried ham and bowls of mashed potatoes and peas to Daed, who sent the food around the table to everyone else. Atlee selected a medium-sized slice of ham and scooped small portions of vegetables onto his plate. Malinda gazed at him from across the table with raised eyebrows, which Atlee promptly ignored. He picked up his knife and fork to start cutting the ham into bite-sized chunks.

"Are you feeling okay, Atlee?" Although Malinda's voice was soft, all seven pairs of eyes around the table turned to stare at him.

"Sure. Why?" He gave up on the ham and forced himself to take a bite of mashed potatoes.

"Your lunch box still had most of the food inside, even the cookies."

He'd meant to empty the box before he set it on the kitchen counter. Now the thing bore witness to his plight. "I didn't feel like eating at lunchtime."

"You?" Malinda gasped in mock horror.

"Are you sure you're all right?"

Great! Now Mamm was concerned. Why didn't Malinda just take out an ad in the *Budget* so Plain folks all over the place could read about him? "I'm fine, Mamm. You know how it is when you get busy and then can't eat in a rush."

If he stretched it, the comment really wasn't a lie. He'd been busy thinking, and then it had been time to go back to work. Thankfully, Aden interrupted the conversation to talk about happenings in school and got him out of the spotlight.

Atlee made it through the rest of the meal and evening prayers without further questions about his health or appetite. He even managed to enjoy a game with Aden until Mamm sent his little *bruder* upstairs to bed. Before he retired himself, he crept to the kitchen for a little snack. His stomach had been reminding him it had missed a meal earlier in the day. A cookie or two or three should tide him over until breakfast. He slipped into the kitchen and silently lifted the lid from the cookie jar.

"Aha! I caught you!" Malinda's hand clamped down on Atlee's wrist, leaving his fingers to dangle inside the jar.

"Guilty."

"I guess if you're sneaking cookies, you really are okay, ain't so?"

"I told you I was fine. Now can I get a few cookies?"

"I suppose I'll let you."

Malinda pulled her hand away so Atlee's fingers could reach farther inside the jar to grasp the cookies near the bottom. "It feels almost empty." He tilted the jar over to peer inside. "*Jah.*"

"Have no fear. I'll bake more cookies tomorrow."

"Whew! That's a relief." Atlee raised a cookie to his mouth and bit off a good-sized chunk that held two fat, juicy raisins. "Mmmm! These are scrumptious."

"I'm making chocolate chip tomorrow."

"Yum."

Malinda replaced the lid on the cookie jar.

"You weren't planning to eat all the rest of these tonight, were you?"

"*Nee*, these three will be fine." Malinda turned to leave the kitchen, but Atlee couldn't let her escape without asking the question that for some unexplainable reason festered in his brain. "Hey, Malinda." He munched to give himself time to figure out what to say.

"*Jah*?"

"Have you talked to Becky since she's been back?" There. He'd begun. He bit into another cookie for fortification.

"Only for a few minutes at Lena's frolic. Why do you ask?"

"Just curious. She seemed, I don't know, lonely or subdued at church."

"Well, you would know about that, not me."

"What does that mean?"

"You were walking with her."

"We weren't exactly walking together—if you know what I mean. I happened to see her walking alone. She looked like she needed a *freind*."

"She may need a lot more than a *freind*." Malinda again prepared to leave the room.

"What do you mean by that?"

Malinda scooted closer and lowered her voice. "Fannie Glick has been telling people she saw Becky leaving the midwife's office."

"Do you think that's true?" Atlee didn't want to reveal he'd heard the same thing.

"I don't imagine Fannie made it up, even though she does like to pass on every tiny piece of news she can find."

"Do you think Becky is, uh . . . ?"

"I don't know, Atlee. I guess we'll have to wait and see." Malinda grabbed her *bruder*'s arm so hard he yelped. "You aren't thinking of taking up with Becky, are you?"

"Me?"

"You seem rather concerned about her. You do remember what she's like, *jah*?"

"*Was* like. Don't you believe people can change?"

"I guess so."

"I've changed. I don't pull pranks anymore."

"I think that's called growing up."

"From just talking to Becky for a few minutes, I think she's grown up, too."

"I hope so. Just be careful, Atlee. You managed to keep from falling into her trap before. Don't let your sympathy and your kind heart lead you down that road."

"I think I can tell genuine from fake. I really think Becky is sorry for the past."

"She did apologize to me at Lena's frolic."

"Did you forgive her?"

"Of course I did."

"Then maybe you and everyone else should give her a chance."

"I'll try, Atlee. She probably could use a *freind*, like you said. She must feel like everyone is watching her and judging her, even though we aren't supposed to judge. Life must be pretty difficult for her right now."

"That's what I was thinking."

Malinda gave her *bruder* a quick hug. "You're a *gut* person, Atlee. I'm glad you're my *bruder*. Just be careful."

Chapter Twelve

Rebecca held the horse to a more leisurely pace even though it was cold and he probably would have preferred to trot briskly to generate more heat. She was in no hurry to reach the dairy. She had offered to finish the baking so her *mamm* could make the trip. She would have rather crawled around on her knees scrubbing floors with her fingernails. But Mamm had her hands in bread dough up to her elbows and a dusting of flour across her forehead where she had swiped at a stray wisp of hair. She didn't want to abandon her chore. Rebecca had even offered to cook something else for dinner, something that didn't require cheese, but Mamm had already started preparing the cheesy potato casserole before she realized she was low on a main ingredient.

Rebecca let out an exaggerated sigh. She'd rather take a beating than walk into the dairy where Isaac Hostetler worked. She hadn't spoken to him since she had returned to Maryland, and she wasn't too keen on having a conversation with him today, either. She had too many other thoughts claiming her attention.

Laurie Allen had confirmed the New York doctor's diagnosis. Rebecca would most likely give birth in late July or early August. She had already accepted the pregnancy. The nausea had given her no choice. She even loved the tiny being growing inside her this very second. It was just the circumstances that troubled her. She would much rather be sharing this experience with a husband. She'd probably never have that chance now, though. How many young men would want a package deal? She wasn't sure she could ever trust another man anyway.

The dairy came into view quicker than she had thought possible. Rebecca sighed again, long and loud. She might as well get this over with, too, and put it behind her. She could always hope Isaac wasn't working today.

Rebecca retied her black bonnet a little tighter so she wouldn't have to chase it down if the wind whipped it off her head. She closed her eyes to offer a quick prayer. She sure seemed to be praying a lot more these days. Maybe that was one *gut* thing about her horrible experiences in New York. They brought her back to her faith and drew her closer to the Lord Gott. They also made her grow up and accept responsibility. Right now she had to be a grown-up and stroll into the dairy as if everything was normal—whatever "normal" was.

She hopped from the buggy and quickly tethered the horse. She could have driven a few more miles to the grocery store to buy cheese, but Mamm would wonder why. She had a strange feeling that Mamm had sent her on this mission more to confront her past than to pick up cheese. Going to the grocery store would only postpone the inevitable. She had to face Isaac sometime. That time might as well be now. "Be right back." She patted the sleek brown horse's head.

Rebecca hurried to the entrance and took one more deep breath before opening the door. At least there were other customers, Amish and *Englisch*, so she shouldn't be too conspicuous. She'd simply march over to the counter, select Mamm's cheese, pay the cashier, and slip right back out to the buggy. It sounded like a *gut* plan.

My plans never work out as I expect. Rebecca's eyes connected with Isaac's as soon as she closed the door behind her. Now that he had spied her, she would have to talk to him, unless he scurried off to avoid her. She wouldn't blame him if he did just that.

Rebecca skirted the *Englisch* woman with her three children and threaded her way through the other customers to reach Isaac just as he turned to leave the area. "Isaac?"

"Hello, Becky."

"H-how are you doing?"

"I'm fine. You?"

She had to force her way beyond this exchange of pleasantries. "I-I'm sorry, Isaac. I was a confused, foolish girl. And selfish, too. I should never have interfered with your plans, your life.

I'm sorry I came between you and Malinda."

Isaac blew out a breath like he'd been holding it forever. "I was mad at you at first, Becky. I'll admit that. I thought you cared about me, but then I realized you only wanted a partner to run off with you."

Rebecca hung her head and watched the toe of her black athletic shoe trace a circular pattern on the cement floor. "I thought maybe you were as adventurous as I was, as eager to see someplace besides St. Mary's County. It was wrong of me to use you. You did the right thing. You stayed and joined the church. I wish I had done that, too."

"You still can."

"I plan to. As soon as possible. I guess you and Malinda . . ."

"Malinda has moved on, and she seems happy. We weren't really that serious about each other." Isaac's eyes roamed the store.

"You'll find someone, the right someone, Isaac. I hope you can forgive me."

Isaac looked back down into Rebecca's eyes. "*Jah*, I forgive you. I hope everything works out for you, Becky."

"*Danki*, Isaac. You, too." Rebecca wandered to the cheese counter. What did Isaac mean about everything working out? Did he mean reuniting with her family and the church, or was he hinting at something else? Most likely Fannie Glick had set the grapevine quivering with news of

Rebecca's visit to the midwife. She knew in her heart Fannie was not mean-spirited. The girl just couldn't keep a single thing to herself. Telling Fannie something was like announcing it to the world. Rebecca would pay for her cheese and rush back to the safety of her home.

Atlee straightened up after stacking more empty crates outside and turned around in time to see a young woman hurrying toward her buggy. Becky. Even though all the Amish girls wore a black cloak and bonnet this time of year, he knew that girl was Rebecca Zook. Before his brain could instruct his feet otherwise, he jogged over to the girl untying the big brown horse. "Becky?"

She jumped and gave a startled cry. Her fingers slid from the hitching post.

"I'm sorry I startled you." Atlee finished untying the horse for her.

"I guess my mind was somewhere else."

"How are you doing?"

"I'm fine, Atlee. *Danki* for asking. Mamm sent me for cheese." Rebecca held out her package as though she needed to show proof her visit to the dairy was legitimate. "I tried to talk her into fixing something else, but she wouldn't hear of it."

Atlee chuckled. "My *mamm* is the same way. If she's determined to do something or cook some-thing, there's no changing her mind. One time she wanted to bake a blueberry cobbler but thought she needed more blueberries. Instead of making muffins or something else, she sent me and Sam out to comb the countryside for more berries. It took us longer to find enough berries than it took her to make the cobbler."

Rebecca laughed. "I bet you enjoyed eating it, though."

"I sure did. I think it tasted extra *gut* since we had to work so hard to find enough berries. In fact, blueberry has been my favorite cobbler and pie ever since."

"I'd better get this cheese home before Mamm thinks I ran off again." Rebecca hung her head.

"I think your *mamm* knows you wouldn't do that, ain't so?"

"I hope she does. I just feel like I have to earn everyone's trust. I let my folks down and worried people with my disappearance. Now I have to prove I've changed."

"You don't have to prove anything, Becky. Just be yourself. You are fine just the way you are."

"*Danki*, Atlee. I'm glad to have you for a *freind*." Rebecca turned to climb into the buggy.

Atlee took her arm and helped her up like she hadn't been getting into and out of buggies all her life. "Uh, would you want to take a walk after church if it's not too cold?" He didn't understand why he asked that or why he was reluctant to let her leave, but something had changed—

either with him or with her or with both of them.

"I-I—uh, sure, Atlee. That would be fine."

Again he didn't know why, but those few words made his day.

Chapter Thirteen

Strands of Lena's dark brown hair escaped her bun and flew around her face as she clapped her hands in exasperation. Her face looked more drawn and even thinner than before.

"Did I come at a bad time?"

"*Ach*, Becky! I didn't hear you over the din in here. These girls are wild today."

"Could you use some help?"

"I sure could, and the sight of a *freind*'s face is most *wilkom*." Lena pushed at her wayward hair and gasped for breath as if she'd overexerted herself merely by speaking. Her two little girls ran shrieking into the room, the older one chasing the younger one until they crashed into their *mamm*.

"Whoa!" Rebecca cried. She grasped Lena, who had wobbled off balance, and held her upright. "Girls!" She lowered her voice to barely above whisper level so the girls had to stop shrieking to hear her. "If you can pick up all those toys"— Rebecca pointed to the assortment of blocks and small toys scattered around the room—"I'll read you a story, and maybe we'll have a little snack. I brought muffins."

The four-year-old flew to gather up toys. Her little *schweschder* toddled along behind her.

"*Danki*. I've been too lenient with them since Joseph passed. I know that. Now I'm struggling to get them back in hand."

"That's understandable." Rebecca gave Lena a quick hug and could practically feel her ribs. She prayed all was well with the new *boppli*, since his or her mamm looked so frail. "I'm sure it was very hard to lose your husband, especially with you expecting again. I wish I had been here to help you then. But I'm here now." Would the old Rebecca have helped a young widow, or would she have merrily gone about her *rumspringa*? She wanted to believe she would have helped. "You didn't sleep well last night, did you?"

Lena laughed. "I must look pretty bad."

"You look tired. Why don't you take a little nap? I'll see to the girls."

"It's ten o'clock in the morning!"

"That's okay."

"I still haven't finished cleaning the kitchen after breakfast, and that was hours ago." Tears filled Lena's eyes, and she sniffed hard.

"Who cares? I can handle that. You go lie down and rest." When Lena didn't budge, Rebecca gave her a gentle push. "Go on now. We'll be fine." At that, Lena relented and shuffled toward the stairs. Rebecca hoped she didn't regret the words of assurance she'd just uttered.

Maybe she should have only offered to do housework instead of tackling the care of two active little ones. She knew next to nothing about taking care of *kinner*, since she had no younger siblings. But if she hadn't exuded an air of confidence, she would never have gotten Lena to leave the room and get some much-needed rest.

"Okay, girls." Rebecca turned and smiled at Mary and Eliza. "You did a fine job. I'll read you one story while you eat your muffins. Then I need your help. Do you think you're big enough to help me?"

Two little heads bobbed before the girls followed Rebecca to the kitchen like ducklings behind a mother duck.

Rebecca had to draw on every resource she could conjure up, but she managed to keep the girls entertained and get the kitchen cleaned, the floors swept, and the noon meal put together. Never before had she taken on such responsibility. Without letting pride overtake her, she felt reasonably satisfied with the results of her efforts.

When Lena, looking somewhat rested and definitely neater, rushed breathless into the kitchen, she stopped in her tracks. "Becky, however did you manage this?"

Rebecca smiled and shrugged. Eliza sat in her high chair happily playing with the pieces of crackers on the tray. Occasionally she popped a bite into her mouth. Mary carefully placed paper napkins at four places on the dark walnut table.

Both girls' dresses were clean and neat. Their hair had been smoothed and braided. No sticky mustaches sat atop their mouths. And they were actually happy and quiet. "I'm not sure how we managed, to tell you the truth, Lena. This was a whole new experience for me."

"Well, you must have some innate talent you've kept hidden."

"It's been hidden from me, too. I've done housework, of course, and some cooking, but I've never had to combine all the tasks with caring for *kinner* at the same time."

"Everything looks *wunderbaar*. And the girls are so, um, subdued."

"They are sweet little girls, Lena. You are blessed."

"I surely am. I know I get overwhelmed sometimes and forget to count my blessings."

"We all do."

"You will make a *gut mudder*, Becky."

"I hope so. I need to learn so much."

"You're a natural."

"Who would ever have thought that? Or that I could even clean a house?" Rebecca laughed. "I never paid a lot of attention to all Mamm tried to teach me."

"It must have sunk in without your being aware of it. Something smells *gut*. Did you cook? I never had time to even think about the noon meal."

"I found vegetables, curly noodles, and canned tomatoes, so I threw together a big pot of vegetable soup. I'm glad my nausea has gotten a bit better. Before even smells sent me running."

"I did that with Mary, but not so much with Eliza or this one." Lena patted her protruding belly. Suddenly a little frown wrinkled her brow.

"Are you all right?"

"Just a twinge. I can't believe I slept like a rock for two hours. I must have been lying crooked, though. I have a little pain in my back."

"Are you sure that's all it is? Because I don't know how to deliver a *boppli*."

Lena laughed. "I don't think you'll have to do that today. I've never had back labor before."

"Why don't you sit down? Mary and I will serve you, right, Mary?"

Mary nodded and smiled, obviously pleased to be helping and to be treated like a big girl.

Rebecca had filled cups only half full of water so Mary could carry them to the table without sloshing liquid everywhere. "*Danki*, Mary," Rebecca said when she handed Mary the last cup. The little girl beamed. "You can carry the biscuits to the table and then go ahead and sit down. I'll bring the soup." Rebecca had only put four biscuits on the plate so Mary could carry it easily. "Mary and Eliza helped me make biscuits," she told Lena as she set the last bowl of soup on the table and wiggled into a chair.

"Really? My girls are growing up! The biscuits look yummy."

After the silent prayer, Mary chattered about making biscuits. Eliza chimed in with excited jabbering as if she understood the entire conversation.

"How did you keep from having a cloud of flour settle over the kitchen?" Lena spread last year's strawberry jam on a biscuit and broke off a piece for Eliza.

"Well, we weren't totally neat, but we worked at the table. They did a pretty *gut* job of keeping their dough on the wax paper. Mary helped me clean up afterward."

"The biscuit is delicious." Lena looked at first one girl and then the other. "I think you will both be fine cooks."

Mary giggled. "Eliza's a baby. She can't cook."

"She helped, though, and that's important." Eliza had mainly played with the dough, but Rebecca wouldn't mention that.

The soup turned out much tastier than Rebecca had dared hope. Maybe she would turn out to be a fine cook, too. Wouldn't her *mamm* have been surprised if she had been a fly on Lena's kitchen wall today?

"It's time for such hardworking helpers to take a rest," Rebecca announced after the meal and cleanup. Mary wanted to help with the dishes, so Rebecca let her stand on a stool and dry the silverware. She even put it neatly in the drawer. Either she was truly eager to help or she had become an expert at dodging nap time. Rebecca chose to believe the former.

When the dishcloth and towel had been hung on a hook, Rebecca lifted Eliza from the highchair, where she had been struggling to keep her heavy eyes open. "You've worked very hard, girls. Let's go take that rest now."

"Will you still be here when I get up?" Mary tugged on Rebecca's hand when they reached the girls' bedroom. She seemed reluctant to enter without assurance of Rebecca's presence when she awoke.

"I think so. I'll see what else I can do to help your *mamm*, but I'll leave plenty of things for you to help with later. Okay?"

"Okay." Mary crawled onto the bed that had been pushed against the off-white wall.

Rebecca laid an already snoozing Eliza between Mary and the wall and covered both girls with the quilt folded at the foot of the bed.

"I'll see you later," Mary whispered. Her eyes began to droop, too.

"Have a nice rest." Rebecca tiptoed from the girls' room and down the stairs.

In the living room, she found Lena sitting in the rocking chair with a mending basket in her lap. She was staring off into space and rubbing her belly in a circular motion. A frown flitted across her forehead but vanished when Rebecca spoke.

"Are you absolutely positive you're all right?" Rebecca perched on the edge of a chair facing Lena.

"*Jah.* I'm just thinking."

"You were frowning. Either you were having deep, serious thoughts or you're still having pain."

"I only have a twinge or two now and then."

"Does it feel like it did when the girls were ready to be born?"

"Not really. I feel achy in my back, not my belly. The baby has been kicking since I sat down. It about kicked the basket off my lap."

"He or she must be *gut* and strong then." Rebecca sat back a little farther on the chair. A hand drifted to her own practically flat belly. She wondered when she would feel her *boppli* kick. Right now she only felt a little bump. "Lena, do you have a plan?" Rebecca finally asked what had been on her mind since she arrived.

"A plan? For what?"

"What if the *boppli* decides to arrive in the middle of the night? You can't send Mary for help, and you certainly can't run for help yourself."

"I've avoided thinking about that. Joseph was here before." Lena's voice drifted off.

Rebecca sat forward again and squeezed the hand Lena had been using to stroke her stomach.

"I know this must be very hard for you. You must feel very alone sometimes."

"I do." Lena's voice came out in a mere whisper.

"You don't have to be alone, Lena."

"I'm not really alone. I have the girls."

"Of course you do. I meant you don't have to face this birth alone and worry what will happen with you or the girls."

Lena turned a questioning look in Rebecca's direction but remained silent.

"I could stay with you until the *boppli* arrives, and after, too, to help out with the girls and house. If you think I'd be more trouble than help, though, I'll understand."

Lena laughed out loud. "Trouble? It would be a godsend. You would really leave your home and stay with me?"

"If you'd like me to. I'd be happy to help. After all, it isn't like I have a husband or *kinner* to care for. I'll be on my own with my little one, too."

"You have your parents."

"I do. And I'm thankful for them. I'm not sure if they've accepted the situation yet, though."

"They'll be fine. Give them time." Lena paused for breath. "It would be absolutely *wunderbaar* to have you here. I don't expect you to do my work, but the moral support would be great."

"You certainly don't think I would stay here and not work! I'll do whatever needs to be done.

You should try to rest up as much as you can before you have three little ones to care for. I can go home, get some things, and be back this evening, unless you think that's too soon to have to deal with me."

"The sooner the better. You are a blessing, Becky Zook."

Rebecca laughed. "I can't recall anyone ever considering me a blessing before. A nuisance, maybe. A troublemaker, maybe. A blessing, never!"

"You are not the same girl."

"Let's be thankful for that!"

Chapter Fourteen

"I think it's a great thing you're doing, staying with Lena and helping her out." Atlee shortened his stride to match Rebecca's. The day was brisk, but the bright sun had sent the mercury higher in the thermometer than it had been for several days. The wind had gentled to a cool breeze. All through the church service Atlee's mind had strayed to walking with Rebecca afterward. It was like Becky was a magnet and he was a nail constantly drawn to her. Malinda would probably say Becky was flypaper and he was the pitiful fly about to become hopelessly trapped.

It was funny that he hadn't been in the least bit attracted to Becky before, when all the other fellows had vied for her attention. Maybe he didn't want to be one of her trophies. Maybe he figured she really didn't care about the different fellows who drove her home from singings. Maybe he was too busy having fun with Sam and his *freinden*.

Something had changed, though. He never really knew Becky before. He doubted anyone, including Becky herself, had really known her. He was beginning to know her now, and the more he learned about her, the more he liked her.

"I'm not doing anything so extraordinary," Rebecca began. "I like Lena and the girls. She's having a hard time right now without Joseph. I know the men take turns helping her with the outside work, and the women often stop by with meals or treats. But she's alone there with two little girls and a *boppli* due any time. I want to help her however I can."

"Well, I think that makes you pretty special, Becky Zook." Atlee reached to squeeze one of her small hands. "You aren't too cold, are you?"

"*Nee.* It feels pretty nice today. I guess today is a little tease before more cold weather."

"*Jah.* We'd better enjoy it while we can."

They walked a bit farther, enjoying the sun shining on their faces. Atlee stole glances down at Becky from time to time. He hadn't realized before how pretty she was with her honey gold hair and big green eyes. She barely reached his shoulder and had a small build. Her size made him feel protective of her, and he found he rather liked that. He cleared his throat. "How is Lena doing?"

"She's been tired. Running after two toddlers has about worn her out, but I suspect the mental stress has played a part in her fatigue as well."

"I'm sure she's glad you're there to help her out. She did look more relaxed today than I've seen her in a while."

"I've been trying to get her to take naps or to at least rest when the girls are napping. I keep telling her she's going to need even more energy when the *boppli* gets here."

"Will you stay with her after the birth?"

"I'll stay as long as she needs me. It will be even harder for her with three little ones."

"What about you? You aren't wearing yourself out, are you?"

"Not at all. It feels *gut* to help someone else." Rebecca looked down at the frozen ground. "You know, I've been a selfish person."

"*Ach*, Becky, don't belittle—"

Rebecca held up a hand to halt his defense of her. "*Nee*, Atlee, it's true. I've only thought about myself and what I wanted. Sure, I helped my *mamm* out around the house, but that was half-hearted, done only because I was supposed to do it. Now I'm doing something because I want to do it. I want to help Lena and her girls. I want to ease her burdens and make those *kinner* laugh. I even want to help my *mamm*. I'm sure she's surprised."

When Becky smiled up into his face, Atlee's heart thumped so hard he almost put a hand to his chest to keep it inside where it belonged instead of flopping out onto the ground like a fish out of water. He smiled back at her. He wanted to take her little hand in his but couldn't decide if he should. He couldn't think clearly at all. Before a logical thought formed, she spoke again.

"It's been a lot of work taking care of the girls and Lena's house, but it's been fun. I fall into bed tired, but it's a happy kind of tired."

Atlee nodded. Then, to his horror, words slipped out before his internal censor could kick in. "Are you sure you aren't doing too much? You don't want to tax yourself too much, ain't so?" If he could have snatched the words back, he surely would have. From the fear that leaped into Becky's eyes, he knew she realized he was referring to her delicate condition—a condition he shouldn't know anything about.

Rebecca's heart lurched. Icy rivers of fear coursed through her veins. Did Atlee know?

Of course, he'd probably heard whatever tale Fannie Glick had passed along. Atlee was intelligent. He'd certainly be able to add clues together and arrive at the correct answer. Soon she wouldn't be able to keep her secret anyway. It would be better to spill her news now and watch Atlee, her *freind* who had been steadily worming his way into her closed heart, abandon her. Better now than later.

She stopped walking, which caused Atlee to halt beside her. She looked up into his green eyes, fringed by dark lashes, and then looked at the sky over his black felt hat. The sky was still blue, and the sun still shone. They would still be there when Atlee fled. The Lord Gott would still be with her. He would never abandon her. She thanked Him for sending Viv to help her make that journey to Him.

Rebecca looked back into Atlee's handsome face and caught her lower lip between her teeth in a moment of hesitation. She released her lip and took in a gulp of crisp air. Best to just plunge right in. "I don't know what you've heard, Atlee, but I'm sure rumors have been flying about me." Atlee opened his mouth to speak, but Rebecca surged on. "I know Fannie Glick doesn't actually have a mean bone in her body, but I also know she can't keep a single thing to herself. She saw me leave Laurie Allen's office. You most likely heard that somewhere along the line."

"Well, *jah*, someone mentioned that."

"Yet you didn't ask me about it?"

"I figured it was your story to tell, if you wanted to tell it. It was none of my business."

Rebecca smiled. "You're a *gut* person, Atlee. Can we sit for a minute? I'd like to tell you the story."

"We can sit, for sure, but you don't have to tell me anything."

"We're *freinden*, ain't so?"

"Of course."

"Then I want to be honest with my *freind*." Rebecca led the way to the trunk of a large pine tree that had fallen some time ago in a storm or strong wind. The needles had long since turned brown and dropped off in clusters around the tree. Rebecca sank down on the trunk near the bottom, where there were no branches. Atlee dropped down beside her, their arms and legs nearly touching.

Rebecca raised her eyes to the sky and silently prayed for strength and the right words to tell her tale. "I visited the midwife because I'm expecting a *boppli*." She paused to search Atlee's face. She saw no horror, no condemnation written there. "Did you hear me, Atlee?" Maybe she'd spoken too softly.

"*Jah*, I heard you."

"And you aren't ready to run as far away from me as possible?"

"Why would I do that? You're my *freind*."

"Let me tell you the rest."

"You don't have to." Atlee fidgeted a bit beside her, his thigh bumping her own.

Rebecca tried to ignore the little shock wave that raced down her leg at Atlee's touch. Even though the touch was as light as a whisper and she wore layers of clothes topped by a heavy cloak, the sensation was keen. "I need to tell you, Atlee. I don't want you to think badly of me. That's important to me."

"I don't . . ."

"Shhh! Let me tell you before I lose my nerve or start crying. You see, Atlee, I actually believed I was married."

Atlee's eyebrows quirked upward. Only a faint "Huh?" escaped his lips.

"I know it sounds pretty preposterous. When I

look back, I can't believe how dumb I was, how naive. I went to the big city and felt like a little minnow thrown into the ocean with sharks. A girl sitting beside me on the bus mentioned a cheap place to stay, so I got a room and started working in a little café."

Rebecca averted her gaze. She couldn't look into Atlee's eyes and tell him about all the mistakes she'd made. She couldn't bear it if she read disbelief or accusation in his expression. Her fingers picked at a loose piece of bark on the tree trunk as she relayed the story of meeting Vinny, the impromptu wedding, the betrayal, the fear for her life, and the flight from New York. "I honestly thought we were married, or I never would have, uh, you know . . ."

"I understand. And I believe you, Becky."

"You do?"

"Why would I doubt you?"

"I was such a flirt before. It would be easy to believe the worst about me. But never would I have done anything inappropriate." Rebecca suddenly yanked her hand away from the tree trunk with a little cry of pain.

"What happened?"

Rebecca held her hand close to her face and searched her index finger. "A splinter."

"Here. Let me see." Atlee tugged at Rebecca's hand and pulled it close to his chest. He probed her finger and gently squeezed it until he could grasp the splinter. Rebecca jerked as he pulled the sliver of wood out. "I'm sorry. I'm sure that hurt." He rubbed her hand between his own.

"It's okay. It's better to get the splinter out. If I'd been wearing my gloves, that probably wouldn't have happened." She also wouldn't have felt the warmth of Atlee's hand holding hers or the tingle of his touch, but she kept those thoughts to herself. She summoned her courage to look Atlee in the eye. "If you no longer want to be seen with me or be my *freind*, I'll understand. In fact, if you want to go back right now, I'll understand. I'll wait a few minutes to return so people won't know we were together."

"Why would I do that?"

"I'm sure everyone has formed some opinion about my predicament. I wouldn't want you to be on the receiving end of any gossip."

"I'm a big *bu*. I can take care of myself. I'm sure people know we went for a walk together again today. That doesn't bother me in the least. I wouldn't be much of a *freind* if I disappeared when you needed support or help, ain't so?"

"I appreciate that, Atlee. I made a big mistake running off like I did. I made a big mistake believing Vinny. But I do love my *boppli* and want to be a *gut mudder*."

"That's what is important, Becky. And I will help you however I can."

"*Danki*. It's okay to tell your family what I've

told you. I'd rather people know the truth than have them concoct all kinds of stories about me. I've told my *mamm* it's okay to tell, too, so I'm sure the grapevine will start quivering. Your support means the world to me."

Chapter Fifteen

"Son, do you think it was wise to be traipsing off alone with Becky Zook?" Saloma asked Sunday evening as she rocked in the old oak rocking chair near the woodstove. Her husband, Rufus, looked up from his perusal of the *Budget*, and Malinda abandoned her crossword puzzle to glance first at her *mamm* and then at her *bruder*. The three younger *buwe* had already headed upstairs for the evening.

Atlee stopped in his tracks. All thoughts of slipping into the kitchen for a handful of cookies fled from his mind. "We weren't exactly alone. I'm sure we were in sight of half the community. Anyone could have called to us or joined us." He changed his direction and reentered the living room to face his family, who all stared at him with mouths agape.

"Are you and Becky . . . ?" Mamm ventured.

"We are *freinden*."

"You steered clear of Becky all the time she batted her eyelashes at first one fellow, then another. Why the sudden interest?" Malinda apparently felt she needed to add her two cents' worth.

"I haven't taken a 'sudden interest' in Becky, as you say. She seemed so lonely and in need of a *freind*."

"I'm sure some of the girls would step up and fill that void. I worry about your getting involved with her." A wrinkle furrowed Saloma's brow.

"What's wrong with Becky? You've always been nice to her, Mamm."

"Of course I would be nice to her. I'm just not sure . . . Have you heard anything about her time away?"

"Are you referring to the story Fannie Glick has been passing along?"

"Do you know about that?"

"Who doesn't? When Fannie knows something, everyone knows something."

Malinda snickered and clapped a hand over her mouth.

"Let's not be unkind," Saloma began.

"I'm not trying to be unkind. I'm being truthful. I know Becky is, uh, in the family way." There. Atlee had confirmed the rumors, but now he had to make them understand.

Malinda and Saloma gasped simultaneously. Rufus's paper rustled to the floor in a heap.

"It's true, then," Malinda whispered. She twirled one of her *kapp* strings around an index finger.

"Maybe your *mamm* is right, Son, about treading lightly as far as that girl is concerned."

"Hold on a minute. I'm not planning on marrying her. I told you we're *freinden*. But you need to know the facts before you judge her."

"We're not judging her, Son." Rufus bent to retrieve his newspaper.

"Do you know the facts?" Malinda asked.

"Actually, I do."

"Can you share that information?" Malinda scooted to the edge of her seat as if eager to hear a story.

"*Jah*, I can. Becky told me the whole story today. I think she needed to gauge the reaction of a *freind* before she told everyone else. She said it was okay to tell you all because she wants people to know the truth rather than invent their own unflattering stories."

"And you truly believe her, or are you a little biased?"

"Malinda! I'm surprised at you. You have always been so sympathetic and forgiving. Are you still bitter because Becky came between you and Isaac?"

Malinda hung her head, but not before Atlee caught her sheepish expression. "Of course I'm not bitter. As it turned out, Becky did me a favor. Isaac was not the right fellow for me." Malinda raised her eyes to meet Atlee's. Her cheeks glowed a fiery red. "I just don't want you to get hurt."

"I appreciate your concern, but I don't think you need to worry. And to answer your earlier question, I truly believe Becky's story." In his peripheral vision, Atlee spied his parents staring openmouthed.

"Okay, Atlee. Please tell me the story. I want to be fair to Becky," Malinda said.

Atlee slowly recited Becky's story, taking care to keep his facts straight. "She even has an authentic-looking marriage certificate she showed to Bishop Menno. He told her he thought it looked real, too." Atlee sucked in a gulp of air at the conclusion of his recitation. Three pairs of eyes stared at him from stunned faces.

"The poor girl must have been devastated to find out the marriage was a lie." Saloma was the first to recover her speech. "She was too trusting, but with *nee* worldly experience, you can't blame her for that."

"And then to find out about the *boppli* on top of the lies, and to fear for her safety, too. *Ach*, poor Becky." Malinda swiped at a tear trickling down her cheek.

"So do you believe her story?" Atlee looked from Rufus to Saloma to Malinda. His parents nodded.

"I do," Malinda said. "Becky may have been a flirt and a bit of a show-off, but I've never known her to lie. Besides, who could make up such horrible things?"

"She really is a different girl now. You'd see that if you gave her a chance."

"There will be some who will doubt her, you know." Rufus folded his newspaper.

"*Jah*, and I think Becky is prepared for that.

145

But the bishop won't tolerate anyone shunning her or criticizing her, ain't so, Daed?"

"We are called upon to show forgiveness, mercy, and love. Any of our young folks could have run off and fallen prey to unsavory people."

"We need to help Becky and her parents get through the difficult times," Saloma added. "Poor Sylvia has lost so much weight worrying about Becky these last months that I feared one of those arctic blasts of air would carry her away."

"Maybe I'll go visit Becky tomorrow," Malinda murmured. "I really am sorry I doubted her. That wasn't fair of me."

"I'm sure she would be glad to see you," Atlee said. "As you know, she's staying with Lena Troyer right now and helping out with Lena's *kinner*."

"That's right. Maybe I'll bake a little treat to take to them, too."

By mid-morning Rebecca had three loads of laundry hanging on the line. A stiff breeze would surely dry the clothes pretty quickly—or freeze them into position on the clothesline. With Lena's help, Rebecca had fed and dressed the girls, cleaned up the kitchen, and swept the floors. Lena seemed to be more tired and out of breath lately.

"Do you think you need to pay a visit to Laurie?" Rebecca briskly rubbed her half-frozen hands together to restore the circulation after hanging wet clothes in the wind.

"I have an appointment later in the week. I'll wait until then." Lena dropped onto one of the kitchen chairs and patted her swollen belly. "This one has sure been making me feel tired and about as big as a barn."

"You didn't feel like this either of the other times?"

"*Nee.* I didn't gain a lot of weight with either of them and was able to keep up with my work just fine. Of course, Joseph was here to do all the hard work. He wouldn't let me overexert myself." A small, sad smile curved the corners of her mouth. Her eyes took on a faraway expression as she apparently gave in to the memories.

"I'm sure this time has been harder." Rebecca squeezed Lena's hand. "You rest as much as you can. I'm perfectly capable of handling the work." She didn't want to worry Lena further by asking if there could be some problem, but she intended to keep a watchful eye on her.

"You don't need to overexert yourself, either. You've got your own *boppli* to think about."

"It's early yet for me. Much of my sickness is gone—not all, I'm sorry to say, but I am feeling more energetic now. Laurie said everything was fine." Rebecca gave her own midsection a little pat. She didn't add that helping Lena and the girls had given her such an emotional lift that she felt better all over.

Lena sighed. "A pie seemed too industrious,

so I was going to bake some cookies. Now even that seems like a chore. I'll rest a minute before dragging out the flour and pans."

"I can make cookies. What kind do you want?" Rebecca crossed the kitchen and opened the cupboard door. She shifted items around to survey the contents of the cabinet. "We can make oatmeal, chocolate chip, or peanut butter cookies."

"You should rest, too. We don't have to have cookies or pie."

"I'm fine. It feels *gut* to stay busy."

"You've certainly been that since you came here. I can't tell you how much I appreciate your help, but I worry about you, too."

"You worry too much, Lena. I am perfectly fine, unless I smell bacon frying or something equally as pungent. Now, what kind of cookies would you like?"

"Lena! It's me, Malinda!"

Rebecca and Lena both turned their heads to see Malinda Stauffer pushing her way through the back door. Her hands held several plastic containers, and a wicker basket swung from one arm.

"Here, let me help you." Rebecca rushed to free Malinda of some of her burdens.

"What is all of that?" Lena began to push herself up from her chair.

"You sit," Rebecca ordered. "I can get this."

"I did some baking this morning and wanted to share with you."

"Some? It looks like you must have been baking all night and used up all your *mamm*'s flour." Lena eased back onto the chair.

"I made three kinds of cookies, an apple pie, and some fudge brownies. I also brought a loaf of Mamm's honey wheat bread and a jar of strawberry jam."

"Malinda, you didn't have to do all of that," Lena protested.

"I feel bad, Lena. I should have helped you out more all this time."

"Many of the women have taken turns dropping by to check on me and the girls. And now Becky is staying with me for a while. Besides, Malinda dear, you've had your own health issues to deal with."

"I haven't had a flare-up of my Crohn's disease in a while now, thank the *gut* Lord."

"But you had a few nasty flare-ups not so very long ago. You need to keep up your strength."

"I feel fine now." Malinda set her basket on the kitchen table.

"I guess I won't need to make cookies today after all, Lena." Rebecca smiled. "Malinda has brought enough to satisfy everybody's sweet tooth for quite a while."

"Becky, would you mind transferring those goodies into my containers and cookie jars so Malinda can have hers to take back home?"

"There's no rush, Lena. We have plenty of containers and jars at home."

"You also have a lot of people in your house. I'm sure you need every spare bowl and basket. Did you leave some treats at home for all your hungry *bruders*?"

Malinda laughed. "Of course. Atlee loves cookies. He made sure I baked plenty."

A little chill rippled up Rebecca's spine again at the mention of Atlee's name. She could imagine him sneaking cookies off the pan as soon as it was pulled from the oven. She would bake him cookies every day just to see him do that. Now, where did that thought *kumm* from? Why would Atlee be watching her bake cookies? *Silly girl!*

"Becky?"

"Huh?"

"You wandered away for a minute. I asked if you'd like a cookie." Malinda held the container full of spicy-smelling gingersnaps out to her.

"Maybe later. *Danki*, Malinda."

"It's *gut* of you to stay here and help Lena," Malinda whispered as she snapped the lid on a plastic bowl.

"I'm glad I could help out. It's been fun, actually."

"You do look a little tired, though, Becky. You don't want to get run-down, either." Malinda kept her voice low so only Becky could hear her.

"Atlee told you?" Rebecca quickly dropped her eyes to the floor she'd recently cleaned. She couldn't bear to see the condemnation on

Malinda's face. Although she and Malinda had never been close, she didn't want Atlee's *schweschder* to think ill of her.

"*Jah.* H-he said it was all right for him to tell."

"That's true. I told him he could tell people. It's not like it's something I can hide forever, and I'd rather everyone know the truth." Rebecca dared to raise her eyes to meet Malinda's dark brown ones. To her amazement, she saw no condemnation. Was it compassion she saw on Malinda's face?

"I think you are very brave, Becky." Malinda reached out to squeeze Rebecca's hand. "You've been through some terrible things, but you returned home to face everyone and to have your *boppli.* I believe you, Becky. My parents believe you. I'm sure everyone else will, too."

"That's what I keep telling her," Lena chimed in.

"I'd like to help you and Lena," Malinda continued. "Did you two hang all that laundry on the line in this bitter wind?"

"*Nee,*" Lena said. "Becky did it all."

"It was not a problem. Most women do all their own housework. Lena would have done it any other day, but her time is getting too close, and she's been having what she calls 'twinges.' "

"You see, Malinda. This stubborn girl won't let me do much these days. She insists that I rest." Lena clucked her tongue.

"Becky is right, Lena. Do you think you need to see the midwife? I could take you, or stay with the girls if you want Becky to take you."

"I don't think I need to do that right now. I've been through this twice before, so I hope I'll know when it's time to see Laurie." Lena gave a little laugh and poked at a loose strand of dark hair.

All conversation ceased when two little girls shuffled into the kitchen. They responded to Malinda's greeting while eyeing the containers of treats.

"You may each have a cookie if your *mamm* says it's okay," Malinda told them.

"Just one," Lena said.

Mary and Eliza each took a fat oatmeal raisin cookie and ran to stand beside their *mamm*. Awkwardly, Lena pulled a girl on each side of what was left of her lap and wrapped her thin arms around them. The girls wiggled to get their balance.

Rebecca laughed at the oddly positioned three-some. "Soon, girls, your *mamm* will have her lap back."

While Lena was preoccupied with the girls, Malinda nudged Rebecca. "Becky, I know we weren't really *freinden* before, but do you think we could be now?"

If she'd been eating a cookie, Rebecca would have choked for sure. She'd figured the purpose of Malinda's visit today had been to help Lena. She certainly didn't expect such an offer from Malinda Stauffer. "I'd like that, Malinda." Truly, she would.

Chapter Sixteen

Rebecca shivered as she peeked out the frosted kitchen window a few mornings later. She had added wood to the stove, but it hadn't yet generated a lot of heat. A magenta stripe in the otherwise dark gray sky provided the only hint that sunrise was on the way. She turned away from the window and tiptoed to the cupboard. Something about a hushed predawn morning always made her want to creep about silently. She'd heard Lena up during the night, so she figured—or at least hoped—Lena was sleeping now. The girls would sleep like little logs until their tummies woke them. There really was no reason for Rebecca to tiptoe, but still she did.

She pulled out the canister of oats and, without bothering to measure, poured some into the pot of water that had just begun to boil on the stove. After all these days of cooking breakfast for the four of them, she could simply eyeball the quantity of oats needed. She stirred the oats around with a long-handled wooden spoon and covered the pot with its metal lid. She had just pulled open the door of the gas-powered refrigerator to remove a carton of eggs when a thumping sound outside caused her heart to thump as well. She left the eggs where they sat on the refrigerator shelf and quickly slid the simmering oatmeal off the heat. What could have made that thumping noise?

Rebecca grabbed a black shawl to throw around her shoulders and eased open the back door. She stared into the semidarkness, willing her eyes to adjust to the dim light. At the next thump, she jumped and turned in the opposite direction. She could just make out a man stacking wood in a rack that was closer to the house than usual. The regular rack, half-empty of split wood, stood at its same spot close to the shed, so this was a different rack the man was filling. Usually the men who brought Lena wood came later in the day or on Saturdays.

Rebecca pulled the shawl tighter against the chill and headed in the direction of the man. His horse, hitched to a wagon loaded with split hardwood, whinnied softly. "*Gut mariye*," she called.

"*Ach*, Becky. *Gut mariye.*"

"Atlee?" Her racing heart told her the man was Atlee even though her eyes had not made that distinction.

"*Jah.* I wanted to bring wood before I went to work."

"Is that a different rack?"

"It sure is. The other one seemed so far away if you or Lena needed wood quickly. I made this one to put closer to the house."

"You made it? *Danki.* I'm sure Lena will

appreciate the convenience. I know I will."

Atlee quickly stacked the wood in a crisscross pattern. "Anything that won't fit here I'll stack in the other holder."

"*Danki*. Would you like breakfast or *kaffi*?"

"I already ate. I wanted to make sure you all were warm. Winter doesn't show any signs of leaving soon. Is there anything I can do for you when I'm done with the wood?"

"I think we're all right."

"Is everything okay with Lena and the girls?"

"So far so *gut*."

"How about you?"

"I'm fine."

Atlee plunked the last piece of wood onto the stack, brushed his hands together to rid his gloves of wood fragments, and hopped across the space between himself and Rebecca. His breath rose in little clouds around his face. He took Rebecca's ungloved hands between his own. "Your hands are nearly frozen."

"I ran out when I heard a thumping noise and didn't take time to grab gloves."

"You didn't grab a cloak, either."

"The shawl was the first thing on the hook, so I took it and hurried out the door." Rebecca attempted to pull her hands away. She couldn't let Atlee get too close. He was only a *freind* and had to stay only a *freind*. Even though his family appeared to be accepting, they would most likely not want him to become involved with a girl who was expecting another man's *boppli*. She needed to protect Atlee—and herself.

"Malinda said she visited you and Lena."

"*Jah.* She was very nice. She brought us lots of treats. Lena's girls were delighted."

"Malinda is a nice girl, even for a little *schweschder.*"

"She said she wanted us to be *freinden.*"

"That's *gut.*"

"She and I can be *freinden* just like you and I are *freinden.*"

"I know I'm not the smartest fellow in the world, but I get the idea you're trying to give me a message."

"Uh, we are *freinden*, ain't so?"

"Of course."

The magenta streak in the sky widened, casting a pinkish glow on the earth. Now Rebecca could clearly see the puzzled look on Atlee's face. She couldn't find the words to tell him they could only be *freinden* and nothing more. What if that was his only intention anyway?

She'd be mortified if she had misinterpreted Atlee's gestures and the tenderness in his expression. She'd be flattered—honored, actually—if Atlee truly cared for her, but she couldn't let their relationship head in that direction. She was going to have a *boppli*. Her attention needed to be focused on that unchangeable fact. She'd have to keep things casual with Atlee. Besides, she didn't know if she could ever trust another man. While he had always liked to joke and tease, Rebecca honestly did not believe Atlee had a single devious bone in his body. But she had thought Vinny was kind and considerate at the beginning, too. *Jah*, it would be best not to take a chance again—for her sake and her *boppli*'s.

Maybe she could encourage Atlee to see someone else. As far as Rebecca knew, her former schoolmate Grace Hertzler was still unattached. Maybe a meeting between the two of them would be something she could subtly orchestrate. Why did that thought send a sharp pain straight through her heart?

"*Danki* for the wood, Atlee, and for stacking it closer to the house for us. I'd better let you get to work." Rebecca yanked her hands free and jogged to the house. She couldn't bring herself to look back or she'd melt at his concerned expression. She did fling "Have a nice day" over her shoulder.

"See you soon, Becky. Maybe we can walk again next church day."

Either Atlee was very persistent or she hadn't conveyed her feelings as clearly as she thought she had.

Chapter Seventeen

Lena perked up the whole week and bustled about doing whatever chores Rebecca allowed her to do.

"I'm glad you're feeling better, Lena, but you still need to take it easy."

"I'm feeling better because you've been doing all the work. You need to rest some and let me do the work. Hmm, I need to make sure everything is ready for the *boppli* and the house is spick-and-span for all the people who will visit once he or she is born, and I need to cook—"

"Listen to yourself!" Rebecca grasped Lena's bony shoulders. "You're talking nonstop, and all those things have already been done at least twice." She gently pushed Lena onto a kitchen chair. "And I think you've lost weight, if your shouder bones are any indication."

"I've always had sharp bones. And I have things I need to tend to." Lena placed her hands on the seat of the chair to heave herself up.

"Sit, Lena!"

"You are a stubborn girl, Becky Zook."

"So are you. I've been reading the pamphlets Laurie Allen gave me. I think you're nesting, Lena, the way women do right before the birth."

Lena looked thoughtful for a moment. "You may

be right. I think I did this with Mary. I was too busy with Mary to do any 'nesting' with Eliza."

"That must mean the *boppli* will be here soon."

"I sure hope so. I'm tired of lugging this big belly around."

"You can talk to me or read to the girls while I prepare food to take to the noon meal after church tomorrow."

The wind whistled around the corners of the Yoders' big barn, where church services were being held. There would probably not be any likelihood of going for a walk today unless the wind suddenly calmed. Rebecca felt relieved and disappointed at the same time. The warring emotions were wreaking havoc on her nerves, not to mention her stomach. The morning sickness had greatly subsided, but now her nerves had her intestines tied in knots.

Despite her best efforts to keep her eyes forward, Rebecca stole a glance at the men's side of the barn. Somehow she knew she'd find a pair of green eyes fastened on her. She couldn't help but smile at Atlee's lopsided grin. Quickly she looked down at her hands interlocked in her lap. She'd better focus on the minister, or the bishop might feel she wasn't serious about joining the church.

Lena twisted on the bench beside Rebecca and shifted Eliza's weight. The poor little girl had fallen into a dead sleep, which seriously chal-

160

lenged her *mamm*'s arm strength. Mary had leaned her head against Lena's other side and looked about ready to drop off to sleep or drop off the bench. Rebecca nudged Lena and motioned for her to pass Eliza over. She figured she could give Lena's arms a little break before she had to catch Mary.

Rebecca found herself gently rocking to and fro as Eliza slept in her arms. Again her mind wandered, but this time to thoughts of her own *boppli*. Would it be a *bu* or a girl? What name would she choose? Who would it look like? How was she going to raise it without a *daed*?

She had her parents for support, of course, but all little ones needed a *daed* as well as a *mamm*. No young man would want to take on a ready-made family, even if she could trust another man. Were Amish men more trustworthy than *Englisch* men?

Rebecca barely caught the sigh before it escaped. She certainly hoped no one asked her what the sermon was about. She needed to force her mind off of worldly concerns. The Lord Gott would take care of her and her little one. She believed that, didn't she?

The wind's whistle had turned into a whisper by the time everyone had eaten and the cleanup had been completed. *Kinner* begged to go outside to play, so *mudders* bundled them into outer clothes, which the older ones would probably shed as soon as they were out of sight.

"Go talk to some of the young folks." Lena elbowed Rebecca. "I've got the girls."

"I don't exactly fit in with them anymore. I'm sure they've all heard my news by now."

"So what? You're still young, and you need to talk to someone besides me."

"I don't feel so young."

"Go!" Lena jabbed Rebecca with a sharp elbow again.

"Ouch!" Rebecca jumped. Out of the corner of her eye, she caught Atlee watching her again. "Maybe I'll go speak to Grace for a minute." She shuffled off in Grace's direction before Atlee could cross the barn to where she stood. Time to put her matchmaking plan into action.

Grace Hertzler had always been a happy, giggly sort of girl. Rebecca hadn't been especially close to her, either, but Rebecca had remained aloof from most of the girls. Or maybe they were leery of her, afraid she'd try to steal their fellows. Shame and remorse washed over Rebecca at the memory of how she'd behaved in the not-too-distant past. She wasn't that person anymore, but she'd probably have to work hard to prove that.

"Hi, Grace."

Grace whirled around to see who greeted her. "*Ach*, Becky. Hello."

Rebecca wished she'd planned a speech so she didn't have to stand here sifting through the web of thoughts swirling through her mind. She needed to raise her head to look into Grace's dark raisin eyes, since Grace was several inches taller. Grace also outweighed Rebecca by ten or fifteen pounds, but she wouldn't be considered heavy, or even plump. *She's probably normal, and I'm too thin.* Rebecca had always liked Grace's chestnut-colored hair with its almost burgundy highlights and the caramel freckles that dotted her nose and cheeks. She coaxed a smile to her lips. "How have you been?" Rebecca could have kicked herself. Honestly, was that the best comment she could utter?

"I'm *gut*, Becky. How about you?"

"I'm fine." This conversation was going nowhere fast. Why couldn't Rebecca think of anything important or even witty to say?

"I hear you're helping Lena out. That's very nice of you."

"I'm glad I can help out." She almost said, *I can be nice,* but she snatched those words back before they fell off her tongue. How was she going to find out if Grace was courting anyone? Lena didn't know, and Rebecca couldn't just ask, especially since they hadn't really been *freinden.* "Uh, are you going to the singing tonight?"

"I expect so. I usually go. How about you?"

"*Nee.* I-it wouldn't be right." Rebecca's voice dropped to a barely audible level. Surely Grace had heard all about her predicament.

"Everything will be okay, Becky." Grace briefly patted Rebecca's arm.

"I hope so." Rebecca had to figure out how to steer the conversation back around to the singing and whether Grace was likely to be leaving with a special *bu*, but she didn't get the chance before Grace's little *schweschder* tugged on her arm and momentarily diverted her attention.

"Hi, Becky."

Rebecca's heart somersaulted at the sound of Atlee's voice. "Hi, Atlee."

"I think the wind has died down enough for a short walk, if you're game. We don't have to go far."

Rebecca would love to walk and talk with Atlee if circumstances were different. But she had to think of what was best for Atlee, and that certainly was not her. She had to give plan B a shot right now. She may never get another opportunity. "Maybe Grace would like to *kumm* along with us. What do you say, Grace?"

Grace's look of surprise rivaled Atlee's. Neither seemed to know what to say. Rebecca turned what she knew for sure was a pleading look in Grace's direction.

"Uh, well, I guess so. If Atlee doesn't mind," Grace sputtered. A red stain crawled up her face, illuminating her freckles.

Poor Atlee. Rebecca had put him on the spot, and he was much too polite to hurt anyone's feelings. He recovered well from the shock. Rebecca had to hand him that. "Well, sure," he replied. "It's not every day I can accompany two young ladies on a walk."

What in the world was going on in Becky's head? Atlee followed both girls outside, trying to figure out how to start a conversation. With just Becky, that wouldn't have been a problem, but how did he address the two of them? Why did Becky invite Grace along anyway? Didn't she want to spend time with him?

"Brrr! It's cold even if the wind has died down." Grace pulled heavy wool gloves from a pocket and thrust her hands into them.

Maybe she'd be too cold and want to go back inside. *That isn't very nice,* Atlee chastised himself. But he had set his heart on spending a little time with Becky, and now that hope had been quashed.

"It is cold, but it's invigorating." It seemed to Atlee that Becky's exuberance was a bit forced.

"As thin as you are, you should be freezing, Becky. I've got lots more meat on my bones, and I'm shivering like the last leaf on a tree in a November wind."

Becky elbowed Grace. "I'm not that skinny."

"Not as skinny as Lena, for sure and for certain, but almost."

Becky heaved an exaggerated sigh. "Well, walk

faster, then. You'll generate more heat. Atlee won't have trouble keeping up, with his long legs."

They picked up the pace and continued in a rather uncomfortable silence. Atlee wasn't sure how much more he could endure. They'd exhausted the topic of the weather, and he honestly hadn't been able to think of anything else to discuss.

"It's not working, Becky. I'm freezing. You two can keep up this arctic walk, but I'm going back." As soon as the words left her mouth, Grace spun around and darted back to the relative warmth of the barn. Becky stared after her.

"Do you want to keep walking, Becky, or are you too cold?"

"I'm okay for a little longer."

Atlee wanted to reach over to take Becky's hand, but he didn't dare. She seemed a bit skittish today, not quite herself.

"Grace is a really nice girl, ain't so?" The words burst from Becky's mouth as if under their own power.

"*Jah*, I suppose so. I don't know her all that well. She was in school with you and Malinda, so I didn't talk to her much."

"You mean we were little *kinner* so you couldn't bother to pay attention to us." Becky playfully punched his arm.

Atlee's eyes slid down to capture Becky's

beautiful green eyes. Her smile did crazy things to his heart. It galloped out of control like a horse eager to race home to its oats. This teasing, smiling girl was the Becky he had *kumm* to know and . . . what? He'd better call that foreign emotion back right now. "You're probably right." He tugged a string of her bonnet, untying the bow. "I was too busy playing ball and thinking about fishing to talk to little girls. Even pretty little girls."

Becky punched him again and quickly retied her bonnet. Atlee thought her pink-stained cheeks looked adorable. Suddenly she switched gears and even shifted over to put a little more distance between them. "So what do you think about Grace? She's cute as well as nice, *jah*?"

Atlee shook his head slightly. Why all the talk about Grace? "I told you. I never paid much attention to Grace."

"Maybe you should."

"And why is that?"

"Well, you said earlier she was nice."

"I said I *supposed* she was nice and that I didn't really know her."

"You could change that. You could get to know her."

"I think my relationship with Grace is just fine the way it is. She's an acquaintance. We speak when in each other's presence. We're polite. End of story. Why are we discussing Grace, anyway?"

"Um, she's a nice person, and you're a nice person, so I thought . . ."

"You thought you'd try to play matchmaker. I don't need a matchmaker."

"You told me before you had changed and were ready to settle down, but you aren't courting anyone."

"Yet."

"Do you mean you have someone in mind but just haven't started courting yet?"

He had someone in mind all right. "Could be." He wiggled his eyebrows at her.

"Atlee! You've been holding out on me. You say we're *freinden* but you haven't confided in me, and here I'm trying to help you." She poked out her lower lip in a pout.

Atlee threw back his head and laughed. "You're pretty cute yourself when you get your feathers ruffled."

Becky impishly wrinkled her nose at him. "Who is she?"

"Huh?"

"This mystery girl you're considering courting?"

Now Atlee did snatch Becky's hand. "I said I had someone in mind. I don't know how she would feel about the whole idea."

"She doesn't know you're interested in her?"

"I think deep down she knows. But she's resisting or not ready or maybe even denying her feelings." He squeezed her hand and shot her what he hoped was a meaningful look. He wanted to wrap his arms around her, hold her close, and tell her outright that she was the girl. He wanted to say he wanted to protect her, to help her, to love her and her *boppli*. Of course, he could say none of these words.

As if realization had suddenly dawned, Becky's mouth opened in an O and all color drained from her face. She slid her hand from his. "I think we'd better go back. Grace was right. It is pretty cold out here." She turned abruptly and sped back toward the barn, nearly at a trot.

"Wait up, Becky!"

Chapter Eighteen

That did not go as she had imagined it would. So much for plan B. Why was it things sounded so perfect, so easy, and so doable in the mind but turned out the complete opposite in reality? Of course it didn't help that she enjoyed Atlee's company so much. If things were different—but they weren't. The *boppli* growing inside her was what was real.

Rebecca's breath came out in pants so loud she couldn't hear if Atlee's footsteps were growing closer. And she didn't dare turn around. That would make it look like she wanted him to catch up with her. She did. She didn't. She couldn't. *Ach*! Life could be so frustrating. Maybe Lena would be ready to leave by now. She surely hoped so.

Rebecca pulled open the back door of the Yoders' house. Most likely Lena would have gone inside, where she'd be warmer and more comfortable. She heard voices from the kitchen—a variety of women's voices, actually. The married women must have all stayed in the house after cleaning up.

She slipped into the kitchen and scanned the room for Lena. With everyone wearing a blue or purple or green dress, sometimes locating the right person could take a moment. There she was sitting on a kitchen chair pulled close to the stove. A big feather pillow was stuffed behind her back, and her feet were resting on a low stool. At least she looked fairly comfortable, judging from her posture. Rebecca would have to see if her face had a pinched or relaxed look to know for sure.

She'd learned the meanings behind Lena's facial expressions during the relatively short time she'd lived in the Troyer household. When Lena bit her lower lip, she was giving serious thought to some matter. When her brow wrinkled, she was worried about something. When that haunted look crept across her face, she was thinking of Joseph. When she had a combination of the three, as she did right now, she wasn't feeling well.

Rebecca skirted around the other women, murmuring polite responses to their comments. She squatted down beside Lena. "Are you okay? Do you want to go home?"

"*Ach*, Becky! You always know my moods, and I think you can read my mind. *Jah*, I'd like to head home now."

"I'll get the girls bundled up. Are they playing with the other little ones in the living room?"

"*Jah*, unless Eliza fell asleep." Lena started to push herself up from the chair.

"You wait right here. I can get them."

"What a blessing you are, Becky Zook." Lena slumped back against the pillow.

A blessing? Her? She supposed she needed to start thinking of herself as "Becky" again instead of "Rebecca." That's what her family and *freinden* called her. Rebecca was who she had been in the *Englisch* world. She was back to being Becky now. Actually, she was a different Becky, a better one, she hoped. At least she liked this Becky much more than the old Becky or Rebecca.

Becky found Mary sitting on the floor playing with some little girls who were several years older. She looked so tired but held her mouth in a determined set as if willing herself to keep up. She looked relieved rather than perturbed when Becky called to her. Poor little Eliza had given up any attempt at playing. She had fallen asleep on the floor, oblivious to the noise and activity around her.

"Poor *boppli*," Becky whispered. She stroked Eliza's face. "*Kumm*, Eliza, let's go home." The toddler's eyes popped open. She held out pudgy arms to Becky, who gently pulled her to a sitting position. "Let's get you ready to go outside." She helped the drowsy child poke her arms into the sleeves of her coat and tied her little bonnet in a snug bow beneath her chin. She stood the little girl on wobbly legs for long enough to tie Mary's bonnet and then hoisted her up onto one hip. She reached her free hand down to Mary.

"My poor tired girls," Lena crooned when

Becky entered the kitchen. She had managed to pull her cloak together over her belly and finished tying her black bonnet. "Whew! You'd think I'd done a day's work, when I only got out of a chair and put on my cloak."

"Are you all right?" Sylvia's expression showed real concern.

"I think so."

Sylvia patted Lena's arm before turning to Becky and asking the same question.

"I'm fine, Mamm."

Sylvia hugged her *dochder* around the two little girls clinging to her. "I'll be by tomorrow to check on you and to help out."

Becky hustled the little family out into the cold. She set Eliza inside the buggy that, surprisingly, had already been hitched, and then helped Mary climb in. She had turned to help Lena when she caught movement from the corner of her eye. Atlee poked his head out of the barn and waved. Now she knew how the buggy happened to be ready and waiting for them.

She kept a watchful eye on Lena the rest of the day. Something seemed different. Lena looked different. "Are you sure you're feeling all right?"

"Sure. I'm just a bit achy, probably from sitting on a wooden bench for three hours."

Becky's own back ached a little from sitting on the backless bench and from lifting the girls, so she could understand. But that didn't account for

Lena's outward change. "You look different. The baby seems lower or something."

Lena's hands flew to her belly. "I believe you're right. I think this little one is getting into postion."

"*Ach*! Should I fetch Laurie or have someone call her or—"

"Relax. I'm not in labor. We don't want to call Laurie before she's needed."

"And we don't want to call her too late." Panic rose, and Becky knew her voice attested to her fears.

"It's okay. I've been through this before."

"I haven't," Becky whispered.

"You will."

Becky's fears increased. How would she get through this when her own time came if she was this nervous for Lena? She had to get a grip on herself or she'd be no help whatsoever to Lena.

Because the girls had only had a catnap and were getting cranky, Lena decreed they'd have an early bedtime. Becky fed them a quick supper of leftover beef stew, bathed them, and had them tucked beneath the covers by the time Lena trudged upstairs to kiss them.

"You didn't eat much supper," Becky observed once she and Lena had settled into chairs in the living room with knitting projects in their hands.

"I don't have a lot of room in here for food anymore." Lena patted the belly that occupied most of her lap. "You didn't exactly make a pig of yourself, either."

"I wasn't very hungry." She didn't mention the fact that what little food she had eaten was churning in her stomach, which was already tied in knots from thinking about Atlee and worrying about Lena.

"You need to eat and take it easier, too. You've been working entirely too hard around here. I feel bad about that. I should have been doing more. Most women handle being pregnant and taking care of their families just fine."

"Most women have someone to share the load."

"I don't know many men who will cook, scrub floors, or wash clothes. Can you see your *daed* doing those things?"

Becky burst out laughing. "I can't say I've ever seen my *daed* do those things, but I think he would help my *mamm* if she needed it."

"Joseph would, too." A pensive look stationed itself on Lena's face.

The two young women knitted awhile without further conversation. The creaking of Lena's rocking chair, the clacking of knitting needles, and the occasional crackling of wood in the stove were the only sounds in the room. Lena's sharp intake of air and subsequent moan rang out like gunshot in a quiet forest.

"*Was ist letz*?" Becky stabbed her knitting needles into the ball of yellow yarn. "Lena?"

Lena's rocking ceased. A knitting needle clattered to the floor as Lena clutched her stomach. "A-a pain," she gasped at last.

"A pain? As in a labor pain?" Becky forced her shrill voice to drop a few decibels. "I-is it time?"

Lena blew out her breath. "I'm not sure. I'll see if I have any more pains."

"Maybe I should go out to call Laurie to let her know what—"

"*Ach!*" Lena sucked in another breath.

Becky dropped her nearly completed baby blanket to the floor and rushed to Lena's side. "Another pain?"

Lena nodded.

"That seemed pretty soon to me, though I'm certainly not an expert."

"It seemed pretty soon to me, too." Lena's breath came in a gasp.

"I'm going to call." Becky ran to grab her cloak and bonnet. "I'll find the nearest phone and be right back, Lena."

"Just wait, Becky. It might be false labor."

"I don't think so." Becky pulled open the heavy front door. "I hear a horse and buggy out on the road. I'll run and try to catch whoever it is. Maybe they can call Laurie and that way I can stay here with you."

Becky flew down the front steps. The brisk wind threatened to snatch her breath away. If it was an open courting buggy she heard, they would be traveling at a pretty fast pace on this cold evening. Becky ran as fast as she could while battling the wind. She called out, but the wind threw the words back into her face. If she could get a little closer, they might be able to hear her. She pushed herself to run even faster and shouted at the top of her lungs. To her relief, she heard a deep voice cry, "Whoa!"

As the open buggy rolled to a stop, a black bonnet poked out around the big man holding the reins. "Becky?"

Becky blinked to get her eyes to focus in the blackness of the winter evening. She should know the voice. She struggled to catch her breath. Her legs, unused to such a sprint, screamed their displeasure at the brutal treatment they'd just endured. "Malinda, is that you?"

"*Jah*, and Timothy Brenneman. Whatever is wrong?"

"Lena. Lena needs Laurie to *kumm* or else we need a driver to get her to Laurie's birthing center."

"We'll stop at the phone shack and call Laurie. Timothy can bring me back here to help and then go tell my *mamm*. Do you have Laurie's number?"

Thankful she had committed the midwife's phone number to memory after her first visit, she rattled it off to Malinda.

Malinda repeated the number over and over. "Okay. I've got it. I'll be right back."

Timothy spurred the horse into a fast trot in the

direction of the nearest telephone. Becky could hear Malinda still reciting the number. At such a time, that cell phone she had discarded would sure be helpful. Her breathing slowed to a more normal rate as Becky returned to the Troyer house. She prayed her own *boppli* had fared okay in her race to the road.

"Lena?" Becky rushed into the living room without bothering to remove her cloak and bonnet. Lena's head was tipped back against the wooden rocking chair, her eyes were squeezed shut, and her breath came in little pants. "Are you okay?" Becky knelt on the floor beside the laboring woman.

"*Jah?*"

"Are the pains closer together?"

"A little, I think."

"Malinda Stauffer and Timothy Brenneman were on their way home. Malinda will call Laurie and return here. She's sending Timothy on to fetch her *mamm*."

"*Gut.*"

"Do you want me to help you move to your bedroom, or would you like me to make you a bed on the couch?"

"Not yet. I'll wait for Laurie. Just stay with me. Talk to me."

"Sure. Let me get out of this cloak, though, and check the fire. I won't leave you." Becky pushed to her feet and began untying her bonnet.

"Wait!" Lena jerked her head up. Her eyes were as big as saucers.

Becky grasped Lena's cool hand. "Another pain?"

Lena nodded and squeezed Becky's hand until Becky feared the bones in her fingers would snap. Becky bit her lower lip to keep from crying out. Gradually Lena relaxed her grip, which allowed Becky to wiggle her fingers and determine that they weren't broken.

"I'm so sorry, Becky."

"Don't apologize. Let me hurry and get out of this cloak." Becky continued flexing her fingers. She never would have guessed that skinny little Lena could execute such a death grip. Maybe she could find some other object—some unbreakable object—for Lena to squeeze when a pain hit.

Chapter Nineteen

Becky quickly tossed her cloak and bonnet onto a nearby chair and added wood to the fire. She brushed her hands together and turned back to face Lena. "Can I get you anything?"

"A cup of water would be great."

"Okay. I'll be right back."

Lena didn't answer. She let her head fall back against the chair again, sucked in deep breaths, and rubbed her belly in time to the rocking of the chair.

Becky snagged her belongings from the chair on her way to the kitchen. She wanted the place to look tidy. Other women would most likely be arriving soon, unless Laurie wanted Lena to deliver at the birthing center. She hoped that wouldn't be the case. Lena seemed too uncomfortable to travel. Becky hung her cloak and bonnet on a hook and raced to get the glass of water.

"Becky?"

Becky whirled around to see Malinda entering the back door. "Hi. I'm getting Lena a glass of water."

"How is she? Is she in bed?"

"She's okay. She's in the living room. She didn't want to lie down. Did you reach the midwife?"

"*Jah.* She said she'll be right over."

"That's a relief. I was afraid she would want Lena to travel to her." Becky heard the squeaks of the rocking chair occurring more rapidly. Another pain must be building. "I need to get back to Lena."

"You go ahead. I'll get the water."

Becky hurried back to the living room to find Lena rocking furiously and moaning softly. "I'm here, Lena." Lena reached out and grabbed Becky's hand like a drowning man would grab a rope. So much for finding an unbreakable substitute. If holding her hand and snapping every one of her fingers brought Lena comfort, she'd suffer the consequences. After all, she was going to be in the exact same position herself in a few months. *Ach*! She'd be suffering like Lena suffered now. How would she manage? She didn't even like to have a splinter dug out of her finger!

When Lena could focus again, she released Becky's fingers. "You'll have to stop holding my hand or your poor fingers will suffer permanent damage."

Becky laughed. "I'm not worried about that. You do whatever you need to do. I'm here to help however I can."

"Maybe so, but a broken hand was not part of the deal."

Becky smiled. "Malinda is here. She said Laurie is on her way."

"*Gut.* I can have the *boppli* at home and won't have to leave the girls."

"Would you like a sip of water?" Malinda had slipped into the room unnoticed. She held the glass out to Lena.

"*Danki,*" Lena said after swallowing several large sips of the cold water. "I needed that."

A loud knock on the front door startled all three women. Usually Amish *freinden* entered the back door without knocking.

"I'll answer the door." Malinda headed in that direction. "It's probably Laurie."

"How is Lena doing?" Laurie bustled into the room with her arms full of supplies. She was a tall, thin woman with a light brown braid sneaking over her shoulder. She moved quickly and had a ready smile.

"She's right over there and seems to be doing well," Malinda answered, pointing toward the creaky rocking chair. "Do you have anything else I can bring in for you?"

"Oh, that would be great. There are two bags in my trunk. It's already open."

"I'll be right back."

Laurie set her armload down and crossed the room to Lena. Becky prepared to back out of the way.

"Stay," Lena whispered.

"It's fine," Laurie said. "I'm just going to ask questions first. Then we'll see how close we are to meeting this baby. If I remember correctly, your previous two labors were pretty short, weren't they, Lena?"

"*Jah.* Seven hours for the first one and five hours for the second one."

"Then I'll ask only a few questions and get your bed ready."

Lena nodded and continued to stroke her belly while she rocked.

"If you tell us what to do, Malinda and I can get the room ready."

Lena turned beseeching eyes on Becky, making Becky hesitant to leave her side, but they had to prepare for the birth. "It's okay, Lena. I'll be right back."

"Malinda and I can ready the room. I've done it plenty of times." No one had heard Saloma enter the house.

Becky's *mamm* slipped in right behind Saloma. "I can help." Becky imagined the grapevine had been vibrating with the news.

"Great," Laurie said. "If you ladies will get the room set up lickety-split, I'll be able to examine Lena." She pulled a blood pressure cuff and stethoscope out of her bag. "I can go ahead and do a few things here." She wrapped the black cuff around Lena's upper arm, placed the stethoscope in her ears, and pumped up the cuff. She finished the preliminary examination by the time the other women trooped back into the room.

"All set?" Laurie turned to look at the women.

"Everything is ready." Becky thought Saloma looked the picture of calm. Having given birth six times herself and assisted with numerous other births, Becky figured Saloma had earned her air of confidence. Sylvia, on the other hand, seemed a bit more nervous. Maybe she hadn't been present at as many births. Or maybe she was pondering the upcoming birth of Becky's *boppli*.

"Can you make it up the stairs?" Laurie's braid flopped over her shoulder again as she leaned down to look into Lena's face. "We'll help you."

Lena nodded. "We'd better move before the next pain hits."

Becky and Laurie each wrapped their hands around one of Lena's too-thin arms and helped her rise from the chair.

"Okay?" Laurie turned concerned eyes on her patient.

Lena nodded again. "I think so. Let's go fast, though."

Becky wanted to move fast—right out the door at top speed. She had never witnessed a birth. That had not been her idea of fun. She was pretty sure she didn't want to witness one now, either. Could she stand to watch someone she'd *kumm* to care about writhe in pain? Could she stand the sight of blood? Would the smells of antiseptic combined with sweat and blood make her sensitive stomach heave? Would she faint?

Please, Lord Gott, don't let me faint. Lena needs me.

There it was. Lena needed her. Lena was counting on her for support. She had to be strong for Lena's sake. She had to cast off her fears. She could not cower in a corner. She had to be calm or she'd be *nee* help at all. She would be a strong woman now, not a whimpering little girl. She would focus on Lena. She would do whatever Laurie asked her to do. She *could* do this.

They made it to the top of the stairs much faster than Becky had thought a laboring woman could move. The look of relief on Malinda's pale face when she'd been assigned the task of sitting in the girls' room in case they awoke almost made Becky laugh out loud. She hoped she didn't look as frightened as Malinda did.

"Let's get you into a nightgown so you'll be more comfortable," Laurie said as soon as they entered Lena's bedroom.

Lena had claimed Becky's hand again as soon as the women had climbed the last step, and Becky had to pry Lena's fingers loose so they could remove her dress. "It's okay, Lena. I won't leave you." Becky made her voice as soothing as possible and was rather surprised she detected no quivering in it. "We need to get your hands through the sleeves and get you settled. Then I'll stay right beside you." She spoke with courage and calm she didn't quite feel.

Her words must have been reassuring, since Lena held out her arms like one of the girls waiting to be dressed. Saloma had already pulled a nightgown from the dresser drawer. Becky and her *mamm* quickly exchanged Lena's clothes for her nightgown. To Becky's amazement, her fingers didn't tremble a single bit. She and Sylvia led Lena to the bed that had been prepared with the special waterproof sheets from Laurie's birthing kit. Sylvia plumped two pillows to tuck behind Lena's head.

"Let me examine you, Lena, and then you can get into whatever position is comfortable for you. You can walk, sit, lie down, whatever, but first let me see how far you've progressed."

Once they got Lena settled on her back in the bed, Sylvia made herself scarce to give Lena privacy. She joined Saloma across the room. Becky didn't have that option, since Lena had latched onto her hand again. Her intent was to look away or even squeeze her eyes shut, but a sudden calmness overtook her, along with an intense desire to watch everything that was happening. She murmured soothing words to Lena during the brief but, most likely, uncomfortable exam.

"It won't be long, Lena," Laurie announced. "You'll be ready to push in no time."

"*Gut.*" Lena's voice came out in a soft gasp.

Laurie disposed of her gloves in the trash bag

Saloma had set up for her and patted Lena's leg. "You're doing fine."

Becky pulled her hand from Lena's grip to rearrange Lena's nightgown. She pulled up a sheet to cover her, though modesty was probably the last thing on Lena's mind at the moment. She took the cold washcloth her *mamm* passed to her and mopped Lena's brow. She pushed loose tendrils of brown hair from Lena's cheek. Lena smiled but then reached for Becky's hand as another contraction swelled.

Laurie pulled out a contraption she called a fetoscope. She positioned one end over Lena's hardened belly and the other in her own ear. "I'm just going to listen to the baby's heartbeat, Lena." After a moment's silence, she lifted her head. "It's galloping along strong and steady."

Becky didn't realize she'd been staring. What an interesting instrument that could allow someone to hear the heartbeat of a *boppli* in the womb! What must that sound like?

"Would you like to listen?" Laurie held the fetoscope out to Becky.

"Could I?"

"Here. I'll show you. The baby's head is down to exit the birth canal. Not all babies are head down, mind you, but thankfully Lena's baby is cooperating beautifully. The baby's heart can best be heard right about here." Laurie pointed to a spot on Lena's distended abdomen.

Becky placed the instrument against Lena's belly and lowered her head to listen. "*Ach*! The heartbeat! I hear it! It's amazing!"

"I always think birth is pretty amazing, too." Laurie took the fetoscope Becky reluctantly gave up.

"You have the best job in the world!" Becky's excited words shot from her mouth before she even finished thinking them. How *wunderbaar* it must be to help bring new life into the world. At a louder moan from Lena, Becky reached for the other woman's hand.

"Breathe through it, Lena." Laurie exaggerated her own breathing so Lena would follow along.

Becky felt her own breathing take on the same rhythm as Lena crushed her fingers. "It won't be long, Lena," she soothed.

"P-push!" Lena cried when the next contraction peaked. "I need to push!"

"Pant with her, Becky." Laurie demonstrated quickly. "Don't push yet, Lena. Let me check." Laurie thrust her hands into a fresh pair of gloves and whisked the sheet out of the way.

Becky panted with Lena. Her excitement mounted. She no longer felt afraid or squeamish. A new life was about to enter the world. Becky barely noticed the antiseptic smell of Laurie's prepared instruments. Her stomach hadn't balked even once. She had been watching Laurie's movements in fascination. Some buried instinct told her when to wipe Lena's brow or when to utter calming words or when to let Lena be.

"Okay, Lena. You can push with the next contraction."

Lena lay with her eyes closed after the contraction ebbed. She gulped in huge breaths of air.

"Did you hear Laurie, Lena?" Becky bent close to Lena's ear. "You can push next time. The *boppli* will be here soon. You're doing great." She swiped the cool cloth across Lena's forehead again.

"Here, Dochder." Sylvia passed a fresh washcloth to Becky and took the now-warm one from her. She nodded at Becky. Her brown eyes showed the pride she, as an Amish woman, could not give voice to.

Becky smiled. She received her *mamm*'s unspoken message loud and clear. Who'd have thought the formerly self-centered girl could selflessly offer aid and comfort during childbirth? She really had grown up. She wiped Lena's face again with the cooler cloth.

"*Ach*! Here it *kumms* again." Lena clapped a hand across her tightening abdomen.

"Okay, Lena, you can push." Laurie positioned herself at the foot of the bed.

Instinctively, Becky supported Lena's head and shoulders as the frail-looking woman summoned enormous strength to bear down with the next contraction.

"Okay, breathe," Becky said encouragingly as

Lena flopped back against her at the end of the contraction.

"You're doing great, Lena." Laurie patted Lena's leg. "You can yell or make noise if you want to. You don't have to be so stoic. We will all certainly understand."

"For sure and for certain," Saloma mumbled as Sylvia nodded. "We've all been in your place."

"Except me," Becky whispered.

"Your time is coming," Sylvia said.

"And you will do just fine." Lena managed to get the sentence out before the next contraction hit. She grunted as she bore down but did not make any louder sound.

"I see the baby's head!" Laurie cried.

Becky couldn't help herself. She stretched to peek at the dark head beginning to crown. She found this whole birth process completely fascinating. Who knows? Maybe Laurie would need an assistant one day, and she could help. First, though, she had to get through her own labor and delivery.

"It won't be long now, Lena, and you'll be holding that little one in your arms," Saloma said encouragingly. She had everything ready to receive the newborn. Sylvia occasionally mopped Laurie's brow or held out a glass of water for her to sip through a curved straw.

Lena still gasped to catch her breath. Her eyes were closed and her brow was furrowed. Becky feared Lena's strength was waning. The poor girl had been through so much. Becky willed her own strength to flow through Lena's veins. "You can do this, Lena." Glancing at Lena's abdomen, she could see the tightening that signaled another contraction. "I'll help you, Lena. Get ready to push." Becky again supported Lena's effort as the laboring woman strained and pushed.

"Okay, Lena, pant now." Laurie panted like a dog.

With her face red from heavy exertion, Lena struggled to imitate Laurie. She raised her eyebrows at Becky but couldn't seem to put voice to her question.

Becky peeked around. Her mouth dropped open in awe. Laurie was using a little blue rubber suction bulb to clear the *boppli*'s mouth and nose. Only the head full of dark hair had emerged. "It's okay, Lena. Laurie is suctioning the baby."

"Get ready, Lena. I'm going to guide the shoulders, and I want you to give a gentle push. One, two, three, push!"

The baby slipped out and immediately began crying in protest at being forced from a warm, safe womb.

"It's a boy, Lena! You have a little boy!" Laurie held the baby up for Lena to see.

"*Ach*, a *bu!*" Tears streamed down Lena's face. She held out her thin arms, eager to embrace her son.

Laurie quickly clamped and cut the umbilical

cord, dried the baby with the soft towel Saloma handed her, and placed the baby on Lena's chest. Sylvia rushed over to cover the baby with a blanket.

Becky observed the whole experience in awe. She absorbed Laurie's every movement and scarcely noticed the tears coursing down her own cheeks. "H-he's absolutely beautiful, Lena." She sniffed and swiped at her tears before they dripped off her chin to splash onto the bed. "That was the most amazing thing I've ever seen."

Laurie nodded. "No matter how many births I attend, I find each one amazing."

Lena, all pain apparently forgotten, stared in fascination at her son. She cooed to him and kissed his tiny hands.

"As soon as I finish up here, Lena, we'll weigh and measure him and get him started nursing."

Lena nodded, but her eyes never left the newborn. Becky couldn't keep her own eyes off him, either, and gently stroked his dark hair.

"Here, Becky. Put this little hat on his head so he doesn't lose body heat." Laurie nodded to the tiny knit hat near her instruments.

Carefully Becky stretched the little blue hat over the baby's head. "There, little one. We want to keep you nice and warm."

"I think he looks like a combination of you and Joseph." Saloma moved closer to the bed to get a better look.

"He has Joseph's mouth." Lena smiled at her son.

"And your eyes." Sylvia crowded in next to Saloma to peer at the new arrival. "What will you name him?"

"Matthew. Joseph and I picked that name when we were expecting Mary. His middle name will be Joseph, for his *daed*." Lena bent to kiss her infant's head.

"I like it. Matthew Joseph Troyer." Laurie stripped off and disposed of her gloves. "Let me wash my hands and we'll see how big this fellow is."

Chapter Twenty

"Six pounds, two ounces, and eighteen and one-half inches," Laurie sang out. "Not bad for a tiny little woman like you. His heart and lungs sound great." Laurie swaddled the infant and handed him to Becky. "I need to press on Lena's belly to check her uterus, and I don't want her to drop him or squeeze him in half." Laurie winked at Lena.

Lena moaned softly through Laurie's brief ministrations, but not even the discomfort stole the peace and joy that lit her face.

"Look at this. Her belly is flat already." Laurie pulled the covers back over Lena.

"That's because she was all *boppli*." Everyone chuckled at Saloma's remark. Saloma and Sylvia busily cleaned up to return the room from delivery room to bedroom.

Becky swayed, gently rocking the *boppli* in her arms. "You are a precious one," she whispered.

"Look at that, Sylvia." Saloma nudged Sylvia and nodded toward Becky. "She's a natural."

"She's a natural at assisting at childbirth, too," Laurie observed. "Are you sure you've never done this before, Becky?"

"I'm positive. I've never even seen a birth before, but it was totally amazing. A miracle."

Laurie helped Lena sit up in bed and propped pillows behind her. Becky reluctantly relinquished Matthew to his *mamm* so she could nurse him. Suddenly she couldn't wait to hold her own *boppli* in her arms. Glancing down, she couldn't even see a bump to indicate she was expecting. She'd have to be patient for a while yet.

"*Kumm*, ladies. We'll leave Lena and Matthew to get acquainted. There's *kaffi* and pie in the kitchen," Saloma announced.

"I'll bring you some," Becky told Lena.

"You go ahead and eat. I'm fine for now. Are the girls still asleep?"

"I'll check on them."

"You don't need to." Malinda cracked open the door and stuck her head inside. "They're both fast asleep. There was never one single peep out of them. Let me have a quick look at the new arrival. I'll get you a piece of pie and some milk, Lena, so these women can rest. Would you like a sandwich, too?"

"*Nee*. The pie and milk will do fine." As Lena positioned the infant to nurse, the women slipped from the room.

Once in the kitchen, Saloma sliced the apple pie she'd brought and plopped a generous piece onto a plate for Lena. "We need to fatten that girl up. Get a tall glass of milk for her, Malinda."

Laurie sighed as she sank onto a kitchen chair

to fill out the necessary paperwork. She wrapped her hands around the steaming mug Sylvia set in front of her and stared into space for a moment before pulling out a folder and an ink pen.

"You did *gut* in there, Dochder." Sylvia squeezed Becky's arm.

"I'll say she did." Laurie looked up from her papers. "I could train you to be an assistant in no time, if you're interested."

"I think I'd like that when Lena doesn't need me any longer, at least until my own little one arrives." Adrenaline still pumped through her, keeping her energy at peak level despite the fact that the hands on the kitchen clock pointed to two a.m.

"Where's Malinda?" Atlee rubbed his still-damp hands on his pants as he entered the kitchen after morning chores.

"Wasn't there a towel for you to dry your hands on?" Saloma looked over the silver wire-rimmed glasses that had slid down her nose.

"*Jah*, there was a towel."

"You chose not to use it?"

"I did use it. My hands didn't get all the way dry."

"So you thought your pants would work better?" Saloma made a little "tsk" sound.

"It's just water. It won't hurt my pants none."

"Says one who doesn't do the laundry."

The telltale twitch in her lips and twinkle in her eyes told Atlee his *mamm* was teasing him, despite the fact she looked pretty tired.

"Where are your *bruders*?"

"They should be along any second. Daed, too. Where's Malinda?" Usually his *schweschder* scurried around the kitchen filling lunch boxes and helping with breakfast.

"I let her sleep. I don't want her getting sick. It was nearly three o'clock when we got home from Lena Troyer's place."

"Lena had the *boppli*?"

"She did. A fine little *bu*."

"Everything went well?" Rufus stomped into the kitchen, followed by Roman, Ray, and Aden. He wiped his hands along his pant leg.

Saloma rolled her eyes. "I see where you got that from, Atlee. I shouldn't bother to hang towels out, since you fellows prefer to dry your hands on your pants."

"It's only water, Fraa." Rufus gave her a quick kiss on the cheek.

"That's exactly what your son said. All of you sit down. Breakfast is ready."

"I'll carry something for you, Mamm."

"*Danki*, Atlee. Just take that plate of pancakes while I dish up the oatmeal. Bacon, butter, and syrup are already on the table."

"Mamm, you should have called me." Malinda raced into the kitchen, breathless from her trot down the steps. Dark circles rimmed her brown eyes, making her complexion appear more pale than usual.

"I wanted you to rest. You were up nearly the whole night."

"So were you."

"I don't want you to have a flare-up."

"I'll be fine. I'll get the oatmeal if you pour the *kaffi*."

"*Jah*, Mamm, you get the *kaffi*," Atlee called. "We don't want Malinda spilling it all over us and scorching us. She's clumsy enough on normal days, but if she's sleep deprived, we could be in real danger."

"I heard that, Bruder. You're so funny."

After the silent prayer, conversation again turned to the previous night's events.

"Did Lena name her *boppli*?" Aden's question came out garbled, since his mouth was full of pancakes. Maple syrup dribbled down his chin.

"Don't talk with your mouth full. You know better." Saloma took a quick sip of the *kaffi*, which was a little stronger than usual. "His name is Matthew Joseph."

"That's a *gut*, strong name." Rufus wiped his napkin across his mouth.

"Mamm, is it my imagination, or does the *kaffi* have an extra kick this morning? I'm not complaining, mind you. I think I need an extra kick anyway." Atlee set his mug down and swirled his last forkful of pancakes through the puddle of syrup on his plate.

"You can always use an extra kick—in the pants," Malinda mumbled.

"Hey!"

Malinda wrinkled her nose at her older *bruder*.

"I thought a little extra caffeine might be in order this morning," Saloma said. "You can always add more sugar or milk."

"*Nee*, this is fine." Atlee took another gulp as if to prove his point. He'd probably stay wired all day.

As he allowed the horse to run at a brisk trot, Atlee's thoughts turned to Becky. From what his *mamm* had said, Becky had been a big help to Lena and was a natural at handling the *boppli*. Maybe all women had natural motherly instincts. He didn't know. But his heart had been strangely warmed as his *mamm* had sung Becky's praises. Of course, Mamm would never say she was proud of Becky. Pride was a sin. Praising anyone but the Lord Gott was a sin. Just the same, his *mamm* did seem pretty happy with Becky's behavior. Maybe she was surprised at seeing this new, responsible Becky, as opposed to the flirtatious girl who had stolen her *dochder*'s fellow.

Atlee wondered if Becky had thought of her own little one while she had helped Lena and the midwife. Had she wondered if anyone would be there to hold her hand and help her through? Surely her *mamm* would be with her. He wished he could be the one to hold her hand and offer her support. He wished he could be the one pacing the floor when the women threw him out of the room to do their work.

Ach! Where did such ideas *kumm* from? Atlee slapped his own forehead to chase the confusing thoughts from his brain. Without any encouragement from him, the horse had picked up the pace. His breath rose like puffs of smoke from his nostrils as he pulled the buggy at a fast clip. He obviously wanted to reach the dairy and get out of the cold wind. Atlee needed to get busy working to keep his mind occupied with mundane, normal thoughts. At least Becky's *boppli* would arrive in warm weather. Becky again! He had to get her out of his head! Like that was going to happen. Maybe he'd stop by Lena's after work to check on, um, everyone.

Chapter Twenty-One

"*Kumm*, girls. Let's let your mamm and new *bruder* rest a bit."

"Again? Didn't they take a nap when we did?"

"They did, Mary, but having a *boppli* is very hard work. Your *mamm* needs to rest up."

"The *boppli* just eats and sleeps."

"That's because he is very tiny. His tummy can't hold all the cookies yours can." Becky reached out to tickle first Mary and then Eliza. "He needs to eat often. Your *mamm* has to get up a lot to feed him, so she's tired. How about if we go outside? We can only stay a few minutes, because it's very cold. When we *kumm* back inside, we'll heat up supper."

Becky smiled at the girls as they nodded enthusiastically at her idea. They'd been inside all day. A brisk outdoor playtime would do them *gut*— provided she could stand the cold herself. Supper would be easy to prepare. So many women had brought casseroles, soups, and pies that she simply needed to pick something and add some vegetables or bread to round out the meal.

She bundled the girls into their coats, scarves, and bonnets and made sure their little hands were tucked inside warm mittens. She dressed the same way herself, took a last breath of warm air, and pulled open the door. "Ready?"

201

The little girls shrieked as they ran around the yard. The brisk wind whipped their cheeks and stained them red. Becky laughed watching their antics and was glad the windows were tightly closed so Lena would not be awakened by the noise. To keep from freezing, she ran around the yard with them. They held hands to play Ring Around the Rosie. Little Eliza couldn't quite get the hang of the game and dropped to the ground at odd times, which sent Mary into fits of giggles. This was what they needed. A little outside time to run off pent-up energy and have fun did them a world of *gut*.

Becky was so distracted she didn't hear or see the approaching buggy until it was halfway up the driveway. She thought she recognized the horse and buggy but couldn't clearly see the occupant. Maybe Saloma had decided to check on Lena, but she should be preparing supper for her own hungry crew about now. Maybe she had sent Malinda over.

A push against her leg snapped her attention back to the girls. Mary's cry of "You're it!" sent her scurrying after them. She pretended she couldn't catch them as they ran in two different directions, squealing in delight. Becky ran after Eliza before she got too far away.

"I got you!" a male voice that made Becky's heart flip-flop called out.

She snatched up Eliza and turned around to see

Mary squirming and giggling in Atlee's arms.

"What are you doing out on such a cold day?" He had to raise his voice to be heard over Mary's laughter.

"The girls have been cooped up inside all day. They needed to run off some energy so they can sleep tonight."

"My *mamm* used to send us outside to do that until I got big enough to be outside doing chores."

"We're a little late getting outside. We should have *kumm* out when the sun was bright. Now that it's setting, it must be ten degrees colder than it was earlier."

"A little playtime is better than nothing. That's what I always thought anyway." Atlee released Mary to run around again.

"Swing?" Mary sidled up to Becky and gave her a hopeful look.

"Okay, for a few minutes. I don't want you two to turn into icicles." Becky carried Eliza to the swing fastened by sturdy ropes to a limb of the big oak tree. The wooden seat was long enough and wide enough for both little girls to sit side by side. Becky plunked Eliza down and had her scoot over to leave room for Mary. "Hold on!" she instructed when Mary got situated.

"I'll push them. You rest." Atlee gently pried Becky's gloved hands off the ropes. "Stand back, Becky. These girls are going to fly high." Atlee made a big show of flexing his arms like he was winding up to pitch a baseball.

"Not too high," Becky mouthed.

Atlee nodded. He took a loud, exaggerated breath, pulled the swing back toward him with a deep groan, and gently let it go. "Look at them, Becky. They're going to touch the sky." He didn't actually swing them very high, but the girls squealed as if they were flying.

A lump swelled in Becky's throat, nearly blocking her breath. Her eyes watered. Atlee would make a great *daed*. He should have a houseful of *kinner*. She wished her little one could have a *daed* who worked hard to provide for him or her but would be fun-loving and willing to play. She wished her little one could have a *daed* just like . . . *Nee*. She hoped Atlee could find the right girl to give him the love he deserved. Grace must not have been the one. She'd have to think of someone else. A single tear escaped from the pool in her eyes and trickled down her cheek. Quickly she raised a gloved hand to brush it away, but she hadn't been quite quick enough.

"Are you okay, Becky?"

"*Jah*. I guess something got in my eye." She continued to rub her eye. She was telling the truth. Something had gotten in her eye. Tears.

"Let me take a look. Be right back, girls." Atlee left the girls gently rocking on the swing and hurried over to Becky. He yanked off his gloves and grasped her chin to tilt her face upward. With his other hand, he carefully pulled down the lower lid of her eye.

Becky's heart thundered so hard she knew Atlee must hear it or feel its vibration. It seemed to her the whole earth shook. She wouldn't be surprised if the ground cracked open and swallowed them. Atlee's breath was warm on her face and smelled of peppermint. He must have eaten a mint before he arrived. His touch was ever so soft but ever so powerful. Her skin tingled all the way down to her toes. She wished he would pull her into his big, strong arms and tell her everything would be all right.

Ach! What was wrong with her? Being in the family way must make her have crazy thoughts. She had never paid much attention to the older, married women before, but she thought she remembered hearing some say they were more emotional when they were expecting.

"I don't see anything, Becky. The wind might have blown a speck of dirt in your eye."

"Probably." She only managed to croak the single word. Did Atlee's hand linger on her cheek, or was it her imagination? *You need to stop this right now!* She tried to be stern with herself. She forced her eyes to leave Atlee's and to look toward the girls. Though they didn't want to budge, she moved her feet back a step. "*Danki* for checking, Atlee. I'd better get these girls inside before they freeze."

Atlee dropped his hands to his sides. "Your cheeks are cold, but they're rosy like they're sunburned."

"From the wind, I guess." That and Atlee's nearness. "Did you *kumm* to see Lena?" Becky couldn't imagine that. Menfolk didn't usually visit new *mamms*.

"I actually stopped by to see if you, uh, if everything is okay. Do you need anything? Do you need wood brought inside?"

"*Nee*. You made us a nice stack near the house, and I already brought enough inside."

"I hope the pieces of wood weren't too big or too heavy. You should, uh, take care of yourself, too."

Becky thought it was sweet of Atlee to care. The bright flush in his cheeks made him all the more endearing. "I'm fine. And the wood wasn't too heavy."

"*Gut.*" Atlee looked at the frozen ground for a moment as if searching for the right words among the clumps of brown grass. "Uh, will you be staying on at Lena's for a while longer?"

"A while, I guess. It's a lot of work taking care of three little ones and the place all alone. I know everyone does as much as possible to help her out, but Lena has a lot of responsibilities."

"I wonder if she's thought of remarrying."

"I don't think she's had much time to ponder that, but maybe she will now that the *boppli* is finally here." Too bad Lena was older or Becky might try to play matchmaker between her and Atlee. Becky sighed. Lena would probably want someone older and more settled and ready to take on three young ones.

"What was the sigh for?"

"Nothing. I'm just a little tired. Even though they would never admit it, the girls are probably ready to get inside and get warm." Becky turned to look at the swing, which barely swayed, all momentum gone. "You girls are going to be frozen stiff. How will your *mamm* like it if you had to walk around stiff as boards?" She exaggerated a straight-legged walk over to the swing. The girls howled with laughter.

"One more swing?" Mary's eyes pleaded, but her teeth chattered.

"Tomorrow we'll try to get outside earlier when it's a little warmer. Now we need to check on your *mamm* and *bruder* and fix supper. Are you hungry?"

"*Jah*!" two tiny voices shouted in unison.

Becky grabbed the swing as Mary jumped off. Then she lifted Eliza to the ground. "You're *wilkom* to join us, Atlee. So many women brought food we'll never be able to eat it all."

"I'd like to, but . . ."

"Please, Atlee!" Mary tugged on his jacket.

Atlee stooped down to Mary's level. "I have to do my chores at home, Mary, but maybe I can *kumm* another day if that's all right with you, your *mamm*, and Becky."

"Okay. Mamm won't mind. You don't mind, either, do you, Becky?"

"Of course not. Tomorrow or whenever you like will be just fine." Now why did she say that and encourage him? Here she'd been trying to match him up with someone else and now her tongue had jumped ahead of her brain and invited him over. She had to start thinking with her brain and not her heart.

"We'll count on tomorrow night, then, *jah*?"

Mary jumped up and down. Eliza joined her, even though she didn't comprehend the reason for Mary's excitement.

Becky almost felt like joining Mary's celebration, too, but maintained her composure, if not her distance. "Tomorrow will be fine. Let's get inside and get warm, girls." Becky took a little hand in each of hers to lead the girls to the house.

"You're doing a great job with them, Becky. They're even lots quieter in church now."

Becky's heart warmed at the compliment. She couldn't stop the smile that tugged at her lips. "*Danki* for stopping by tonight."

"See you tomorrow."

Despite her intention to distance herself from

Atlee, her smile broadened at his merry whistling as he strode toward his buggy. Her heart did a little dance and her feet wanted to follow along at the mere thought of seeing him again tomorrow.

Chapter Twenty-Two

Becky took the girls out to play earlier the next day, while the sun still peeked through the clouds. She let them run and play until they began to droop. The poor little things could barely hold their eyes open to eat the noon meal, so as soon as they finished eating, Becky tucked them in for a well-deserved nap. She should have plenty of time to think of a supper menu.

"Don't we still have tons of food left?" Lena shuffled into the kitchen after laying Matthew in a cradle in the living room.

Becky stood in front of the pantry surveying its contents. "*Jah*, we still have some things, but I wanted to make something fresh. The only thing is I'm not a very experienced cook."

"Ah! We need to impress the beau, I see."

Becky turned to face Lena, her fists on her hips. "Atlee Stauffer is not my beau. I am not in the market for one of those. I happen to think when someone has a guest for a meal, it's proper to cook something fresh. I just don't know what to cook that won't turn out a disaster."

"I see." Lena smirked, and her eyes crinkled. "Well, you've certainly cooked for all of us before the *boppli* arrived and we were bombarded with casseroles. None of us died or got sick."

"That's reassuring."

"You're a fine cook, Becky. Honest."

"I don't have a very extensive repertoire, as the *Englisch* say."

"Most of us make things up as we go."

"What should I prepare?"

"Your beef stew is yummy, and we should have plenty of vegetables. Your meatloaf was tasty, too. I'm not sure what you added to give it a different flavor, but it was far better than mine."

"Maybe I'll do the stew since I can always keep it warm on the back burner. We have cornmeal, so I can bake corn bread."

"That would be nice. Beef stew is a hot, stick-to-your-ribs food and would be perfect for this cold day." Lena shivered and briskly rubbed her thin arms.

Becky glanced at the clock centered on an otherwise bare wall. "I should have time to make a batch of fudge brownies, ain't so?"

"Sure. I'll entertain the girls when they wake up. It's time for me to resume my responsibilities so you can get on with your life."

"*Ach*, there's no rush." Becky reached out to squeeze Lena's hand. "I truly have enjoyed staying here and helping you and the girls and Matthew. I'd be at loose ends if I weren't here."

"You could always take Laurie up on her offer. You'd make a *wunderbaar* birthing assistant."

"I don't know. Maybe. But I've got my own

childbirth experience to get through first."

"You've got at least four or five months yet."

"True." Becky absentmindedly tapped one black-shod foot on the linoleum floor. "You know, maybe I should think about Laurie's offer—and stop thinking about Atlee Stauffer." The last part she declared practically under her breath, but Lena heard her anyway.

"Atlee's a nice fellow. He'd probably make a *gut daed*, too."

"To his own *kinner*."

"Hmmm. He may surprise you. It's not hard to love a *boppli*, especially if you love his or her *mamm*."

"*Ach*, Lena!" Becky clapped her hands to her overheated cheeks. "Don't talk of love!"

For all her protesting that this supper was nothing special, nothing more than a way to return kindness, Becky's fingers fumbled often, and a whole flock of butterflies took up residence in her stomach. She barely rescued the brownies from the oven before the edges burned, and she almost forgot to put salt in her beef stew. How bland would that have been?

To top things off, when she cracked an egg to stir into the cornmeal, pieces of shell fell into the cup while the egg slid onto the counter in a gooey mess.

"Are you okay?" Lena entered the kitchen from which she'd been banished in time to hear Becky muttering as she wiped up the egg mess. Lena cradled Matthew in her arms.

"*Jah.*" Becky blew out an exasperated sigh. "I just seem to be all thumbs today."

"Do you need some help?"

"*Nee.* If I can get this corn bread mixed up and into the pan without glopping it everywhere, I should be okay."

"It sure smells *gut* in here. My stomach has been rumbling." Lena patted her already flat abdomen.

"You're always hungry because you're nursing the *boppli.* You'd probably eat a mud pie if I sliced it up."

Lena burst out laughing. "Hey, I'm not that much of a pig."

Becky smiled and forced herself to relax. "*Nee,* you're not. And you're just as skinny as ever."

"I never keep my weight on after delivery."

"I hope I'll be able to say the same thing."

"What weight? I don't think you've gained any. You've probably lost weight instead. You must be growing a peanut in there."

Becky laughed. "I've got a long way to go. But I don't have a lot of time left to get this supper pulled together. Atlee will be here soon." She raised an arm to brush a stray strand of hair from her brow. She cracked another egg. This one made it into the cup without shell fragments. She whisked it into the dry ingredients in the big ceramic mixing bowl.

"But this supper is nothing special. Right?"

Becky looked up in time to catch the teasing gleam in Lena's eyes. "Oooh, you! If I had another hand, I'd throw the wet dishrag at you."

"Let's be glad you aren't an octopus, then. Would you like Mary to set the table? She's been wanting to help, but I don't think you could use her cooking assistance right now. You seem to be flustered enough without an inquisitive little girl under your feet or making a mess."

Becky wrinkled her nose. "Sure, Mary can set the table."

"You might want to wipe the cornmeal off your nose before our esteemed guest arrives."

Becky poked out her tongue in Lena's direction.

"Very mature response!" Lena's laughter filled the room.

It did Becky's heart *gut* to hear Lena laugh, even if it was at her expense. During the weeks before Matthew's birth, Lena had been alternately excited and apprehensive. Becky assumed that was normal for women about to give birth. But Lena also struggled with sadness. The loss of her husband loomed large. Naturally, Lena wished he could have been with her to greet their new *kinner*. And then Lena had feared all the grief she'd experienced had harmed the unborn *boppli*, despite the reassurances of the other women and even the midwife that that would not be the case. With the delivery behind her and a healthy little son added to her family, Lena had perked up considerably. So Becky would gladly endure Lena's teasing.

A clomping up the back steps told Becky Atlee had arrived. Hastily she brushed at her dress. She snatched up a big stainless steel serving spoon and held it close to her face so she could see her reflection in it. She turned her head this way and that way and squinted but couldn't see any remnants of cornmeal on her nose. That Lena! Becky raised an arm to wipe her sleeve across her nose just in case.

"Hello," a deep male voice boomed, sending a little shiver up Becky's spine.

"*Kumm* on in." Becky grabbed a thick dish towel, opened the oven door, and pulled the corn bread out. It looked like perfect timing, for once. The golden corn bread, barely crispy around the edges, smelled as *wunderbaar* as it looked. Becky hoped the taste matched. She also hoped she had remembered to add all the necessary ingredients.

"It sure smells *gut* in here." Atlee entered the kitchen, rubbing his hands together. "It's getting even colder, and the clouds have thickened. I wouldn't be surprised if we had snow tonight."

Becky shivered. "Brrr! I hope not. Snow is pretty, but I'm ready for warmer weather."

"*Jah*, I think we're all itching to get outside again. It's about time to start working on the fields."

215

"Hello, Atlee." Lena inched her way into the kitchen. She carried a swaddled infant in her arms while the girls clung to her dress, making walking a challenge.

"Hey, girls. You remember me. We played on the swing only yesterday."

Mary grinned and let go of Lena's dress. "*Jah*, Mamm. We flew way up high." She hopped up to demonstrate.

Eliza caught Mary's excitement and jumped up and down, flinging her arms skyward.

"Whew! I can move again." Lena took two tiny steps back from the hopping little girls. "And this is Matthew."

Atlee peeked at the sleeping infant and smiled. "He looks like a big strong fellow, ain't so?"

"Girls, are you hungry?" Becky immediately got their attention, so the jumping and squealing ceased. "Go sit at the table, please."

Mary, like a little *mamm*, took Eliza's hand and led her to the big oak table.

"That was delicious. It just hit the spot on such a cold evening. I'm full up to the top." Atlee patted his full stomach. He'd polished off two bowls of beef stew and two big chunks of corn bread. Becky's blush at his words made him smile. She sure was pretty, and that little blush was adorable. Would she ever forget the past and give him a chance?

"There are brownies for dessert," Mary announced.

"Did you help make them?" Atlee turned his attention to the dark-haired little girl who looked so much like her *mamm*.

"*Nee*, but I can help eat them."

Atlee laughed. "I'm sure you can."

"They're chocolate fudge brownies," Becky said.

"Mmmm! Those are the best kind, ain't so?"

Mary nodded vigorously, her brown eyes sparkling.

"Well, I think I can find room in my belly to fit in a brownie. How about you?"

Mary nodded again. This time Eliza nodded along with her.

Lena smiled at her girls, and Becky laughed. Becky's laughter was music to Atlee's ears. It was funny he'd never noticed how soft and pleasant her voice was or how her laughter brought joy into a room. Had she really changed so drastically, or had he? Maybe they both had made monumental changes. Whatever it was, Atlee decided he liked the changes in himself, and he definitely liked the changes he'd observed in Becky since her return from her city adventure.

Before he could call it back, Atlee's mind wandered off on its own adventure. What would it be like to sit at the table with Becky every evening with their *kinner* spread around the table with them? They'd sit together in the living room after supper for Bible reading and prayers. He and Becky would work together on their own farm and take turns pushing their little ones on a swing or chasing them around their yard. They'd tuck them into their beds and then have some precious time to themselves. They'd . . .

"Atlee? Atlee?"

"Huh?"

"Your brownie?" Lena held out a small plate with an enormous chocolate fudge brownie in its center. How long had she been holding the plate in front of him? "You look like your mind has gone visiting somewhere and forgot to take your body along." Lena didn't bother to try to hide the smile on her face. Her eyes traveled to where he'd been staring.

When he abruptly returned to his senses, Atlee realized he'd been staring at Becky, whose face had flushed a deep crimson color. "Uh, I guess I was kind of, uh, lost in thought."

"Uh-huh." Lena waggled the plate a bit.

"*Danki.*" Atlee took the plate and set it on the table. He stared at it as if it was the most important thing in the world and waited for his own face to cool. "This is a big brownie. Mary, I might have to get you and Eliza to help me finish it."

"Okay," Mary agreed quickly.

"Okay," Eliza parroted.

Atlee made a big show of how full he was.

"This brownie sure is tasty, but my poor belly can't hold it all." He broke off a chunk and cast a questioning glance at Lena. When she nodded, he looked at Mary. "Do you think you could help me with this bite, Mary?"

"*Jah.*"

Atlee stretched to lay the treat on Mary's plate. He broke off a slightly smaller piece. "What about you, Eliza? Can you help me, too?"

The little girl nodded and giggled.

Both girls murmured, "*Danki,*" before devouring treats while the adults talked and laughed.

"I'm going to get these girls cleaned up and ready for bed. Just leave the dishes for now, Becky. I'll help with them later."

Becky started to push back from the table. "I can see to the girls, Lena. Then I'll do the dishes. You can rest while Matthew is sleeping."

"I'm not an invalid, Becky. I've been resting off and on today. You've been spoiling me terribly. It's time for me to do more now. I can take care of the girls. You visit."

"I'll help Becky with the dishes, Lena. You go ahead with the girls." Atlee saw through Lena's ploy. It was *gut* of her to give him some time alone with Becky.

"You? Help with the dishes?" Becky looked as if he'd just said he'd stick his head in the woodstove.

"Why not? I think I can handle the job. How

about if you wash and I'll dry. I surely can't mess up that task."

"I didn't mean you weren't capable of doing the job. I just meant . . ." She twisted her hands and looked completely flustered.

"I know. Men don't do kitchen chores, but I don't mind. I've helped out plenty of times at home." He winked at her and watched the color rise in her face again.

"Let's go, girls." Lena lifted Eliza from her chair and took Mary's hand.

"But, but . . ." Becky sputtered.

Lena took no notice of Becky's protest. She jabbered to the girls as she led them from the kitchen.

"Are you ready to get started?"

"*Ach*, Atlee. You don't have to help. I can clean up. You must be tired after working all day. If you need to head home, I'm fine."

Was she trying to get rid of him? Didn't she want to be alone with him, or was she afraid? Atlee couldn't quite read the expression on her face. "I certainly have time to help, unless you don't want me to stay."

"It's not that." Becky started to reach out a hand to touch his arm but drew it back before making contact. "It's just, uh, well, let's get busy, then." Becky snatched up plates and silverware and carried them to the sink. She turned on the water and squirted in liquid dish soap.

"You're really cute when you're flustered."

"Atlee! You shouldn't say such things."

"I shouldn't be truthful?"

"Of course you should be truthful. You just shouldn't be so, uh, forward."

"Forward? I'm simply saying what I see and what I feel."

Becky scrubbed a plate until Atlee feared it would crack in half. He took it from her hands and rinsed the soap off. "It's okay for us to be alone, you know."

"Is it?"

"Why wouldn't it be? Besides, Lena is right upstairs."

Becky stared at him for a moment with those beautiful green eyes. She quickly looked away and plopped another plate into the sudsy water, sending bubbles flying through the air. A glob of soap landed smack on her slightly upturned nose. Before she could react, Atlee tilted her chin up to wipe the soap away with his free hand. A tingling sensation traveled from his fingertips up his arm and straight into his heart. What was happening to him?

Chapter Twenty-Three

Time stopped. Becky feared her heart had stopped as well, but then it thumped so hard she nearly gasped. With Atlee's hand on her chin, she had nowhere to look but up. Up into his eyes as green as her own, eyes with laugh crinkles at the corners, eyes filled with . . . *Ach*! She had to look away from those eyes before she drowned in them. She had to get away from his touch that sent warmth through her entire being. But she felt nailed to the spot. Her eyes, her feet, nothing would obey her brain, her logic. Her heart wanted to rule, but she couldn't let it. *Do not become involved with Atlee or with anyone. Look where that got you before.* Her brain screamed the warning.

"Um, *danki*." Becky's voice came out whisper-soft. She forced herself to take a step back from Atlee and to look away from his penetrating, mesmerizing eyes. "We'd better finish these dishes." She picked up the plate and scrubbed it.

"What are you afraid of, Becky?"

Atlee's deep voice was low and right beside her ear. Little shivers ran down her body. "I-I'm not afraid of anything."

"You act afraid of me. I wouldn't hurt you, Becky."

"I never thought you would. I've never known you to hurt anybody or anything, unless you've changed drastically in the months I was away."

"I have changed, Becky, but in a positive way, I think."

Becky dared to raise a questioning glance, careful not to get caught in Atlee's eyes again.

"I guess I've grown up. About time, my *mamm* would say." Atlee chuckled. "I'm ready to settle down now, and—"

"That's *gut*, Atlee." Becky feared what he would say next, so she didn't give him the chance to finish. "I suppose we all grow up at different times and in different ways." She had been forced to grow up instantly when she had foolishly run away and found there was nobody else to take care of her. She'd learned many hard lessons. One of those lessons was to keep her distance from others. She could trust her parents and perhaps her *bruders* and their wives, but she couldn't be sure of anyone else. She had to protect herself and her *boppli*. She rinsed the cup she'd been washing and set it in the drainer.

Atlee snatched her hand before she could plunge it back into the dishwater. "Look at me, Becky. Please."

She hesitated and kept staring at a cup bobbing in the water like a rowboat in the pond.

"Please?"

She couldn't stand it. That plaintive note in his

voice grabbed her soul. She had to look at him again. She had no strength left to resist.

"You feel it too, *jah*?"

"I don't know what you're talking about." Becky attempted to pull her hand from Atlee's, but his grip was too strong. The grip wasn't painful at all, but it was firm, like he'd never let her go. She didn't want him to let her go. Wait. She did want him to let her go. He had to let her go. She tried to look elsewhere, but his eyes were two green magnets drawing her gaze to them.

"I think you do, Becky. You can trust me. I wouldn't hurt you."

"I know that. *Freinden* don't hurt each other, and you're a *gut freind*." There. She got the words out.

"We're more than *freinden*, ain't so?"

Her heart wrenched in two. It wanted her tongue to agree with Atlee, but her brain tried to squeeze in reason at the same time. "H-how can we be?"

"Easy. We spend more time together and get to know each other better. Haven't you enjoyed our walks and talks?"

"Of course, but . . ."

"I feel I already know you well, but we can take all the time you need."

All the time she needed? Soon she'd be bulging with child; another man's child. She cared too much to saddle Atlee with such a burden. "I-it's impossible."

"Nothing is impossible if we believe."

This time when she yanked she was able to free her hand, though it suddenly felt cold and lonely. Could a hand be lonely? *Get a grip on yourself, girl.* "You know my, um, condition." She could barely hear her own words, but apparently Atlee heard them.

He nodded but his eyes, full of concern and compassion, never wavered from her face. "I fully understand your condition, and it truly doesn't matter to me."

"Atlee! You can't mean that! In a few months, I'll be as big as a barn."

Atlee chuckled. "Somehow I doubt that, but even if you were, you'd be even more beautiful."

"You aren't thinking clearly. What would your parents, your family, your *freinden* say? They'd say you had taken leave of your senses, for sure and for certain."

"*Nee.* They would not think I'd lost my mind. They'd be happy I found someone to care about." He captured her hand again.

"They'd be horrified and would tell you to run away from me as fast as you can, as well you should."

"I'm not running anywhere."

"Atlee." Becky paused to gather her thoughts. She felt like she was trying to simplify some concept for Mary and Eliza to understand. She gently squeezed his hand as if to transfer strength from him. "I'm going to have a *boppli*. Another man's *boppli*." A tear escaped and tracked down her cheek. Atlee halted it with the thumb of his free hand. Such a tender gesture nearly made Becky sob aloud. She could not let this *wunderbaar* man throw his life away on her.

"If you married me, the *boppli* would be mine, too." He left his work-roughened hand on her cheek.

"*Ach*, Atlee. You don't know what you're saying."

"I certainly do."

"Then you need to think about this some more. Then you'll see how impossible such an idea would be." Becky tried to put distance between them. With the edge of the kitchen counter biting into her back, she had no further escape route unless she pushed Atlee aside and ran from the room.

"I have thought of little else since you returned. And I've prayed about this a lot."

"Maybe you should discuss this with your *daed* or *mamm*. They should be able to talk some sense into you."

"You know that's not our way. Relationships are between the two people involved."

"It could never work, Atlee." Becky kept her voice gentle. She didn't want to hurt him.

"Give me a *gut* reason why it couldn't."

"Your family would be absolutely horrified.

They would think you were making the biggest mistake of your life."

"Anyone who cares about me would care about my happiness."

"What makes you think we would be happy together?"

"I can feel it. I knew when we took our first walk together that you were the girl for me. I know you feel it, too, ain't so?"

Becky didn't want to lie, but neither did she want to further encourage Atlee in his preposterous dream. She bit her lower lip so hard trying to formulate a reply that she cringed at the metallic taste of blood.

"You can't answer me, so I take that as agreement."

"Atlee, I-I'm not *gut* enough for you, and you know that."

"I don't know any such thing. Don't go running yourself down."

"I'm, um, tainted."

"Whatever gave you that idea? Has anyone said something like that to you?"

Becky smiled at the protective expression that crossed Atlee's face. "Of course they haven't said anything *to* me. But I've seen people whispering behind their hands and heard snippets of conversations that halted abruptly when I entered the room. Some folks don't believe I thought I was married. Some prefer to believe the worst about me. I suppose I can't blame them, based on my former behavior. You don't need that in your life."

"I need you in my life, Becky. Please don't shut me out. Please give me, give us, a chance. I can't change other people's thoughts and beliefs. I don't much care what others think. I care about you and the *boppli*." His eyes slid briefly to her midsection. "I believe you told the truth, and that's all that matters to me."

"You're too *gut*."

"*Nee*, but together we could have something very *gut*. And we could provide a *gut* home for the *boppli*."

The sound of approaching footsteps caused Atlee to back up, but not before placing the whisper of a kiss on Becky's cheek. "Think about it, about us." He cleared his throat and raised his voice as Lena entered the kitchen. "*Danki* for supper, Becky. I'll be heading home." He turned toward the door but not before throwing a pleading look at Becky. "*Gut* to see you again, Lena. That's a fine son you've got." Atlee slipped past Lena and out the back door, leaving Becky to stare after him, her hand on her cheek.

"My word! Do you care to explain that look?"

"What look?" Becky pulled her eyes from the space Atlee had just vacated to focus on Lena.

Lena huffed an exaggerated sigh. "That hang-dog expression Atlee shot you before he did his disappearing act. If his face was any longer, he'd have tripped over it."

Becky couldn't help but laugh. "He asked me to think about some things, that's all."

"What might those things be?"

Becky hesitated, weighing the pros and cons of confiding in Lena. Maybe another opinion would help her put things into perspective. Or better yet, maybe Lena would have some ideas how she could discourage Atlee. She certainly hadn't been successful at that on her own.

"It's okay." Lena shook Becky's arm, thereby jerking her out of her reverie. "You don't have to tell me. I'm teasing you."

"You did that on purpose, ain't so?"

"I did what on purpose?"

Becky stomped her foot. "You know very well what I'm talking about, so don't play all innocent."

Lena raised her eyebrows and mouthed, "Me?"

"You deliberately left the room to leave me alone with Atlee."

"The girls needed to get cleaned up and ready for bed before they fell asleep at the table."

"I could have cleaned them up."

"I told you before; I need to resume my duties. You need to be free to get on with your life. Besides, being alone with Atlee wasn't such a terrible thing, was it? You have to admit he is quite nice-looking." Lena winked and smiled.

"I have *nee* business speculating whether some-one is nice-looking."

"I'd like to know why not?"

"In case you've forgotten, I am expecting."

"That doesn't hinder your eyesight. You are also a single, young *maedel*."

"A man deserves a chaste woman, not a woman who is expecting another man's *boppli*."

"Becky, you are too hard on yourself. Are you planning to remain single all your life and raise your little one all alone?"

Becky shrugged. "I have my family."

Lena took Becky's hand and towed her into the living room to sit on the couch near Matthew's cradle. "Men and women who already have *kinner* marry all the time."

"True, but they are widows and widowers."

"It's sort of the same situation with you."

"Ha!" Becky clapped her hand over her mouth, afraid her loud exclamation might have woken Matthew. A quick peek at the cradle told her the infant was still sleeping peacefully and soundly, completely oblivious to the two women in the room with him. "My situation is hardly the same."

"Sure it is. Your *boppli*'s *daed* has passed on." Lena held up a hand to prevent Becky's inter-ruption. "You believed you were married. You can't help it that the man you believed in and trusted lied to you. When he died, that sort of made you a widow."

"You have strange logic."

Lena shrugged her bony shoulders. "Anyway, it wouldn't hurt you to give whatever matters Atlee mentioned some serious thought and prayer."

"I can't let Atlee throw his life away on me. You've got to help me."

"Atlee Stauffer couldn't possibly find anyone better than you. I firmly believe that. I won't do anything to cause him to think you aren't a *wunderbaar* person."

"You could help me find him a special girl to care about."

"Atlee has found one all on his own. You need to think about that. And don't take forever, either. You don't want to let such a *gut* man slip away." Lena nudged Becky with her elbow. "And stop touching your cheek."

Chapter Twenty-Four

"How was your supper?" Saloma dried her hands on a blue-checked dish towel as she turned to face her son.

"Fine. It was fine."

"Did you get enough to eat? I just put leftovers in the refrigerator."

"I got plenty to eat."

"Did Becky actually do the cooking?" Malinda asked.

Atlee fixed his sister with a glare. "*Jah*, Malinda. Becky did the cooking. We had beef stew and corn bread and fudge brownies for dessert."

"It sounds like a nice meal," Saloma said soothingly.

"I wasn't trying to be mean," Malinda clarified. "I didn't know if Becky knew how to cook."

"Everything was tasty. Lena's son looked healthy." Atlee hoped to steer the conversation away from Becky.

"Is Lena getting along well, then? I need to get over to see her again." Saloma hung the towel on a hook.

"She seemed to be fine. I think I'll head upstairs." Just a few more minutes and he could be out of sight of the two intuitive women who had the uncanny ability to read him like a book.

He threw in an exaggerated yawn for effect.

"*Gut nacht*, Bruder." Malinda squeezed Atlee's arm as he scooted by her on his way out of the kitchen.

Atlee almost made it out the door when another hand on his arm stopped him in his tracks. He tried to brace himself for whatever his *mamm* intended to say to him.

"Are you sure of what you're doing, son?"

"What do you mean?" Playing dumb wouldn't buy him much time, but maybe he'd get a few seconds to collect his thoughts.

"I mean getting involved with Becky Zook."

"I simply had supper with Becky, Lena, and Lena's girls."

"Somehow I don't think it's Lena Troyer you are interested in."

Words failed him. Atlee couldn't meet his *mamm*'s eyes nor could he deny his interest in Becky. It simply wasn't in him to lie. "I thought you forgave Becky and believed her story."

"I have nothing against the girl, Atlee. We all did foolish things in our youth, and we've all made mistakes. From what I've seen, Becky has matured into a fine young woman. I wonder if you've thought through a relationship with a woman, uh, in the family way. You would be taking on a big responsibility. You would be an instant *daed*—that is, if you took the relationship further than simply being *freinden*."

"I understand all that, Mamm."

"Do you? Pray about it, Atlee. That's all I ask."

"Pray," she said. I've prayed and thought so much my brain hurts. Atlee closed the door of the bedroom he used to share with his older *bruder*. Now Sam and Emma Swarey were happily married, if their constant smiles and tender looks were any indication. More and more often he'd found himself wanting to share such smiles and glances with someone special.

Atlee flopped on his bed. How did Sam know for sure Emma was the right girl for him? He wished his big *bruder* was here right now to listen to his ramblings in the dark and to help him sort things out. But Atlee was on his own. It was totally up to him to make sense of his jumbled thoughts. It was his decision. His and the Lord Gott's.

Atlee wanted to do the right thing, and he firmly believed pursuing a relationship with Becky was the right thing. He was convinced of it. The thing was, he had to convince Becky they were right for each other. His *mamm* and family would *kumm* around as long as he was happy. They were a warm, loving bunch. They'd accept Becky.

Becky. He had never given her a second glance before. Sure, he'd noticed her honey gold hair, big green eyes, and pretty face, but he had never taken her seriously. In fact, he'd been rather amused at her less-than-subtle flirtations with half the fellows her own age and even a few older ones. He'd pitied the poor fools who thought Becky actually cared for them. They'd been too blind or too besotted to see it was all a game to Becky. He and Sam had shared a few laughs over the whole business and had congratulated themselves for being smart enough to avoid Becky's hooks.

Now, without even trying, without any of her old flirtatious ways, Becky had reeled him in. And to his dismay, she kept trying to cast him away. For his own *gut*, she'd said. She believed she was tainted and not *gut* enough for him despite his trying to convince her otherwise. She truly had changed from that carefree, playful girl into a caring, serious woman—a woman he now thought about constantly. Dare he say a woman he loved?

Atlee wrapped the feather pillow around his head as if he could snuff out the tormenting thoughts. If only it was that easy to empty his brain. *Lord Gott, what do You want me to do? I never gave her a second thought before, but ever since our first walk together after she returned, I've been drawn to her like a hummingbird to sweet nectar.* Atlee prayed for guidance. He prayed for peace. He wrestled with the pillow all night long as he wrestled with his thoughts.

How ridiculous! Becky had washed her face as she prepared for bed, careful to avoid a certain spot on her cheek. She paused in brushing her hair to put a finger to that very spot. A little tingle ran down her spine at the memory of that whisper of a kiss.

Stop it, Becky! She dropped the hairbrush onto the dresser. Quickly she braided her thick, waist-length hair, berating her fingers all the while for their trembling. After a little more fumbling, she secured an elastic band around the end of her braid. She padded barefoot across the cold wood floor, extinguished the lamp, and crawled beneath the covers. She wiggled into a comfortable position and tugged the covers up to her chin. She sighed, squeezed her eyes closed, and waited for sleep that refused to claim her.

Think, Lena had told her. She couldn't turn off her thoughts. Her body might be weary, but her brain remained wide awake and flashed one picture from her life after another. It reminded her of walking through Walmart, where every gigantic television displayed a different scene. She quickly shut off the images of New York. That horrible chapter of her life was behind her. She didn't have any desire to revisit those memories.

Did she want to spend the rest of her life alone? She had her *boppli*, of course. Her right hand slid over to stroke her barely rounded belly. She loved him or her, but did she want it to be just the two of them forever? Well, until her *boppli* grew up and got married. Then she would be completely alone. Could she raise him or her by herself? Of course she could! Look at Lena. She now had three little ones to raise, but Becky believed Lena would remarry in time.

It would definitely be nice to have someone to share the joys and struggles with. It would be nice to give her *boppli* siblings. How could she do that when she couldn't trust another man?

Atlee had proven trustworthy, though, hadn't he? He had been very caring, very concerned, very sweet. Again her fingers strayed to her cheek. She had no reason to doubt Atlee's trustworthiness or his sincerity. He had been open and honest, and he treated her with respect. It was she who didn't deserve him. How could she let him ruin his life? He needed to find a nice girl who hadn't made such a mess of her life as Becky had.

She turned onto her side, rearranged the covers, and groaned. Why couldn't she extinguish all the images swirling in her brain like the *Englischers* switched off their televisions? One screen in her mind depicted her rocking an infant in the creaky swing on her parents' front porch. Her parents would give them a home, for sure and for certain. She loved her parents, but she didn't want to live with them all her life. She wanted a home of her own. Maybe they could build a small attachment onto their home for her.

Another screen displayed her standing beneath

a tall oak tree in the yard of some unrecognizable two-story house. A host of *kinner* ran around her playing tag while an infant snuggled in her arms. She could possibly marry some widower who needed a woman to care for his little ones. She could hope to grow fond of him in time. She didn't know of any such man in her district, and the thought of leaving home again gave her goose bumps.

The largest screen in her mind showed only one person—a tall, muscular young man with dark brown hair and kind, caring green eyes. Atlee. He filled her heart the same as he filled her mind. His image forced out all the others. Why had he sought her out on her return home? Why had he been so nice to her? She had never flirted with him or Sam. She had never tried to get his attention. She had never tried to get him to like her. For some reason she had steered clear of the Stauffer *buwe*. They were a bit older. She had had her twentieth birthday while she was in New York. That must make Atlee twenty-two, since he had been a couple of grades ahead of her in school. Why couldn't she get him out of her mind? Why were her thoughts so mixed-up?

Had Atlee been right? Had Gott put them in each other's path for a reason? Was it His will for them to be together? Atlee had been so sure he could love her *boppli* and be a *daed* to him or her, but would he be able to do that when the time came? What if they married and had other *kinner*? Would he treat them differently?

The bed squeaked in protest as Becky flipped over yet again. She tugged at the covers that had wound themselves around her and bound her like sausage in a casing. She had to get some sleep. The new day would be dawning, and Mary and Eliza would awaken with boundless energy. Lena had been growing stronger and soon would not need her to care for the house and girls. Then Becky would have to go home to await the birth of her infant. Would Atlee visit her at her parents' house?

Ach! Atlee again! He invaded every single thought. What should she do? If she examined her heart, she knew she cared deeply for Atlee. That was just it. She cared too much to have him face ridicule or endure whisperings because of her. Was it love to care that much about someone else's well-being? She bolted upright. Did she love Atlee? Dear Gott, what was she to do?

Chapter Twenty-Five

"You look like you've been wrestling with demons all night."

"I feel like it, too," Becky mumbled. She knew her puffy eyes must be rimmed with dark circles, but there was nothing she could do about it. Splashing cold water on her face had not made her feel any better. She had only dozed off for a few moments all night, and that had been right before it was time to get up. Now she was late getting downstairs and Lena was already pulling out pans to cook breakfast. "I can get this. You should rest."

"Honestly, you look more in need of rest than I do. I, at least, slept in between nursings. You look like you didn't sleep a single wink."

"My brain wouldn't shut down." Becky took the pan from Lena's hand and held it under the faucet to fill it with enough water for the oatmeal. She set it on the stove to heat and kept her back to Lena. For some reason, tears threatened to spill and she needed to keep them at bay. If she saw compassion in Lena's eyes, it could be her undoing.

"I'm sorry, Becky. I shouldn't have pushed you to think about your feelings and options. It was none of my business. I certainly didn't intend for you to stay awake all night."

"It isn't your fault that my jumbled thoughts tormented me all night. I thought and prayed and thought some more." Becky grabbed the box of oats and dumped in enough for four people.

Lena stepped closer and grasped Becky's upper arm. "Did you *kumm* to any conclusions?"

"*Ach*, Lena, I-I don't know. I . . ." She sniffed hard.

Lena pulled Becky into her arms and patted her back in soothing circles. "You don't have to tell me anything, but I am a *gut* listener whenever you feel like talking."

Becky nodded against Lena's shoulder. "I do care for Atlee. I can't deny that. I care too much to let him be saddled with me."

"I'm sure he doesn't see it that way."

"He's not thinking clearly. People will talk about him because of me. They might not say anything to his face, but they'll whisper." Becky pulled away from Lena's embrace and swiped at her eyes.

"I believe you underestimate us."

"I didn't mean you, Lena." Becky sniffed again and wished she had stuck a tissue in a pocket or up her sleeve.

"I think most people will feel exactly as I do. They would be happy for you and Atlee and the *boppli*. You'd make a great little family."

"The *boppli*! That's another thing. Atlee says he'd care for him or her, but what about later if we had our own *kinner*? Would he still feel the same way? Would he treat my *boppli* the same as ours?"

"Now you underestimate Atlee. Your *boppli* would be his, too. You don't stop loving your *kinner*, no matter what."

"It wouldn't really be his . . ."

"If you marry, you are family. All of you. That wouldn't change if you added two dozen more little ones."

"Marriage! I don't know if any relationship with Atlee is right."

"For him or for you?" Lena said, then suddenly rushed to check on her infant, who had begun to fuss in the cradle near the stove in the living room.

For him! Becky would be happy to be Atlee's *fraa*—she had reached that conclusion—but she needed to protect him and spare him any embarrassment or pain.

"Whew, Bruder, you look like you slept under the back wheel of the buggy, or maybe underneath a thrashing horse."

"Well, don't you look lovely yourself, dear *schweschder*." Atlee playfully punched Malinda's arm, causing her to drop the apple she had been about to add to Aidan's lunch box. It plunked off the kitchen counter and rolled across the floor.

"Now look what you made me do!"

"I'll get it." Atlee bent and captured the apple in mid-roll. He wiped it on his shirt and tossed it into his little *bruder*'s lunch box. "There. *Gut* as new."

"Atlee! You didn't wash it off."

"Do you honestly think Aiden cares? He eats dirt and grass half the time."

"He does not."

"He certainly does! Haven't you ever seen him playing horse in the yard? And I'm sure he's eaten many a treat just after holding a toad in his grubby hands." Atlee wrinkled his nose and made a disgusted face.

Malinda burst out laughing. "You've got a point there, but I'm sure you did the same thing."

"I might have eaten cookies after holding some critter, but I don't remember ever eating dirt."

"You did wash your hands after coming inside from doing chores, didn't you?"

"Of course. I do have *some* manners."

"Hmmm. Why the raccoon eyes?"

"I beg your pardon?" Atlee had hoped all the joking would have diverted Malinda's attention from his sleep-deprived appearance.

"I believe you know exactly what I'm talking about."

"Since I don't go around looking at myself, I'm sure I don't know what you mean."

"I'm sure you do."

"We all have restless nights, ain't so?"

"I suppose, but usually there is a reason for such nights."

Atlee shrugged. "Is breakfast ready?" He snatched a crisp strip of bacon from a plate near the stove.

Malinda swatted at his hand. "What's yours?"

"What's my what?"

"Why are you deliberately avoiding the subject? I meant what is your reason for your sleepless night?"

"I couldn't get comfortable." Atlee turned aside so Malinda couldn't look directly into his eyes. Didn't they say the eyes were the windows to the soul? He didn't need Malinda looking into his soul or picking his brain. He should make his escape from the kitchen right now. A hand clamped firmly on his wrist caused a glitch in that plan.

"You know you can talk to me, Bruder."

"I talk to you all the time."

"I mean if you have something troubling you, I can listen. Who knows? Maybe I can even help."

Atlee seriously doubted that. "I'll keep that in mind." He threw a half-hearted smile at her. "Now what do I have to do to get something more substantial than a flimsy piece of bacon to eat?"

"You have to be patient and go sit at the table with everyone else."

Atlee stomped off in mock frustration. "You

have to be patient." Malinda's words rattled around in his brain. Perhaps he'd have to exercise patience with Becky, but he'd really like to be a part of her life now and be a *daed* to her *boppli* from the very beginning.

"You do *not* need cheese, Lena." Becky poked around the pantry, sorting through the cans and boxes on the shelves. "There are plenty of other things in here to fix."

"But the *kinner* want macaroni and cheese. I've kind of got a hankering for some, too."

"Then I'll put cheese on the grocery list to pick up on the next trip to the store."

"You know the cheese from the dairy is ever so much better than that store-bought stuff that's been wrapped in plastic packaging forever and a day."

"Cheese is cheese, especially when it's melted over noodles." Becky backed away from the pantry and turned to face her *freind*. She couldn't stop the laugh that bubbled up at the sight of Lena's forlorn expression. "Don't give me that fake pitiful look," she gasped out between giggles.

"It's not fake."

"Then you go to the dairy and fetch your cheese. I'll stay here with the *kinner*."

One of Lena's thin hands flew to her chest. "Me? I'm still recovering from childbirth."

"How convenient!"

"Are you going to nurse Matthew?"

"He'll sleep while you're gone.

"You can't be sure of that."

"Since you are no longer expecting, you should be over your food cravings now. I'm still expecting, and I do not crave cheese."

"Aw, Becky, I haven't had macaroni and cheese in ever so long. Cheese has lots of calcium and protein."

"So does milk. I'll pour you a glass."

"You're mean." Lena poked out her lip in a pout that could rival any of Mary's.

"You're *narrisch*!"

"What's crazy about wanting a yummy, gooey, cheesy, stick-to-your-ribs food?"

Becky rolled her eyes and then smiled at Mary, who entered the kitchen towing Eliza behind her. "I'm sure the girls would like macaroni and cheese for supper, too," Lena said.

Mary jumped up and down, pulling Eliza with her. "*Jah! Jah!*" she cried. Eliza echoed her squeals.

"No fair, Lena. You can't heap guilt on me by involving the girls." Becky squeezed her eyes shut and clapped her hands over her ears. "I can't see you or hear you." A tug on her skirt caused her to crack open one eye.

"Cheese?" Eliza stared up at Becky and grabbed a hunk of Becky's dress in her fist.

"*Ach*, Lena, you've created a monster." She crouched down to look Eliza in the eye. "How

about if you help me find something else?"
She scooped the child into her arms and swung
around to search the pantry again. "We can make
a green bean casserole or . . ."

"Cheese?"

"Face it, Becky. Nothing else will do."

"This is all your fault, Lena." Becky whirled
back around in time to take in Lena's smirk. "And
you only want me to go to the dairy because you
want to play matchmaker."

"That, and the girls want cheese."

"They didn't before you set them off."

"How can you refuse these adorable, sweet
little girls?"

"Okay. I give up. Let me get my cloak, bonnet,
and purse." Becky set Eliza down beside Lena
and stomped from the kitchen.

"And don't you dare go to the Food King. We
want dairy cheese!"

Becky grumbled as she fought the wind to hitch
the horse to the gray buggy. "Cold enough out
here to spit snow or sleet or both." She cast a
wary glance skyward. Sure enough, thickening
gray clouds threatened to snuff out any rays of
sunshine that might possibly send a smidgen of
warmth to the earth. "We'd better hurry." She
patted the horse's neck and climbed inside the
buggy, which provided a respite from the wind
but not a lot of warmth.

After she got the horse trotting at a brisk pace, she fumbled to cover her legs with the wool blanket beneath the buggy seat. This would be a test. How quickly could she slip into the dairy, make her purchase, and race home? Part two: Could she slip in and out without being detected by a dark-haired, green-eyed man who made her heart do crazy, uncontrollable flips?

Apparently Lena's big, dark horse was as anxious to complete this mission as Becky was. He stepped lively, pulling the buggy quickly along the blacktopped road. His breath puffed out in a cloud around his head. Becky wiggled her fingers inside her heavy wool gloves in an attempt to get the blood to flow and the tingling to stop. She wondered if being pregnant made her more sensitive to the cold. She didn't remember feeling so cold during previous winters. She thought she recalled other women complain about being hot when in the family way, but maybe that had been in the summer. She was freezing—all for macaroni and cheese. *Nee*, all because Lena wanted to throw her at Atlee.

Becky's icy fingers fumbled to tie the horse to the rail outside the long white one-story building. She promised him she would return as quickly as possible so he could get home to his feed and warm stall. The big horse stomped, snorted, and shook his massive head as if he understood her words. Now to sneak into and out of the building.

A gust of wind threatened to tear Becky's black bonnet off her head and send it flying, despite its being snugly tied beneath her chin. She hurried across the gravel parking lot to the entrance, glad to see several cars parked near the building. The more people, the better. An approaching car's tires crunched on the gravel behind her, snagging her attention.

Becky hurried to get to the door. She glanced over her shoulder to see a big, dark car. She sucked in a breath and barely squelched a scream. The car's tags told her the occupants were from New York. She'd observed the same kind of tags on vehicles that had whizzed by her as she scurried along the city's sidewalks. Her heart thundered, and her stomach rolled over. She had to get inside. She had to hide.

Chapter Twenty-Six

Becky pushed the door open in a panic and nearly bowled over the *Englisch* couple about to exit. She mumbled an apology and scooted out of their path.

The woman gave her a polite smile and said, "That wind is really something, isn't it?"

"*Jah*, it's pretty cold." Becky didn't have time to exchange further pleasantries. She had to get out of sight. Her eyes darted around in search of a hiding place. Her heart still pounded so hard it made her already rolling stomach even queasier. Where should she go? Unless someone let her pass through the employee door and into the back, she had no place to hide. If she crouched behind a display case, she would still be in view of anyone who stepped up to the counter. Maybe she should run out the back door and try to escape to the trees behind the dairy. No one would think to search there, would they?

She could only hope the people in the car didn't get a close enough glimpse to recognize her. From the distance, she would look like every other Amish woman. She whirled around to flee and crashed into a broad, hard chest. She only barely managed to stifle a scream as she struggled against the two hands clamped around her upper arms.

"Becky! Becky! It's me. What happened?"

"*Ach*, Atlee!" She wanted to sink into his embrace, but she had to run. Those people would be out of their car and walking through the front door any moment. "I-I have to go. Quick!" She glanced behind her at the still closed door. "Please, Atlee, let me go in back. Now!" She raised her eyes to meet his questioning ones. "Please. Right now!"

"*Kumm.*" Atlee kept his hand wrapped around one of Becky's arms and hustled her through the employee door.

As soon as the door shut behind them, Becky exhaled the breath she'd been holding. "Nobody can *kumm* back here, can they?"

She couldn't force a sound louder than a whisper, so Atlee had to lean close to hear her.

"Just employees. What's wrong, Becky? You're as white as fresh snow and trembling like the last leaf on a branch in a windstorm."

"I-I got scared."

"Of what? Did you have a problem with the horse on the road?"

"*Nee.* A car."

Atlee looked at her as if she'd lost her mind. "Huh?"

Becky knew she wasn't making any sense. She took a shaky breath and tried again. "In the parking lot, Atlee. There was a big, black car

251

with New York tags. I know those tags. What if . . ."

"I'll go and check it out."

Becky clung to Atlee's arm. "Don't leave me."

"I don't want to, but I want to see who came in. I'll be right back. Just stand over here out of sight in case someone opens the door."

Becky allowed Atlee to steer her to a corner away from the door. "Hurry!"

Atlee nodded, patted her hand, and strolled through the door, acting as if everything was perfectly normal.

Becky shrank back into the corner, berating herself for cowering like a helpless *boppli*. She moved a hand to her midsection to where her little one grew safe in her womb. She had to protect him or her. The door swung open so hard it banged against the doorstop. Becky nearly jumped through the ceiling. How had they found her?

The employee who zoomed through the door stopped abruptly, almost as startled as Becky. "What . . . ?"

Becky interrupted, keeping her voice low. "I'm sorry I scared you. I-I'm waiting for someone."

"You aren't supposed to be back here. Employees only."

"I know. I'll leave in a minute. I promise. I wasn't feeling well and didn't want to stay out there with all your customers." It wasn't really a lie. She did feel sick—scared, mostly—but the fear turned her stomach upside down and made her feel faint.

"I can get you a chair." The young man, who Becky didn't know well because he was from another district, changed his tone and became more concerned.

"That's all right. I'll be okay in a moment. I don't want to keep you from your work."

"Are you sure you're going to be okay?"

Becky nodded. "My *freind* had to check on something but will be back in a minute. I'm starting to feel better." Becky tried to smile and wished that last part was true. She only felt slightly better being out of sight. She'd feel much better if Atlee would hurry back to tell her all was well.

"Are you positive I can't get you anything?"

"*Nee*, but *danki*."

The *bu*, who was maybe a couple of years younger than Becky, nodded, retrieved the supplies he had come into the room to fetch, and left her alone with her mounting fears. Where was Atlee, and what was taking him so long? She yanked off her gloves and stuffed them into a pocket. She straightened her bonnet, which the wind had blown cockeyed, and nibbled at a fingernail. She knew it had only been a few minutes since Atlee had left, but those minutes felt like decades. Had something bad happened to Atlee?

She would never have returned to Maryland if she thought trouble would follow her here. She never should have left home in the first place. Why had she wanted to experience the big city before deciding to join the church? And if she was going to go off on her own, she should have at least been smart enough not to get involved with someone almost as soon as she reached New York. *Dummchen*, that's what she was. Too naive to spot a liar and a swindler.

Sure, Vinny had been so kind and sweet when he had waltzed into the café on her very first day. She'd been so nervous and all thumbs. It had been a miracle she hadn't dumped *kaffi* or food all over someone. But Vinny had smiled at her and told her she was doing a fine job. He had come every day for a sandwich or just to chat. He'd walked her to the cramped room she rented, to make sure she was safe, he'd said. Right! *He* had turned out to be her biggest danger.

But Becky hadn't known any better. She had believed the best about people. She'd never met someone she couldn't trust, someone evil, so she'd had no experience to draw upon. Vinny had sent her flowers and bought her little gifts. He'd confessed that he had fallen hopelessly in love with her at first sight. Huh! He wouldn't have known love if it crawled up his arm and bit him on the neck. She could see that now.

She had been flattered at the attention and

overwhelmed by his pretty words. Vinny had known what he wanted and known she believed in marriage, so he had arranged that phony ceremony. He'd even bought her a pretty lace dress to wear and a little bouquet of red roses. She had happily signed the marriage license, or what she had believed was a marriage license. The first two weeks had been blissful, but then Vinny's true colors began to emerge.

Nothing Becky did was *gut* enough. He even called her a dumb hick. When he demanded to know what was wrong with her after she had raced to the bathroom clutching her belly, she confessed her suspicion. She'd thought he would be happy. After he slapped her, cursed at her, and belittled her for not knowing how to prevent a pregnancy, he told her to "take care of it" or they were through.

When she told him she didn't believe in divorce, he threw his head back and laughed a harsh, evil laugh. That's when he told her they weren't really married.

"We signed the paper," she said. "We had a ceremony."

"All fake." The words cut her to the core. She could still see his sneer. "That minister was my pal Jimbo, no minister by any stretch of the imagination, and that license was printed off the Internet." He laughed and laughed as tears poured down her face. Then he told her to get out and not return until she'd taken care of the mess she'd gotten herself into.

She wandered up and down the sidewalk until Julie, a coworker, spotted her and took her in. She stayed with Julie until she could gather enough courage to retrieve her few belongings from Vinny's apartment. Unfortunately, she chose the wrong time to return. She arrived to find Vinny dead and his horrible *freinden* standing over him. When they tried to force her to go with them, she fled again.

She had thought she would be safe at home. After all, she hadn't seen what had happened in New York. She couldn't be any kind of witness, so those men didn't need to worry about her going to the authorities. Had they really tracked her down? Why? Would she have to run away again to protect her loved ones?

Atlee's senses all went on high alert. Somehow, without looking obvious, he needed to figure out which customers had gotten out of the car with New York license plates. It would be easy if a couple of evil-looking men stomped around searching the place, but Atlee felt pretty sure that wouldn't be the case. And what would he do if he spotted suspicious-looking characters? Confront them? Accuse them of scaring a defenseless girl?

Atlee rubbed a hand across his smooth jaw. He

would do whatever he could to protect Becky, short of violence. The Amish did not believe in violence. If someone started after Becky, though, he would have an awfully difficult time making himself remember that fact. He took a deep breath, released the tension in his shoulders, and tried to look casual. He'd do a quick survey of the shop before mingling. More customers had arrived, making the crowd similar to a Saturday morning crowd. That might be to his advantage.

The *Englisch* women shopping alone and the elderly couples Atlee ruled out altogether. He tried to wander among any groups of males, pausing long enough to eavesdrop on conversations. Most people were repeat customers, but he did linger near a couple of strangers who spoke with a slight accent. Granted, some local folks spoke a little differently, especially the watermen and some of the longtime farming families, but this couple's accent was different from what he'd heard before.

The men Becky feared could have brought a woman along to provide a cover. Now where had he heard that before? His younger *bruder* Ray must have mentioned something like that. The *bu* was always reading, and his choice of reading material was not always to *mamm*'s and *daed*'s liking.

"The cheeses all look so good and fresh," the

woman said with a wide smile. "We're glad our neighbors told us about this place."

"Are you new to the area?"

"We're from New York. Greg is in the military, and we just got transferred here." She turned her smile on the tall, sturdy-looking man beside her.

"*Wilkom* to Maryland. Take your time." Innocent. Atlee sighed in relief as he shuffled in another direction. The New York car belonged to legitimate customers. Becky would be so relieved. He glanced over his shoulder a final time. The couple were still perusing the cheese cases. No one pulled out a gun or issued any threats. Nothing seemed out of the ordinary. He needed to calm Becky and convince her that no one was after her.

Footsteps sounded outside her hiding place. If she could have crawled inside a cabinet, she surely would have done so. She held her breath as the door opened much slower than it had earlier. She sucked in a gasp and paused in her nail nibbling. She should have run out the back door when she had the chance. She shouldn't have involved Atlee at all, that was for sure and for certain. She'd never forgive herself if he got hurt. She wanted to cry or scream, but instead she waited silently for the person to enter and discover her.

The door opened just far enough to allow a person to slip through. Becky wished she could blend in to the wall. There was no time to hide, even if she could find a place. She clapped both hands to her face and peered through the slots between her fingers. She sucked in another breath and held it. She wouldn't be surprised if her heart stopped beating, too.

"Becky?"

The whisper made her widen the cracks between her fingers. Atlee's face was the most *wilkom* sight in the world. Her breath whooshed out in a little sob.

Atlee crossed the room in two long strides and pulled Becky into his arms. "*Shhh, liebchen.* It's all right."

Becky tried to squirm away. "Where are they?" She looked around Atlee toward the door.

"There isn't anyone here to hurt you. There is a couple from New York. They are shopping for cheese. You know, with the military base close by, we get people here from all over the place."

"There aren't any horrible men here to grab me?"

"*Nee.* You're safe. I don't think you need to worry about anyone tracking you down."

"Safe." Becky echoed the word and willed herself to believe she was truly safe. She heaved a huge sigh of relief before collapsing into Atlee's arms.

Atlee patted her back and murmured soothing words, not all of which Becky could decipher.

Tears of relief raced down her cheeks and splashed onto Atlee's shirt. After a moment, Becky pulled herself together and realized she was in Atlee's arms. Scarier was the realization that she enjoyed being in Atlee's arms. She didn't want to move, but she had to tear herself away. Was Atlee right? Was it ridiculous to think those men would pursue her? Was she putting her *freinden* in any danger, or were they all perfectly safe?

Freinden. That's all she and Atlee could be. Why did she keep forgetting that? Did he really call her "*liebchen*" a few minutes ago? That could never be. She pulled back from Atlee's embrace and immediately experienced an intense chill. Loneliness enveloped her like a shroud. She swiped at her tears with the back of one hand. "I-I'm sorry." She pointed at his damp shirt.

"That's all right."

"I'd better get Lena's cheese and get back to her house." Becky couldn't bring herself to look into Atlee's eyes. "Maybe I shouldn't have returned."

"To the dairy?"

"To Maryland."

"Do you want to leave?"

Becky detected a note of sadness in his voice. "I don't want to leave, but I don't want to bring harm to any of the people I care about."

"I don't think those men will track you here, if they even want to find you at all. They probably don't remember what happened if they had been drinking or using drugs. They might be in jail by now. Your *freinden* and family want you to stay here forever. *I* want you to stay."

Chapter Twenty-Seven

"Becky's back!"

Becky heard Mary's shout before she'd even gotten all the way inside the house.

"It's about time! You must have found someone to talk to at the dairy." Lena removed the pot of noodles from the stove and turned to face Becky. Immediately the smile fled from her face. "What happened?"

"N-nothing." Becky's gaze took in the two little girls staring at her. She mouthed, "Later," to Lena and pasted on a wobbly smile for the *kinner*.

"Cheese?" Eliza tugged on the black cloak Becky hadn't yet taken off.

Becky reached down to hug the tiny girl. "*Jah*, I brought cheese, you little mouse." She held up the bag for Eliza to see and smiled a genuine smile at the little girl's excitement.

Lena carried the pot of noodles to the sink to drain the water. She pulled out a saucepan and began to assemble the ingredients she needed.

"Let me wash up, and I can do that for you." Becky tossed the bag of cheese onto the counter and shrugged out of her cloak.

"I'm not an invalid, you know."

"I am well aware of that, but you've been

chasing after these two rascals while I was gone. Besides, I think I hear Matthew stirring."

"Ugh. I just nursed him an hour ago. There's nothing wrong with his appetite, for sure and for certain."

"I'll be right back." Becky untied her black bonnet and pulled it off. She peeked in at the *boppli* on her way to hang up her cloak. Sure enough, he fidgeted a bit before popping a tiny fist into his mouth.

"I hear you, Matthew!" Lena called.

Becky washed her hands and hurried back to the kitchen. Maybe she could enlist the girls' help with something and give Lena a few minutes to quietly nurse Matthew.

"Now, suppose you tell me what had you looking like a scared rabbit when you got home?" Lena rocked as she knitted. The needles made a soft clacking sound in time with the squeak of the chair.

Home. Lena's house had been home to Becky for weeks. A pang of sadness struck when she thought of leaving. "I believe it's time for me to let you and your *kinner* have your house back to yourselves."

Lena stopped rocking and laid her knitting in her lap. She leaned forward to look directly into Becky's eyes. "We've discussed this before. You know we love having you here and consider you family. I don't think this is what has you looking so nervous. You've been jumping at every sound since you got home."

Becky flinched and lowered her eyes. "Sorry."

Lena reached over to clasp Becky's hand. "What is it, Becky? Look at me. You can tell me anything."

Becky looked up hesitantly. "I-I don't want to put you and your *kinner* in harm's way."

Lena squeezed Becky's hand. "How could you ever do that?"

"What if those men from New York try to find me? They are bad people."

"They haven't done so in all this time you've been back. What makes you think of this now?"

Becky relayed the incident at the dairy. Her nose tingled as she struggled to hold back the tears that were building up.

"That turned out to be perfectly innocent. Atlee was right. We have a lot of out-of-state people in the area."

"But don't you see? It could easily have been those bad men. I could lead them right to your door. When Atlee didn't *kumm* back right away, I thought those men had hurt him. I couldn't live with myself if something happened to any of you because of me. I probably shouldn't even go back to my parents' house."

"Pshaw! I'm not worried one whit."

"You should be."

"I've got too much to do to worry myself over shadows that might be chasing me. And I've still got plenty for you to help with if you're willing to stay."

"It isn't that I don't want to stay. I've told you before how much I enjoy living with you. I just don't want you to be hurt. If I have to go away to ensure your safety, I will."

"Go away where?"

"I don't know. Some place far away so I can't be tracked down and so the people I love can't be hurt."

Lena smiled. "So are you going to live under a log and not associate with anyone?"

A smile tugged at Becky's lips. "*Nee.*" She giggled at the image of a pregnant woman slithering beneath a log. She shared her thought with Lena, and both women dissolved in fits of laughter that dispelled the tension in the room. "I don't know where I would live," Becky gasped when she could catch her breath.

"Well, I do. Right here. If you want to move back to your parents' house, that's well and *gut*, of course, but I'd much rather you stay here. It's been ever so nice having you here. I don't mean you have to stay to take care of the house and *kinner*. I'm quite capable of doing that. Almost capable, anyway. I enjoy your company, and, well, you've become family."

Becky threw her arms around Lena's bony

body. "I'd love to stay here, but if there's even the hint of danger, I'll be gone in a flash."

"Fair enough, but I think you're worrying for nothing. Those horrible men have moved on to other pursuits by now. How about a piece of pie to celebrate?"

Becky jiggled Lena's skinny arm. "I think you need the whole pie."

Atlee tossed and turned, unable to find a comfortable position. He might as well have been sleeping on a bed of nails. He lifted his head just enough to yank the feather pillow out and flipped it over. He punched it once and then dropped his head back down. Maybe the coolness of this side of the pillow would calm him. Atlee hated feeling out of sorts. He hated being unable to fall asleep. Most of all, he hated feeling helpless.

He knew Malinda suspected something was wrong. He had only snatched two of the chocolate chip cookies she had baked that afternoon instead of his usual handful. When he had refused her offer of a bedtime snack of peach pie, she'd raised her eyebrows. At least she hadn't barraged him with a zillion questions or asked if he was sick. That would have propelled Mamm into action—fetching the thermometer, feeling his forehead, fussing over him like he was a little *bu*.

The questions would begin in the morning, for sure and for certain, if he stumbled into the

266

kitchen all bleary-eyed after punching his pillow all night. He turned over once again and snatched up the covers he'd kicked off moments before. What would he do if Becky left?

Atlee wasn't sure when or how Becky had crept into his heart, but she was there to stay. No matter what Mamm or Malinda said, he couldn't change his feelings if he wanted to. And he didn't want to. Becky had become very important to him. Even when she tried to discourage him, his feelings couldn't be swayed. Her concern for him only endeared her more to him. He had to make her understand he truly cared for her and her *boppli*. He had to make her see she was safe here.

He bolted upright in the bed. Becky wouldn't steal away in the night, thinking she had to do that to protect everyone, would she? She'd sneaked off before in the dark. But she was a different person now. She stole away for herself before, following a childish whim. She was a woman now, a caring, selfless woman who wanted to do what she thought was right.

It certainly was not right for her to leave her home and loved ones. Atlee flopped back down. His head sank into the pillow. He prayed Lena could make Becky listen to reason, since he doubted he had succeeded in doing so.

He understood her momentary trepidation when she had discovered the car from New York. She had experienced some horrible things. Seeing that car had probably triggered those awful memories and fears. But he honestly believed those men had long forgotten about Becky. Somehow he had to make her believe that as well. He had to make her see he would do everything he could to protect and care for her. He had to make her see he loved her. What? Atlee jerked upright again as that lightning bolt jolted through him. *Jah*, it was true. He loved her.

Becky wasn't sure if it was the late-night sliver of apple pie that didn't agree with her or if it was the fear that had been tying her intestines in knots for days, but something made her stomach awfully queasy. It churned relentlessly as she readied herself for bed. She'd thought that once she'd made the decision to stay, she'd feel at peace.

Was she doing the right thing? Was she endangering her community? Lena didn't seem worried. Neither did Atlee. But they hadn't seen those cold, evil eyes. They hadn't had to run for their lives, afraid that at any second a hand would grab them and drag them off. Just the memory aroused panic and terror.

Enough! She couldn't keep reliving that awful time. She had to calm down, for her sake as well as her *boppli*'s. She patted her stomach before sinking to her knees beside the bed and propping her elbows on the mattress. *Am I doing the right thing, Lord Gott? I want to stay here, but I don't want anyone to be hurt. Please take away my fears and give me your peace.* Becky continued to pour her heart out to the Lord. When no more words came, she dropped her head into her hands and listened. Silence. Not a scary silence, but a peaceful, calming silence.

"For I the Lord thy Gott will hold thy right hand saying unto thee, Fear not: I will help thee." Words from Bishop Menno's sermon surfaced in her brain. Becky stretched forth her right hand. A tingling began in her fingertips and ran up her arm straight into her heart. A strange warmth spread throughout her body. She felt wrapped in strong, loving arms. Peace flooded her mind and soul. Tears of relief spilled down her cheeks, and she brushed them away with her left hand.

Gott cared about her. Gott was bigger than any fear she had—real or imagined. Gott would surely help her. She need only to cast her cares upon him. Suddenly Becky felt like a great burden had been lifted from her. The tension drained from her neck and shoulders. Her stomach settled down and behaved itself. Becky crawled beneath the covers and fell into a blissful sleep, cradled in the warmth of Gott's love.

Before any hint of sunrise tinted the black sky, Becky had the teakettle whistling and the oatmeal simmering on the stove. Lena would no doubt be up again soon to nurse Matthew. Becky had slept like a newborn herself and awoke feeling lighter and more at peace than she could remember feeling in a long, long time—maybe ever. She softly hummed a tune from the Ausbund as she pulled out a loaf of banana bread and cut thick slices.

"Someone is in a much better mood." Lena shuffled into the warm kitchen with Matthew snuggled in her arms.

"Would you like a cup of tea?"

"That would be *wunderbaar*. This little fellow had me up and down all night. He must be going through a growth spurt."

"Well, it's herb tea for you, then. Little Matthew definitely doesn't need any caffeine."

"*Nee*, but his *mamm* could sure use a big dose of it."

"I will be here to handle things, so you can take a nap as soon as you get him back to sleep."

"I may have to take you up on that offer today."

The day had been almost too busy to think. Washing three loads of clothes, cooking meals, baking crusty wheat bread, and entertaining the girls indoors since it was too cold to go out for long had eaten up the hours in a flash. She'd finally convinced Mary and Eliza to build a block tower on the living room floor near where Lena was rocking a fussy Matthew. She'd shoved a big piece of wood into the stove to make sure they all stayed warm before she headed out into the cold to drag in the clothes from the line.

Becky's previous experience with caring for a house and *kinner* had been quite limited. She'd helped her *mamm* with chores and occasionally watched little ones at some community function, but she'd never had total responsibility like she had at Lena's. Lena naturally made major decisions, but running the household fell to Becky. She kept everyone warm and fed. She felt pretty pleased with herself but tried to quash any niggling of pride. One thing that never ceased to amaze her, though, was the amount of laundry one tiny *boppli* could generate.

Her cloak whipped around her as soon as she stepped outside. Gray clouds raced across a darkening sky, and bare tree branches swayed back and forth reaching for those clouds. Becky's nose stung and eyes watered from the cold. She hurried toward the clothesline, where little blankets and white cotton diapers flapped like sails. Tiny nightgowns and little girls' dresses filled the rest of the line. So many items for such little people! She'd better get used to it. Soon her own *boppli* would make just as much work.

Over the howl of the wind, Becky's ears barely picked up the sound of wheels rolling up the gravel driveway. She had no fear, only curiosity, since the familiar sound of a horse and buggy was totally different from the sound of an approaching automobile. Maybe Mamm or one of the other women had stopped by to check on Lena. A little blanket wrapped itself around her face before she could identify the visitor.

"You're here!"

Becky's heart leaped at the voice that sounded so relieved. She clawed at the blanket and pulled it down to look up into Atlee's face. The worry creases across his forehead smoothed when their eyes locked. "Did you think I had run off again?"

"Not like before, but I was afraid you might have decided to vanish to protect everyone."

"You know I don't want to leave, Atlee. I would only do that if I thought I would cause harm to visit anyone. I hurt people when I left before. I never want to be the source of pain and worry again."

"People who love you will always be concerned about your well-being. It's a part of caring, but we aren't worried you'll cause problems."

Did Atlee mean he loved her? Becky's heart did a little dance. She felt warm despite the biting wind. Words escaped her, and her cheeks burned. She couldn't look at Atlee's face. She couldn't let him see how his words affected her. She couldn't let him see her heart mirrored in her eyes. She tossed the blanket into the big wicker laundry basket and reached up to release the next blanket from the wooden clothespins clipping it to the line.

"I'll help."

Atlee snatched the next blanket down. He stood so close that Becky would be in his arms if she turned around. She willed herself not to do that, even though the desire to throw herself into his arms was strong. Her face burned hotter. She shouldn't have such thoughts. She was supposed to be discouraging Atlee.

"You don't have to help, Atlee. I can get the clothes in."

"You'll freeze out here—if you don't blow away first."

He moved down a ways and quickly yanked down tiny clothes. Becky immediately felt chilled without his closeness, like when a bright, sunny day suddenly turned cloudy and cool. Her cold fingers fumbled to unpin the clothes as she moved down the line.

"Little ones sure have a lot of clothes. I'm surprised Lena doesn't have one of those lines on a pulley so you can draw the clothes in to remove them."

"She said Joseph always meant to put one in but never got around to it. Usually a regular line is no problem. It's these cold, windy days . . ." A gust of wind stole her voice and her breath.

"Maybe that will be the next project for Lena's house."

"I'm sure she wouldn't want to be a bother. She's grateful for all the men do around here."

"That's what *freinden* and neighbors are for, ain't so?" Atlee lifted the full basket and started for the house.

"I can take that, Atlee. I appreciate your help."

"I don't mind carrying it inside, unless you're trying to get rid of me." When Becky didn't answer, he gently nudged her with his elbow. "Are you trying to get rid of me?"

Becky searched for the right words, but they wouldn't seem to materialize. Atlee needed an answer, so her unfiltered thoughts tumbled out. "*Nee*, that's not it at all. I just don't want to encourage you."

"I don't need encouragement."

"You need to be spending your time looking for the right girl to settle down with."

"What if I told you I'd already found her?"

Chapter Twenty-Eight

Atlee couldn't tell if it was surprise, shock, or disbelief he saw on Becky's face. At least it didn't look like horror or repulsion. That had to be a point in his favor. Either of those expressions surely would have devastated him. How would he ever convince Becky to give him a chance? Whenever he sensed she may be drawing closer, she pulled into her shell like a turtle.

"Maybe you should keep looking."

The wind grabbed Becky's words, tossed them into the air, and plunked them down on Atlee's head like a limb falling from the big oak tree. He stopped walking and lowered the laundry basket to the ground beside him. He reached for Becky's arm to stop her. "Look at me, Becky." At first she simply stood stock-still. Was he going to have to force her to look at him? "Please, Becky."

Slowly she looked up at him with what Atlee thought were the saddest eyes he'd ever seen. "Atlee . . ."

"Shhh!" He pressed an index finger to her lips. "Listen to me."

Becky pulled his hand away from her mouth. "*Nee*. You listen to me. We've been through this, Atlee. I am not the right person for you. I'm too much of a risk. I've made too many messes. You could even be in danger."

"I'm not afraid."

"Maybe you should be."

"Don't you trust the Lord Gott to take care of you and everyone else?"

"I do, but those men could be a threat, Atlee, and they don't care about anyone. I can't let them hurt people I care about—my *boppli*, Lena and her *kinner*, my parents, you."

"Aha! You do care about me, since you lumped me in with that group." Atlee smiled and tweaked her nose, hoping to bring even a slight smile to her face. "You have to let go of this fear, Becky. Those guys are not going to *kumm* here. I'm sure they gave up their pursuit of you as soon as you got out of their sight. They aren't going to expend the effort or spend any precious drug money searching for you."

Becky shrugged. She bent to retrieve the laundry basket.

Atlee pulled her back up straight and kept his hands on her shoulders. He leaned closer. "Look into my eyes, Becky, and tell me you don't care for me. Then I'll walk away and leave you alone." He truly hoped she didn't call his bluff. Unless his vibes had been all wrong the past few weeks, he felt certain she couldn't deny her feelings for him without lying. *Please, Lord Gott, don't let her send me away. Please let me be right about this. Let her give me, give us, a chance.*

Becky squirmed, but Atlee held her firmly, not allowing her to put distance between them. She dropped her gaze, as if the laundry basket was the most interesting thing in the world. A blast of wind ruffled the small dress on top, nearly giving it a life of its own. Atlee moved one hand to gently grasp Becky's chin, tilting her head up. "You can't tell me that, can you?"

"*Nee.*"

Atlee pulled her against his chest and held her tight. He wanted to hold her forever. He feared he was crushing her but couldn't bring himself to let her go. The very fact that she didn't break away gave him hope.

"Hey, would you two like to *kumm* in for some hot chocolate or tea, or are you already frozen there?" Lena's head poked out the back door. A huge smile split her face.

Becky jumped back like she would have if she'd grasped the hot oven rack with her bare hand. "*Ach*, Lena! We were just . . ."

"I see!" Lena chuckled.

"Lena!" Becky reached down again to snag the laundry basket, but Atlee beat her to it.

"*Danki*, Atlee, but I can take it." She yanked the basket from his hands. Her face burned, and not from the wind. How could she have let herself stay in Atlee's embrace? What message did that send him? It certainly wasn't the same message her mouth had conveyed moments earlier. What in the world was wrong with her?

"You can't just send him off in the cold, Becky, after he's been standing out there with you for ages."

"It hasn't been ages," Becky muttered.

"Maybe, but it seems like a long time ago that you went out to gather the laundry."

Becky peeked at Atlee's face, which blazed as red as hers felt. She shifted her gaze to catch Lena's smirk.

"*Kumm*! It's cold!" As Lena drew her head back inside, the wind caught the door and slammed it closed.

Becky jumped at the loud bang and nearly lost her grip on the wicker basket. Would her nerves ever settle down?

"Here, I'll get this." Atlee easily lifted the basket into his arms. "Just tell me where you want it, and I'll be on my way."

"*Nee.* I mean, you don't have to leave. Please have some tea or something to warm you up."

"Are you sure you want me to?"

"Of course." Becky turned and led the way inside before Atlee could see the confusion sure to be written all over her face. She'd never be able to explain the meaning of it since she didn't understand it herself. One minute she wanted Atlee to stay forever. The next minute she tried, albeit half-heartedly, to drive him away for his own *gut*. Was it for *gut*, though? Why did things have to be so complicated? Life would have been so much easier if she'd never left Maryland.

Atlee scarcely got into the kitchen before Mary sidled up to him with a shy smile on her face. "Can you play with us?"

Atlee stooped down to Mary's level. "I'd like to play, Mary, but my *mamm* is expecting me home soon."

"Atlee is going to have something warm to drink, Mary," Lena said. "You can go play with Eliza."

The little girl's shoulders slumped but she obeyed. "Okay."

"You could sit with me while I drink some hot chocolate, if you want." Atlee tickled her under her chin.

Instantly Mary brightened. She giggled and bobbed her head up and down so hard that Becky feared she would injure her neck.

"Why don't you put these napkins on the table, Mary?" Lena handed her the stack of paper napkins.

"Cookies, too?" Mary ventured.

"Not now. It's too close to supper time."

Lena set two steaming mugs of hot chocolate on the table while Becky and Atlee shrugged out of their coats. Suddenly chilled, Becky crossed over to the woodstove, hoping to absorb some heat. Her fingers were icy from the wind, but she wasn't sure the chill could be entirely attributed to the cold.

Seeing Atlee with Mary and watching him smile as Eliza toddled into the room did strange things to Becky's heart. She would never have guessed Atlee was so fond of *kinner*, but then she had never taken the time to get to know him before her mad dash from Maryland. Would Atlee be as gentle and caring with other little ones, with her *boppli*? She couldn't imagine he wouldn't be. *Stop it, Becky. You're freinden, nothing more. Remember that.*

"Are you okay?"

Becky shook off her disturbing thoughts. She looked up to find Atlee watching her. Though he jostled a little girl on each hip, the concern etched on his face was directed at her. What a *wunderbaar* image to hold on to—Atlee surrounded by smiling *kinner*. It nearly brought tears to her eyes. Becky nodded and cleared her throat. "I'm fine." She rubbed her hands together and forced a smile. "I just needed to warm up my hands." The worry lines eased from Atlee's forehead.

"Girls, you need to get down and let Atlee drink his hot chocolate. You may each have a half cup of your own. I don't want you to spoil your appetites for supper." Lena wagged a finger at them.

Atlee lowered the little bodies to the floor. The

girls scrambled to climb into chairs to await their treat. Atlee sat opposite them.

"Look what I found!" Becky held up a bag of miniature marshmallows. "Who wants some?"

"Me! Me!" two little voices cried in unison.

"Me!" a deep voice chimed in. "Me, too!"

Becky and Lena laughed as Atlee bounced in his chair the same way the girls did.

"Maybe he doesn't need the extra sugar," Lena said as she set cups in front of Mary and Eliza.

"Pretty please?" Atlee poked out his lower lip.

Mary and Eliza burst into giggles at Atlee's antics. Becky gave each of the girls a small handful of marshmallows, which they played with before dunking them into their cups. She placed a larger handful in front of Atlee and dropped five tiny marshmallows into her own mug. She sealed the plastic bag and returned it to the pantry lest the girls be tempted to ask for more.

"He'd make a great *daed*," Lena whispered as Becky passed her.

"Shhh!" Becky hissed as she nudged Lena with her elbow. What if Atlee heard? Becky's cheeks burned, and not from the heat of the stove. She hoped the girls' babblings had distracted Atlee. Determined to act nonchalant, she pasted a little smile on her face before turning back toward the table. Atlee's grin told her he had indeed heard Lena's words. Becky's cheeks practically burst into flames.

Becky slid onto the chair next to Eliza. She grabbed the little girl's fingers just before she plunged them into her hot chocolate to fish out the bobbing marshmallows. Becky withdrew the spoon from her mug and scooped out a marshmallow for Eliza. "Here, Eliza. Let's get them out this way." Eliza popped the marshmallow into her mouth and squished it between her teeth. Little bits of the sticky white goo squirted out. Mary giggled, causing Eliza to laugh and spew out the rest of her half-eaten marshmallow.

"Ew!" Mary giggled so hard she nearly fell off her chair.

"I think you two need to leave the table." Lena frowned at the girls.

"I'll be *gut*, Mamm." Mary straightened on her chair and looked down at her cup.

Becky glanced at Atlee, who worked hard to hide his own amusement. "Maybe Atlee brings out their impish side, Lena."

"Me? What did I do? I'm just sitting here, minding my own business and drinking my hot chocolate."

"For now." Becky took a tiny sip from her mug.

"You are done, little one." Lena grabbed Eliza's hand, which was again heading for a floating marshmallow. She wiped Eliza's face and hands and set her on the floor. "You can help me with Matthew," Lena added when Eliza's lower lip protruded and her face scrunched up as if she was about to howl. Lena took the little girl's hand and propelled her from the room. Over her shoulder she called, "Why don't you stay for supper, Atlee? We still have some scrumptious macaroni and cheese."

"The cheese I risked my life for," Becky mumbled.

"It's nice of you to ask, Lena, but I need to get home today."

How could Becky feel relieved and disappointed at the same time? It would definitely be better if Atlee did not stay for supper. Lena needed to stop pushing them together. Atlee had enough fantasies of his own without Lena adding fuel to the fire.

"Maybe another time?" Atlee winked at Becky as he pushed back from the table. "I need to help my *daed* tonight, but I'd like to share a meal with you again."

"Any time," Lena hollered from the living room where she and Eliza tended to Matthew.

How had Lena heard? Atlee hadn't spoken that loudly. She had been trying to find a way to politely discourage Atlee when Lena yelled. That woman could probably hear a gnat whisper in the next county.

"You don't seem especially happy about the idea." Atlee laid a hand on Becky's arm.

"I, uh, it's not that. Of course you are *wilkom* here." His hand seared her arm.

He leaned close. "I'm not going to give up on

you, Becky, or on us." Atlee's low voice in her ear sent shivers down her spine. He tucked a hand under her chin to raise her head. "Remember that." He winked again and tickled Mary as he passed her. He slipped out the back door, whistling as it closed behind him.

Atlee's whistle died off once he settled himself inside the buggy and headed home. His confidence waned as well. He'd told Becky he wouldn't give up. Maybe he should. Maybe he should just lie low and not push. He didn't want to push Becky away altogether. Maybe he should wait for her to make the next move. But what if she never did?

If only he had someone to talk to, someone with some experience with women. He could use a little advice about now. He couldn't go to his *mamm* to get a woman's opinion for fear she'd only try to discourage him. Though he truly believed she held no grudges toward Becky, he got the feeling she didn't exactly want him to get involved with her. He'd always been close to Malinda and able to talk to her about all sorts of things, but he wasn't sure how objective she would be when it came to Becky Zook.

Maybe he should seek out another man's advice. He could try talking to Daed as they worked, provided his younger *bruders* weren't within earshot. Or it might very well be time to pay Sam a visit. After all, Sam had just been through a courtship. He certainly seemed happily married now. Granted, Emma hadn't had any of Becky's issues, but Sam would understand Atlee's feelings, wouldn't he? Atlee would think on it.

Right now he needed to wipe all traces of worry off his face. His horse, eager for food, warmth, and rest, trotted briskly up the lane toward the barn, where Daed would no doubt be finishing up chores. Atlee ran a hand across his face as if he could physically remove the wrinkles from his brow. He resumed whistling as he pushed open the door and jumped from the buggy.

"Is Atlee gone?" Lena trudged into the kitchen with Eliza on one hip and Matthew in the crook of her other arm.

Becky stood in the same spot where Atlee had whispered into her ear. Mary still sat at the table finishing her hot chocolate.

"Becky?"

"Huh?" Becky gave her head a little shake. "Uh-huh, Atlee had to go home."

"That's too bad."

Becky reached out to take Eliza. "You're going to give yourself a hernia or something carrying the two of them."

"I used to carry Mary and Eliza together."

"I'm sure your back was delighted with the situation."

"Probably. How about your situation?"

"Which situation would that be?" Becky lumbered toward the refrigerator to pull out supper fixings. "You are definitely getting heavy, little Eliza."

"Don't try to change the subject or play dumb. You know very well I'm talking about Atlee."

"There isn't anything to talk about. Atlee is a nice person and a *gut freind*."

"*Freind*, my foot!"

"Don't you think a man and a woman can be *freinden*?"

"Of course, but that isn't the kind of relationship Atlee has in mind."

"You can read minds now?"

"I can read faces. You are one stubborn girl."

"I am determined, not stubborn. I don't want Atlee to be hurt. I will only cause him pain and problems with his family. You've got to stop playing matchmaker, Lena. It isn't making things easier for me."

"Sometimes the course of love isn't easy, but once you get over the bumps, it's smooth sailing."

" 'Love'? Who said anything about that?"

"Can't you tell that Atlee is in love with you?"

"You're *narrisch*, Lena. It looks to me like Atlee really loves *kinner*. Maybe you should consider him for yourself. Mary and Eliza sure are thrilled when he visits."

"Mary and Eliza like anyone who pays attention

to them and plays with them. Besides, I'm much too old for Atlee, but if there was an older version of him around, I might very well be interested. You, my dear Becky, are not being honest with yourself. If you were, you'd acknowledge the fact that Atlee jumps at the chance to help you, that he shows true concern for your well-being, and that he worries about you and your *boppli*. If you were truly honest, you'd admit your feelings for him."

"And what makes you think I have those?"

"If I was blind and unable to see the meaningful, loving looks you exchange, I would still pick up the vibrations and feel the electricity between you two."

"*Ach*! You really are *narrisch*, Lena, or else you've been reading romance novels."

"I am not crazy and I haven't had time to pick up a book other than the Bible and the Ausbund in ages."

Unable to lift a heavy pan from the refrigerator with one hand, Becky lowered Eliza to the floor.

"Mary, please take Eliza into the living room to play for a few minutes while Becky and I get supper on the table." Mary obediently grabbed the younger girl's hand and did as her *mamm* asked.

Becky set the pan of leftover macaroni and cheese in the oven to warm. She pulled out the big plastic canister of flour and measured out enough to make biscuits. If she kept her hands busy, maybe her brain would focus on what her hands were doing and stop conjuring up thoughts she did not want to consider.

Lena opened two jars of home-canned green beans and dumped them into a pan. She shook in salt and pepper and set the pan on a back stove burner. She touched Becky's arm. "I'm not trying to upset you. I care about you, Becky. You've become like a *schweschder* to me. I just don't want you to be sorry later if you turn Atlee away now."

Chapter Twenty-Nine

Atlee knew he should have gone straight upstairs after supper, but he had to talk to someone. Sam and Emma didn't live that far away. Maybe a brisk walk on such a frosty evening would help him organize his thoughts. Would they have already gone to bed? There was only one way to find out.

The temperature must have dropped several more degrees since he'd gone inside the house for supper. His walk turned into a jog. If he didn't see any lamplight when he approached Sam's house, he'd turn back around and jog home. He prayed he'd see at least one lamp still glowing. He needed to talk, for sure, but he needed to warm himself even if only for a few minutes.

Relieved to see a glow in the windows of the old two-story house Sam had bought from an elderly couple who had moved to live with family, Atlee slowed his pace to a brisk walk. He struggled to control his breathing and to gather his thoughts. Now that he was here, he didn't have a clue what to say. How should he approach the topic he wanted to discuss? Should he blurt out his reason for such a late visit as soon as he entered the house? Could he pour out his heart in front of Emma? He hadn't thought about that. He couldn't very well ask Emma to leave the room. It was her home, after all. Why hadn't he considered these things on the way here? "Because my brain is frozen, like the rest of me," he muttered into the wind.

Atlee climbed the steps to the front porch. Since light seemed to be coming from the living room, he'd use the front door instead of using the back, as he usually did. His heart was still pounding from his jog, and his breath came in gasps. He forced himself to take slow, deep breaths before raising his hand to knock on the door. The sound of heavy footsteps told him Sam was approaching the door. Emma certainly wasn't big enough to make that much noise.

"*Wilkom*, Bruder." Sam opened the door wide and practically pulled Atlee inside. "What brings you out on such a cold night? Is everyone all right?"

"Who is it, Sam?" Emma shuffled down the hall and peered around Sam. "Atlee! *Kumm* in and get warm."

"Everyone is fine. I'm sorry to drop in so late."

"It's fine. Go in the living room by the stove and warm yourself. I'll go get you a cup of tea." Emma hurried toward the kitchen.

"Don't go to any trouble, Emma. I won't stay long."

"It's not any trouble at all. The kettle is still hot since I had a cup of tea a few minutes ago."

Atlee followed Sam into the living room and immediately strode over to the woodstove. He held his hands out, turning them this way and that way to thaw them. Sam dropped onto a worn armchair near the stove.

"Here you are." Emma handed Atlee a steaming mug. "It's chamomile, always nice to have at night."

"*Danki*, Emma." He was pretty sure it would take more than herb tea to calm him, but he was grateful for a hot cup to wrap his hands around and hot liquid to thaw his insides.

"I'm going to go upstairs and let you two talk. It's *gut* to see you again, Atlee."

"You too. *Gut nacht.*"

Atlee lowered himself to sit on the edge of the wooden rocking chair on the other side of the stove. He ventured a small sip of the tea to moisten his suddenly dry throat. "How is everything going? Are things busy at Swarey's Furniture Shop?" Sam had worked at Emma's *daed*'s shop for years, and Atlee knew the place usually stayed very busy. Pretty lame beginning, but Atlee hadn't yet figured out how to talk about his true reason for visiting. He took a gulp of tea that ignited a fire all the way down to his stomach.

"Everything is fine. Emma and I are getting the house in shape. Swarey's is busy, as usual." Sam leaned forward. "I don't think you came here on a cold, dark night to ask about business. Do you want to tell me the real reason for your visit?"

Atlee coughed and clapped a hand across his mouth to keep from spewing out that second boiling gulp of tea he'd just taken. He carefully set the cup on a cherry end table to keep from spilling its entire contents. "Nice table," he mumbled.

"I just finished that for Emma. Now, enough chitchat. It isn't that I don't like seeing you, Bruder, but I don't think this is a social call. What's going on?"

"Nothing is going on, actually. Not yet, leastways." Without the mug to occupy his hands, Atlee wasn't sure what to do with them. He drummed his fingers on the wooden chair arms, but the noise sounded like thunder in the otherwise quiet room. Sam stared at him, waiting for him to spill whatever was on his mind. *Help me out here, Sam,* he begged silently.

"Would this be about a girl?" Sam urged.

"I, uh, I suppose so."

Sam settled back in his chair. He crossed one ankle over the other knee and rubbed a hand across the short beard he'd been growing since his marriage.

Atlee suddenly felt overcome with embarrassment. He shouldn't have bothered Sam. His poor *bruder* worked all day at the shop and worked around the house when he arrived home. He was probably beat, and Atlee was keeping him from his sleep. He needed to say what was on his mind or leave. Right now, leaving sounded like the best choice.

"I'm taking that as a *jah*. Do I have to guess who it is or are you going to tell me?"

Atlee sighed. "Becky," he mumbled.

"Becky Zook." It was a statement, not a question.

"*Jah*. You don't act very surprised."

"Should I be?"

"I didn't think my interest in her was so obvious."

"Maybe not to anyone else, but your family picked up on it pretty quick."

"You mean Mamm and Malinda have been discussing me with the rest of the family. Is that it?"

"Not with everyone. I doubt Aden and Ray would be interested."

"Funny. So what did Mamm or Malinda tell you?"

"Why don't you tell me what you feel?"

"I'd kind of like to know what they think."

"I think they are concerned about you. They care about you and want you to be happy. But they want you to make the right decision."

"So they don't think I'm thinking clearly. They aren't exactly thrilled that I, uh, might be interested in Becky, ain't so?"

"They don't want you to be hurt, and Mamm

doesn't want you to take on more than you can handle."

"Translation: Mamm thinks because Becky is, uh, well, she thinks a ready-made family will be too much for me." Atlee rubbed his hand across his face. "I thought Mamm and Malinda would be fair. They both said they didn't hold a grudge against Becky."

"Becky did steal Malinda's beau."

"Isaac wasn't right for Malinda. She even said so herself. She has Timothy now. I thought she would want me to find happiness, too."

"That's just it, Bruder. They do want you to be happy."

"They don't think I can be happy with Becky? Tell me what you think, Sam."

"The important thing is what do you think? What does your heart say?"

"It's really hard to explain. I don't even understand it myself. You know I never paid attention to Becky before she left. You didn't, either. We just thought she was a silly flirt and all the other fellows were foolish to be taken in by her."

Sam nodded. "I only had eyes for Emma."

"That's true. And I wasn't thinking about any girls in a serious way." Atlee paused. A frown crossed his face as he scratched his head. "But something changed, Sam. I changed. Becky changed."

"Are you sure she has—other than the obvious, I mean?"

"*Jah.* I believe her story."

"I didn't say I didn't believe her. I think we can all understand how a young, innocent girl could be easily deceived. She was able to trust people here, so she naturally assumed she could trust people everywhere. But has she changed in here?" Sam thumped his chest.

"She has. I've gotten to know her well. We've taken walks, and I've visited at Lena's. She's truly sorry for the way she acted before and for running off. She regrets what happened in New York, but Sam, she loves her *boppli*. She wants to do the right thing. She's planning to join the church as soon as she can."

"Those are all *gut* things. I don't think anyone took her flirtations that seriously. A few fellows might have felt a twinge or two of pain. Some girls, including our own Malinda, might have harbored some jealousy or anger, but I think they've all gotten over those feelings and moved on."

"I think so, too. Malinda and Isaac have. I'm not sure how thrilled Mamm would be to *wilkom* . . ." Atlee stopped abruptly. He'd revealed more than he intended.

"How serious are you about Becky?"

Atlee reached for his tea and swigged another gulp. At least the liquid had cooled and no longer scalded his tonsils. "I, uh, I care a great deal for her."

"Have you thought this through, Bruder? Are you ready to be a *daed* right away?"

"I've thought and prayed until I'm blue in the face. And I already care about the *boppli*, too."

"Are you sure you aren't letting your heart run away with your head?"

"I don't believe I am." Atlee thought for a moment, considering how to phrase his next question. Drawing a blank, he simply blurted, "How did you know Emma was the right one for you?"

Sam uncrossed his legs, slumped back in his chair, and closed his eyes for a moment. A smile played with his lips. "That was easy. Emma was always the nicest girl in school. Prettiest, too. She stole my heart when we were still scholars."

"You were *kinner* then. How did you know as a grown man? Did your heart trip over itself at the thought of her? Did your breath catch at a glimpse of her? Did you feel a strong urge to protect her and take care of her?"

Sam slapped his knee and chuckled. "It sounds like you already know exactly how it was. How it is. I'd do anything for Emma, and I want to make her happy however I can. Gott first, and then Emma."

Atlee nodded in complete understanding. "*Jah.*"

"I think you've got it bad, Bruder. Now what are you going to do about it?"

That was an excellent question. What was he going to do about it? If Becky didn't share his feelings there would be absolutely nothing he could do. He couldn't force her to care. But he had a very strong hunch she did care. She just needed to conquer her fears. How did he help her do that?

Sam broke in on his thoughts. "Does Becky feel the same way as you?"

Atlee drummed his fingers on the chair arm again. "I hope so. I think so. I don't know."

"You must have some idea."

"My gut says she does, but Becky is afraid she'll make trouble for me. Whenever she seems to draw closer to me, she jumps back. She thinks she'll tarnish my sparkling reputation or cause problems with Mamm and Daed."

"Has either of them hinted they would be less than pleased if you courted Becky?"

"Like you, Mamm worries about my taking on the responsibility of a *fraa* and a *boppli*. She still sees me as a happy-go-lucky little *bu*, but I'm not a *bu*, Sam. I'm not even the same fellow I was a few months ago. Sure, I still like to laugh and look at the bright side of things, but I've grown up."

"Finally!"

Atlee tossed the little needlepoint pillow behind him at Sam's head.

"I suppose we'll always be *buwe* to Mamm." Sam tossed the pillow back.

"Probably. How'd she ever let you go? You were her firstborn."

"I'm sure it was hard for her."

"You were always the serious one, though, so she probably trusted your judgment a whole lot more than she trusts mine."

"I don't think it's that she doesn't trust you. She most likely wants you to be sure you've thought everything through before you take such a big step."

"I've thought so much it's a wonder my brain hasn't exploded. It isn't like I'm getting married tomorrow. Becky hasn't even joined the church yet. Besides, she may not even want me." Atlee felt his brow wrinkle. That wasn't a thought he wanted to entertain.

"Well, I'll tell you, Bruder. I've observed you and Becky at gatherings, and I've seen the same light in her eyes when she looks at you as I see in your eyes just sitting here talking about her."

"Really? Then why did you ask me if she cared?"

Sam stroked his short beard. "I wanted your impression. I'm just an observer. Look, Atlee, if you truly care about Becky and you feel it is right, then you need to listen to your own heart. Anyone who has any qualms will have to deal with it."

"That's our *mamm* you're talking about."

Sam laughed. "Our *mamm* is a fair-minded, caring person. She wanted me to be sure Emma was right for me."

"She did?"

"For sure. I think it *kumms* with the territory of being a *mamm*."

"Mamm never had any problems with Emma, did she?"

"*Nee.* She only wanted me to be sure, since marriage is forever. I never had any doubts. Emma has always been the girl for me."

"I don't have doubts, either, not about myself at least. I just need to convince Becky to give us a chance."

"Give her time, Bruder. I've seen signs that she cares, but she's been through a lot. Be patient."

"Be patient. Be patient." Atlee mumbled Sam's words over and over as he began the trek home. First Malinda told him to be patient, and now Sam said the very same thing. Two little words. Easy to say. Hard to do. If he had his horse and buggy, he might head over to Lena's to talk to Becky right now, despite the late hour. Hope. That's all he needed. A little encouragement. Some sign that Becky would give him a chance. Preferably sooner rather than later.

He would never have believed he, Atlee Stauffer, fun-loving jokester, would want more than anything to settle down. He felt absolutely sure now. He wanted to marry Becky. He wanted to be a *daed* to her little one.

Atlee shivered and increased his pace to a slow jog. If he had his horse and buggy, he wouldn't be freezing right now. The bright stars and big moon shining in the inky sky were sure pretty, but the lack of clouds had made the temperature plummet. If he didn't want to turn into a block of ice, he'd better speed his jog up to a full run.

If only Lena Troyer's house was on his way home. Maybe it was better it wasn't, though. Not being able to stop by would force him to be patient. He didn't think he'd be able to be patient for too long, but he'd give it a try. He prayed Becky would realize he wasn't concerned about what anyone else thought or said. He wasn't worried those guys from New York would show up here. Southern Maryland was so far off the beaten path, the chances of them ever locating Becky were slim, even if they wanted to find her.

His lungs burned from the frigid air and from his sprint the last half mile home. The dim light burning in an upstairs window was a *wilkom* sight, even if it did mean someone was still awake. Atlee counted the windows. Just what he thought. It was Malinda who was still awake. He wondered if he could slip into the house and into his room without her ears picking up a sound.

Blessed heat wrapped itself around Atlee in a

bear hug as soon as he stole into the house and eased the door closed behind him. He crept into the living room to stand against the woodstove for a few minutes before sneaking upstairs to his cold bedroom. He held his hands out toward the stove and would have dropped them onto the metal if he could avoid burning them. Since they were numb at the moment, he feared he would burn them without even noticing. Instead he rubbed them together briskly to restore circulation.

When adequately warmed, Atlee picked his way up the stairs, stepping lightly to prevent the wood floor from creaking. He paused at the landing to listen for a second. Maybe Malinda had fallen asleep with the lamp burning. Doubtful. Maybe she was absorbed in a book and wouldn't hear him. A little more likely. He tiptoed down the hall and slipped into his room. Before he could get the door fully closed, he heard the soft voice.

"Atlee?"

Apparently Malinda had been wide awake and waiting for him to return home. He pulled the door open wider and pressed a finger to his lips.

In two steps, Malinda was beside him, pushing him into his room. She held a small lamp in one hand. "Where have you been?" She closed the door behind them and set the lamp on the chest of drawers.

"I didn't realize I had to check in with you."

Atlee's lips twitched as he tried to hold back a smile.

Malinda playfully slapped his arm. "I was worried about you. You took off without saying anything."

"It doesn't look as though Mamm and Daed were worried. They've gone to bed."

"Mamm was worried all right. Daed convinced her you were a grown man and could take care of yourself. At least she acted convinced and followed Daed upstairs."

"But you aren't convinced?"

"I know you're grown up all right."

"But you don't think I can take care of myself? I'm crushed at your harsh opinion of me." Atlee pretended to wipe away a tear.

"Did you go to visit a girl? Are you courting?"

"Do I ask you about Timothy's visits?"

Even in the dim lamplight, Atlee could see the color spring into Malinda's cheeks. "*Nee*, but . . ."

"Then why am I not extended the same courtesy? Why do I have to tell all?"

Malinda shrugged but didn't budge. She obviously wasn't going to leave the room before extracting some sort of information from him. Atlee sighed. Fatigue threatened to swallow him. Morning would be here in the blink of an eye, and he needed to try to get a little sleep. "For your information, dear *schweschder*, I went to visit Sam."

"So late?"

"They were still up. I needed to talk to him about something."

"It must have been awfully important if you couldn't wait until tomorrow."

"Sam and I both work all day and have chores before and after. Exactly when would we find other time to talk except in the evening?"

"Was it about a girl? Was it about—"

"You are a nosy little thing. Do you know that?"

"I'm not nosy." When Atlee's eyebrows shot upward, Malinda amended her statement. "I'm concerned."

"Right."

"You can trust me, Atlee. Did you talk to Sam about Becky?"

"Now why would you ask that? Do I ask you what you and Mamm discuss all day?"

"We talk about the house or the chores we're doing or community happenings. Some things are private."

"My point exactly."

Malinda huffed out a breath. "I only want to help, Atlee. You're my favorite big *bruder*." She smiled and batted her eyes.

Atlee laughed. "I'm the only big *bruder* you have around right now to harass."

"I'm a great listener, Atlee, and maybe I can give you some insight if you have girl troubles."

"The only girl trouble I have is you."

"Funny. Then why did you go to talk to Sam about Becky?"

"You said that. I never mentioned her at all." Atlee faked a yawn. "It's getting late, you know."

"*Nee* you don't. I didn't wait up for nothing."

"Maybe you shouldn't have waited up at all. You could have been getting your beauty sleep."

"Atleeeeee." Malinda drew out his name. She poked out her lip in a pout.

"Go to bed, Malinda."

"Not until you talk to me."

"We talked. I'm tired. Go to bed."

Malinda stomped her foot. "You're infuriating, but I'm not giving up."

"You will when I toss you over my shoulder, carry you to your room, and throw you on your bed."

"Atlee, talk to me."

Atlee sighed louder. Clearly Malinda wasn't going to go away unless he did toss her out. "Malinda, it's late. We have to get up early."

"I like Becky."

"What?" Atlee shook his head and pulled at an ear, thinking he hadn't heard her clearly.

"Your ears are fine, Bruder. I said I liked Becky."

"After she lured Isaac away from you?"

"If Isaac had truly cared about me, he wouldn't have been tempted by Becky's flirtations. I don't think Isaac could handle my illness. Sometimes

304

my Crohn's disease can get pretty bad. I'm not sure Isaac could deal with a girl who has a chronic illness."

"Timothy can." It wasn't a question. Atlee had been *freinden* with Timothy forever. He knew Tim had cared about Malinda for years and had waited patiently for her to grow up and think of him as someone other than her *bruder*'s *freind*.

"*Jah*, Timothy can deal with any flare-ups I might have."

"If Timothy can deal with you, any flare-ups would be easy as pie."

Malinda punched Atlee's upper arm. "We were talking about you, not me."

"*Nee.* We were talking about going to bed before the rooster tells us it's time to get up." Atlee doubted sleep would visit him tonight, but he did want to pray and think. Alone.

"Actually, the last thread of our conversation— before you changed the subject, that is—was about me liking Becky. You know, if we girls had tried harder to be *freinden* with her when we were scholars, things might have been different. Becky always sort of stayed to herself. We all figured she thought she was better than us, but I'm thinking maybe she was really shy and didn't know how to make *freinden*."

"And when did you start analyzing everyone's behavior and motives? Have you been studying psychology on the sly?"

305

Malinda swatted him again. "I'm trying to be totally serious and you jest."

"Okay. So you think Becky was shy because she kept to herself."

"Possibly. Or she could have lacked confidence in herself. She might have tried to get all the fellows' attention to prove she was worthy, or something like that."

"Hmm. It sounds like you've been doing research. Did you sneak off to the library and get the librarians to look stuff up for you?"

"You're impossible. I'm trying to tell you I'm on your side, and you won't be serious."

"You're on my side for what?"

Malinda rolled her eyes as if to say he was the biggest dunce in the world. "I'm on your side if you want to court Becky."

"What made you decide that?"

"I've watched Becky with Lena and her little girls. Becky has been loving and kind. Lena's girls obviously adore her. But they respect her, too. Sometimes she can get them to behave when Lena can't. I think Becky will make a fine *mamm*."

Atlee nodded but kept silent, studying his *schweschder* in the flickering lamplight. He found no trace of teasing. He could tell she spoke honestly, from her heart.

"And I've seen Becky with you."

Atlee swallowed the wrong way and coughed. "Exactly what have you observed?" He could kick himself for asking, but he needed to know if he had any chance with Becky. He knew what he had observed, but he could be seeing only what he wanted to see. Input from an unbiased party may help. Was Malinda unbiased? He hoped so.

"Wouldn't you like to know?" Malinda gave him a sly smile and turned toward the door.

"I don't think so." Atlee grabbed Malinda's arm to keep her rooted to the spot. "You started this. Now finish it."

"My, but it is late." Malinda exaggerated a yawn. "I should let you get some rest. You know that old rooster will be crowing soon."

"I'm going to throw that old rooster on you to peck your eyes out if you don't start talking."

"Such violence, Atlee. You know that's not our way."

"You're real funny, Malinda. Thanks to a certain pesky little *schweschder*, I am now wide awake, so let's finish the conversation."

"I've always loved teasing you."

"I may be grown up, but I'm not above short-sheeting your bed or sticking a toad beneath the covers."

"I believe you've done that a time or two. I'm not fond of sleeping with toads, but I'm not scared of them."

Atlee kept hold of Malinda's arm and fixed her with a stare. He tapped his foot as he waited for the mischievous grin to slide from her face.

"Okay, Atlee. I'll be serious. You can turn me loose now."

Atlee released his grip on Malinda's arm and waited, toe still tapping.

"Atlee, I have seen Becky look at you with all the love in her eyes a person can show."

"And when was this?"

"On more than one occasion. Sometimes during church my gaze wanders a bit."

"To someone besides Timothy?"

"Ha ha! I'm usually sitting somewhere behind and to the side of Becky, so I see when she turns her head to look at the men's side of the room. Her face lights up if her eyes happen to connect with yours."

"You've observed all this in the few seconds when people take their eyes off the minister?"

"What can I say? I'm a very observant person. Besides, girls are very in tune to these things."

"More so than men, I suppose."

"Do you mean to tell me you haven't seen how much Becky cares by the way she looks at you?"

"I've been afraid to trust my own judgment. I've been afraid I'm transferring my own feelings onto her, that I'm imagining she cares."

"I'm not imagining things, Bruder. I can tell you truly that Becky never looked at the other fellows the way she looks at you. That was all play. This is real. I know in my heart Becky cares for you."

"But what do I do about it? She's afraid to let me into her life."

"Give her time, Atlee. She's been hurt, and she's scared."

"That's about what Sam said."

"Listen to us, then. Keep helping her, walking with her after church, and visiting her. She'll learn she can trust you. You are a *wunderbaar* person. I hope Becky realizes what a gem she has in you." Malinda squeezed Atlee's hand. "*Gut nacht*, Bruder."

Chapter Thirty

"How did your visit with the midwife go?" Lena stood at the stove stirring vegetable soup. "Would you like some soup? The girls and I have eaten, and they're both down for a nap."

"I'm sorry I wasn't here to help you."

"Don't be silly. I'm perfectly capable of handling the meal alone. Besides, your appointments are important." Lena tapped the large wooden spoon against the side of the pan and replaced the lid. "So would you like a bowl of soup to warm you up?" Lena turned to look at Becky. "*Ach*! What's wrong, Becky? You look like you lost your only *freind*. Is everything all right with the *boppli*?" Lena grabbed a kitchen chair and dragged it close to the stove. "Here. Sit." She took Becky's arm and led her to the chair.

"The *boppli* is fine. Laurie said everything was progressing normally, except for my weight. She said I need to gain more weight. That's hard to do when I often don't feel like eating."

"I know, but you are feeling a bit better now, ain't so?"

"*Jah*. I still feel queasy, but usually I'm able to eat at least a little."

"Well, then, let me dish you up some soup."

"I'll try to eat a little, Lena, but I can get it myself."

"Relax. You took care of me. Now I can take care of you."

"Me and three *kinner*? I don't think so."

Lena lifted a bowl from the cabinet and ladled soup into it. "Enjoy being waited on for a change. So if your appointment went well, why the long, gloomy face?"

Becky sighed. She scooted her chair back under the table. She gulped as Lena set the bowl of steaming soup in front of her. Although the soup, with its chunks of carrots and potatoes, green beans, corn, and tomatoes, looked and smelled delicious, Becky wasn't so sure her stomach could handle it.

"Take the spoon in your hand and put a bite into your mouth. Or I can feed you." Lena picked up the spoon, loaded it up, and raised it toward Becky's mouth.

Becky wrinkled her nose at Lena and grabbed the spoon. "You've been around little ones for too long. I think I can feed myself."

"When I was expecting Mary, I remember Laurie telling me that an empty stomach can make you feel sicker."

Becky blew on the spoonful of soup and popped it into her mouth. "It's *gut*." She lowered the spoon into the soup and propped it against the edge of the bowl. "I visited my parents after my appointment."

"Didn't that go well?"

"It was fine. I was glad to see them and to talk to Mamm for a little while."

"But?"

"But they're planning to move away from Maryland." To Becky's horror, she burst into tears. She covered her face with her hands and sobbed harder than Matthew when he was impatient for a feeding. Becky heard Lena scoot a chair over beside her and felt Lena's thin arms encircle her to hold her close. For some reason, the empathy and comfort made her cry harder, until she hiccupped and gasped for breath.

"Take a few deep breaths. Give that *boppli* some oxygen."

"*Ach*, the *boppli*!" Becky pulled away from Lena in a panic. "Did all that crying hurt the *boppli*?"

"I'm sure it didn't. I cried rivers when Joseph died, and Matthew turned out fine. I think something about being in the family way makes us more sensitive. I know I teared up at the drop of a hat all three times."

Becky sniffed and swiped at her nose and eyes with the paper napkin Lena had pressed into her hand. "I-I'm sorry, Lena. I shouldn't have carried on so." Her breath still came out in little jerks.

"Everyone needs a *gut* cry now and then. I think it helps. It's kind of a release and a relief. Then we can pull ourselves together and move on. You've certainly had plenty of reasons to cry, and I don't think you've ever given in to the urge, so you were about due, ain't so?"

Becky gave Lena a small, wobbly smile. "You're *gut* for me, Lena."

"I try to be. Now, tell me about your parents. Why are they moving, and why so suddenly?"

"I'm not sure if it's sudden or not, but they never mentioned anything to me before today."

"Where are they going?"

"My *grossmammi*, Mamm's *mamm*, has lived with my *mamm*'s *bruder* for years. My *onkle* and *aenti* have taken care of her since my *grossdaddi* passed on."

Lena nodded. "Where do they live?"

"They lived here. Then they moved to Indiana when I was a little girl. My *aenti*'s family was from Shipshewana. I didn't get to see them often after they moved, but we wrote letters. Anyway, Grossmammi fell and broke her hip. She's been having a lot of problems, and it's hard for my *aenti* to care for her alone while my *onkle* is working. Mamm feels she should help. She says she wants to spend as much time with her *mamm* as she can." Becky paused to blink back more tears.

"That's understandable."

"I do understand that. Really I do. I think Mamm should be with Grossmammi. I know I'm being selfish, but I want my *mamm* to be with me, too." Becky began shredding the napkin.

"That's understandable, too, Becky. And it's not selfish. It's natural to want your *mamm* here when you have your *boppli*. I wish my *mamm* could have been here for me. Are your *bruders* planning to move, too?"

"I don't think so. They all have families and businesses or farms here, and I don't believe they want to uproot and start over." Becky dropped the bits of napkin onto the table beside her soup bowl.

"I'm almost afraid to ask, but what about you, Becky? Do you plan to move with your parents to start over in Indiana?" Lena's fingers played with the pile of shredded paper on the table.

Becky looked into Lena's stricken face. It was plain to her that Lena loved her as a *schweschder*. And she considered Lena the big *schweschder* she never had. "*Nee.* Maryland is my home. I left once and don't want to leave again."

"Shipshewana would be an Amish community, you know, not a big city like New York."

"I know, but home to me is here, even if my parents leave."

"I certainly don't want you to leave, but I don't want to be the reason you stay. Think about what you truly want, Becky, about what is best for you."

Becky swiped at a stray tear. "I thought and prayed all the way here. I know in my heart my home is here. This is where I belong. I'm just not sure where I'll live."

"What will your parents do with their place?"

"My oldest *bruder*, Emanuel, has always eyed the place. His house is small for his growing family. I believe Daed will work things out with him. I suppose I could keep my room there, but I wouldn't want to be in Sally's way. Sally is a nice person and perfect for Emanuel, but I'm sure she and I do things differently. It would be very hard for me to see the changes she would have every right to make. Besides, I'll have the *boppli* in a few months, and they certainly don't need that extra burden."

"Your *boppli* would never be a burden. I'm sure Sally would love your little one."

"I know she would, but she has enough of her own and will probably have more *kinner* herself." Becky tapped her fingers on the table.

Lena filled the spoon with soup and held it to Becky's lips. "Eat."

Obediently Becky opened her mouth. She chewed the soft vegetables and swallowed. "Speaking of *kinner*, I'm not one." She took the spoon from Lena's hand.

"I know, but you keep forgetting to eat. You'll never gain the weight the midwife wants you to gain if you don't eat."

Becky plunged the spoon into the bowl and swirled the potatoes and carrots around. "I'll try."

"You can live with me, you know. The *kinner* and I would be overjoyed if you and your *boppli* stayed here."

Becky patted Lena's arm. "That is so nice of you to offer, but I don't want to be in your way, either."

"In my way? You've been a godsend to me."

"But you are back on your feet and, uh, you'll probably remarry, and . . ."

"You don't see anyone shining a light in my window, do you? There aren't any men falling over each other to court me."

"They will, Lena. It's just a matter of time. You're a *wunderbaar* person, and your *kinner* are adorable."

"I'm not sure I'm ready to even think of remarriage, even though I know it's expected."

Becky squeezed Lena's hand. "I know. I'm thinking of in the future."

"I have a feeling you'll get married long before I do."

Becky gasped. "I have *nee* plans to get married. Why would you think that?"

"I know a certain young man who, I believe, is just waiting for some sign from you."

"I don't think so. I fear if you offer me a home here, you may be stuck with me for a long, long time. You may want to give your offer further thought."

"I don't need to do that. I consider you family. Unless you'd rather live with one of your *bruders*, I would like very much for you to stay here."

"I'm sure my *bruders* and their *fraas* would *wilkom* me, but I think they would consider it their obligation to do so. It wouldn't necessarily be their desire. I'm afraid I would be more an intruder than anything else."

"They all seem nice enough to me. Surely they would be happy to have you, Becky."

"They are nice. I love all my family members. I just don't think I'd be comfortable living with them. I'd feel like a guest in their homes, and you know guests tend to wear out their *wilkom* after a while."

"I can assure you that you would never wear out your *wilkom* here. I hope you haven't felt uncomfortable."

"Never, Lena. You've made me feel like part of the family from the beginning, but the plan was for me to help until you got back on your feet again. I don't want you to feel obligated to let me live with you, either. I suppose I could live alone, until my *boppli* arrives, that is. Surely someone has a *dawdi* house not in use."

"*Ach*, Becky! You don't want to be alone! Let me help you now that I'm mostly recovered."

"I want you to feel free to marry again when the right man *kumms* along. I don't want to hold you back."

"Like I told you, I have *nee* plans to marry. How about this? You live here and consider this your home until either of us marries."

Becky laughed. "I can see us now. Two crotchety old women rocking in chairs beside the stove. Our *kinner* are grown and gone."

Lena smiled. "I don't think you'll be rocking beside me. I see a husband in that chair next to you."

"Don't count on that."

"Do we have a deal? You will stay here? I don't mean as my helper. This will be your home. You can *kumm* and go as you please. You don't have to take care of my *kinner*."

"I love taking care of your *kinner*."

"They love you, too, but I don't want you to feel responsible for them. We can work together and help each other, but you will be free to live your own life. Does that sound like a *gut* plan to you?"

"I want you to be sure, Lena. Up until just a little while ago, we expected I would soon go back to my parents' house. I don't want you to make a spur-of-the-moment decision that you'll regret later."

"It really wasn't a quick decision. I've been thinking for a long time how nice it would be if you could stay here. I didn't know you that well when you first came here, but right away you felt like family. If you need time to think, that's fine. If you want to live with a *bruder*, I'll understand. I just want you to know I'd love to have you stay as long as you'd like."

Becky threw her arms around the older woman in a quick hug. "*Danki*, Lena. You and your little ones have become family to me, too. If I stay, will you promise to tell me any time you want me to leave?"

"That won't happen."

"You never know. Promise you'll tell me if I get in the way or you want your house back to yourself. Do you promise, Lena?"

"All right, but it's an empty promise. We've gotten along splendidly all this time. I can't imagine anything changing. But you have to promise me something, too, Becky."

"What's that?"

"When that young man convinces you to marry him, you'll do it without worrying about me."

"I don't have plans—"

"Promise me, Becky!"

"All right, if that makes you happy."

"It does." Lena picked up the spoon and pressed it into Becky's hand. "Now eat your soup."

Chapter Thirty-One

Early the next morning, Becky sat in the rocking chair in the dark living room and leaned her head back against the worn cushion. The house was silent except for the wood crackling in the stove and the soft creaking of the chair as she gently rocked back and forth. Only a faint shaft of light from the lamp she'd lit in the kitchen allowed her to discern the shapes of the furniture in the living room. She'd already made *kaffi* for Lena, who allowed herself only one or two cups per day since she didn't want a hyperactive *boppli*, and had set a mug of raspberry tea on a woven coaster on the little round table beside the rocking chair. She pulled the blue, black, and white crocheted afghan lying across her lap up to her shoulders and closed her eyes.

She'd been so weary last night, but sleep played games with her overactive mind. She was done crying over her parents' imminent departure, at least until she actually waved them off. The hurt she'd felt because they wouldn't be here for her and her infant gradually subsided. Although it made her sad, she understood her *mamm*'s need to go.

Becky thanked the Lord Gott for Lena and her generous offer to share her home. She could have lived with one of her *bruders'* families, but that idea did not appeal to her. She could live alone with her *boppli*, but that idea scared her a little. She could move to Indiana with her parents, but as she'd told Lena, she considered Maryland her home.

Her one venture outside of the state had proved disastrous. Sure, she'd have her parents with her this time if she left, but something held her here. And it wasn't only the fact that everything was familiar here. She felt safe here. She liked the slower-paced life in St. Mary's County and appreciated it even more after living in the city for even a few months.

Her community was her extended family. She knew some probably doubted the story of her New York adventure, but they accepted her back with open arms. At least she hoped they did. She knew for sure and for certain a dark-haired, green-eyed young man did, but she wouldn't let him waste his life on her.

Becky sighed. This was where she wanted to raise her little one. Her *boppli*. She smiled and snaked a hand under the afghan to gently rub her barely rounded belly. Was it a *bu* or a girl growing inside of her? Would he or she have dark hair like Vinny? She hoped not. She'd tried so hard to push Vinny and New York from her mind. She'd almost succeeded in forgetting what he looked like. Maybe her *boppli* would be a little girl with honey-colored hair. Whatever it turned out to be, she already loved him or her with the fierceness of a *mudder* lion. She would do everything possible to protect her *boppli*.

She leaned over to take a sip of the sweet raspberry tea that Laurie had said would be *gut* for her body. She dropped her head back against the cushion again and offered a prayer of thanks for her blessings—her little one, her home with Lena, her community. Bishop Menno was willing to review all the baptismal classes with her. She had attended them previously but had run away instead of joining the church. Shame still crept in to scald her at the memory of bolting from the service at the very moment she was supposed to answer the baptismal questions. She truly believed she had been forgiven for her foolish mistakes. She was ready now, and Bishop Menno said she wouldn't have to wait for the next baptismal class.

Despite her lack of sleep last night, Becky didn't feel that drowsy now. Instead, she felt at peace. She'd wrestled with the pros and cons of her options and made the decision she knew was right for her and her *boppli*. She'd almost been swayed by the memory of her *mamm*'s sad eyes when she'd told Becky of the plans for moving. Mamm had urged Becky to leave with them, but her staying in Maryland would be easier for all of them. Her parents would be spared the necessity of explaining why their *dochder* was expecting and not married. She would be spared dredging up the past again in order to explain. Besides, if she stayed here, she would not be subjected to the physical and emotional hardships of moving.

Emerald eyes had peeked into her thoughts during the decision-making process and had lent some weight to the pros of staying put. Her best efforts at ignoring those eyes had been futile, but she would be careful to make sure the owner of those eyes remained only a *freind*. A *gut freind*. A caring *freind* who selflessly considered her needs above his own.

Becky smiled as she rocked. She was content—dare she say happy—in her small, secluded community. She reached to swallow another sip of tea and then tucked her hand back under the afghan. She closed her eyes and listened to the stillness of the sleeping house. When she blocked out the ticking of the kitchen clock and the creaking of the rocking chair, she heard only the thrum of silence. If serenity was an object, it would be a warm, fuzzy blanket enfolding her in comfort as she sat in the predawn darkness.

She sighed. She had made the right decision to stay here with Lena for as long as the arrangement worked for both of them. The faint sound of Eliza mumbling *boppli* talk in her sleep reached Becky. The mumbling, sweet jibber-jabber ceased as quickly as it had begun. She pushed against the handles of the wooden chair to boost herself to a standing position. She'd creep back up the stairs to check on the girls. Poor Lena had been up and down most of the night with a fussy Matthew. Becky hoped she would be able to catch the girls before they rolled out of bed and trounced into Lena's room.

She tiptoed up the stairs with only the beam of a small flashlight to light her way. A quick peek in the girls' room told her Eliza had settled back into sleep. Mary lay as still as a stone. She poked her head into Matthew's room and found him squirming and sucking on a tiny fist. If she could change him without totally awakening him and swaddle him firmly, maybe she could rock him back into a deeper slumber to give his exhausted *mamm* a few more minutes of sleep.

Becky crept downstairs with Matthew snugly wrapped in his blue blanket. She settled herself in the rocking chair again and hummed softly as she rocked. She lowered her head to inhale his sweet fragrance. In a few months she would be cradling her own newborn, but the weather would be warm, so she wouldn't need to sit beside the crackling woodstove.

"I wondered where my little man went." More than an hour later Lena shuffled into the living room with the girls on her heels.

"I thought if I could catch him before he fully

awoke, I could soothe him so you could sleep a while longer."

"It looks like your plan worked." Lena nodded at the sleeping infant. "I was about beat. That little fellow had me up most of the night."

"I know. That's why I wanted to let you sleep."

"I'm sorry we kept you awake. You need your sleep, too."

"You didn't keep me awake. My brain didn't want to stop churning."

"Is everything okay?"

"More than okay. Staying here is the right thing for me—as long as you haven't changed your mind."

"Absolutely not. Hey girls, Becky is going to keep living with us! Isn't that *wunderbaar*?"

"*Jah!*" Mary jumped up and down. Eliza imitated her.

Matthew jerked in Becky's arms, startled by the sudden noise. Becky rocked him as Lena hushed the girls. When he popped the little fist back into his mouth and began sucking vigorously, Becky figured they wouldn't be able to stall a feeding much longer. "I think you'd better get ready, Lena. I changed him before I brought him downstairs, so he's ready."

Lena reached to take the squirming infant in her arms. "Let's go, my fussy little one. It's time for you to eat."

"Well, girls, should we make pancakes for

breakfast?" Becky looked first at Mary and then at Eliza.

They squealed their delight and jumped again.

"I wish I awoke with their energy," Lena mumbled as she settled herself in the chair on the other side of the stove and prepared to nurse Matthew.

"Let's get the pancakes started so they're ready when your *mamm* is finished feeding Matthew." Becky took a little hand in each of hers and ushered the girls into the kitchen.

"Can we help?" Mary squeezed Becky's hand.

"You certainly can." Becky squeezed back. She surely loved these little girls. Staying in Maryland with Lena was definitely the right decision.

By the time Becky had a plateful of golden-brown pancakes ready, Lena had finished nursing Matthew and tucked him into the cradle near the stove. Becky had let the girls take turns stirring the batter with her hands over theirs on the big wooden spoon.

"It sure smells *gut* in here, and I'm starved." Lena rubbed her hands together.

"I helped stir, Mamm. Eliza did, too!" Mary couldn't wait any longer to share that news.

"I'm sure the pancakes will be extra *gut*, then." Lena hugged each of her girls. "Let's get you two seated."

After enjoying their breakfast, Becky carried sticky plates to the sink, while Lena wiped maple syrup off of two little faces. Becky glanced out the window while the sink filled with water. "It's snowing!" Mary and Eliza ran to check.

"I can't see!" Mary wailed and tugged on Becky's dress.

Becky lifted the little girl in her arms so she could look out the window.

"Me! Me!" Eliza chanted, tugging on the other side of Becky's dress.

Becky leaned down to snag Eliza and hoisted her to the opposite hip. All three stared out at the big, twirling snowflakes. "If it keeps snowing, we'll go out to play in it later, if it's okay with your *mamm*."

"If what's okay with their *mamm*?" Lena returned to the kitchen after checking on Matthew and adding a piece of wood to the stove.

"I told the girls we'd play in the snow later, if it's okay with you. Even if it doesn't stick, we can catch snowflakes on our tongues and have fun."

"Snow?" Lena crossed to the window. "I'm ready for spring. And what in the world are you doing holding both of these big girls at once? Here." She extracted Mary from Becky's arms. "You shouldn't be lifting so much."

"The girls are like you, Lena. Together they don't weigh as much as a barn cat we used to have."

"It must have been a cougar! These girls weigh

too much for you to haul around, especially both of them at the same time."

"You worry too much." Just the same, Becky lowered Eliza to the floor.

"You two go play." Lena shooed them out of the kitchen. "And don't bother your *bruder*." Lena picked up the dish towel to dry the dishes Becky had stacked in the drainer. "I need a break while he's sleeping, so I don't need little fingers poking at him and setting him off again."

"Why don't you go back to bed for a while?"

"*Nee*, I'm up now. I'll rest later if all three of them nap at the same time."

"That snow is really falling fast." Becky leaned closer to the window to get a better look at the yard and driveway.

"I want to be done with winter. I don't like being cold." Lena shivered and rubbed her arms. "Maybe this is just a squall that will pass soon."

"I don't think so. It's already sticking to the grass. This may be winter's last big effort. I'd better fill the wood boxes as full as I can get them, just in case."

"In case of what? Don't you dare say what I think you're going to say!"

"In case we're snowed in!"

"Bite your tongue, girl. I want to plant geraniums and petunias and peas and beans."

"You're anxious to start weeding, picking, and canning?"

"It's better than shoveling snow, that's for sure and for certain."

"You might have a point. I'll shovel if we need to."

"You definitely will not!"

"Are we going to let it pile up to the windowsills?"

"Funny. I'm still hoping this will all blow over and the sun will be shining before the noon meal."

"You'd better hope hard."

"Just what do you think you're doing?" Lena asked a short time later.

Becky tugged on an old pair of gloves. "I'm going to bring in a few armloads of wood. Have you looked outside lately?"

"I've been trying to ignore what's happening outside." Lena ran to the window. "I don't think I'm going to get my wish. I suppose winter is not ready to leave us alone." She sighed. "But you don't need to be lifting a bunch of firewood."

"I don't think I can coax it inside on its own. Besides, I've been bringing in the wood."

"But you're getting farther along."

"Not much farther than last week, and I brought in wood just fine then. I'm not even showing much." Becky patted her barely rounded stomach.

"That's because you don't eat enough to sustain a flea."

"I'm doing better."

"I suppose you are, but you're still too skinny."

"Now there's the pot calling the kettle black. Have you ever looked at yourself?"

"But I eat like a horse."

"Uh-huh."

"Let me get a coat and gloves, and I'll help you."

"I can do this. You can hold the door for me."

"Then get that wood from the pile close to the house. Don't go all the way out to the big woodpile."

"I'll leave that wood in case the snow piles up and I can't get out to the big woodpile."

"Do you really think we'll get that much snow?"

Becky shrugged. "I don't know, but it's snowing hard and already starting to pile up."

"Just what I didn't want to hear. I think I'll make some vegetable soup for later."

"That sounds great. I'll chop vegetables when I finish bringing in wood."

Becky ventured outside only to be met by an arctic blast of air and fat snowflakes plopping on her cheeks. She filled the wheelbarrow as full as she could and grunted through three trips to the house. She piled the wood boxes high with as much wood as they would hold.

"That should last a while." She stripped off her wet gloves and held her hands out to the stove. "We may get to build a snowman later, girls."

Mary and Eliza cheered from the spot on the

floor where they were playing with their dolls.

"Would you like to bake some chocolate chip cookies to have when we come inside? You know, building a snowman is hard work, and we'll probably get as hungry as bears." Becky winked at Lena.

"I'd like to see you as hungry as a bear," Lena mumbled. " 'Barely hungry' may be more like it."

Becky wrinkled her nose. She would have poked out her tongue but two little pairs of eyes were watching her, and she didn't want to be responsible for instilling a bad habit. "Laurie says I'm doing fine."

"Let's make sure we keep it that way, *jah*? I'll start the soup if you want to make cookies. We can't have two hungry little growly bears later." Lena tickled each of her girls.

A warm kitchen smelling of chocolate made the idea of going out into the cold very unappealing, but Becky had promised the girls she would take them out in the snow. The last batch of cookies were now cooling on wire racks, so as soon as she washed the cookie sheets and bowls, she'd have to fulfill her promise.

"It looks pretty raw out there. The wind is blowing the snow all around."

Becky peeked out the window over the sink. "There must be about four inches on the ground already. It sure piled up fast."

"You don't have to take the girls out in this.

Surely we can distract them with some other activity."

"*Nee*, I promised them. I can't break a promise. We might not stay out there long, though."

"You don't need to get chilled and get sick."

"I won't get sick from getting cold. As Laurie says, germs make people sick, not the weather."

"So you listen to Laurie, huh?"

"She knows a lot. And she doesn't talk in medical talk. She makes things easy to understand."

"Do you think you'll take her up on that offer to be her birthing assistant?"

"I think I'd like that, but I'll have my own *boppli* soon."

"Maybe you'll have a husband, too, and he might not want you to do that."

"I'm definitely not planning on acquiring one of those, so the decision will be mine."

"We'll see."

"Don't go getting any wild matchmaking ideas or I'll do the same for you." Becky dried her baking pans and put them away. "Let's get the girls ready to go outside. I might as well get this over with, since conditions might be worse out there later."

"If you want to change your mind, do it before we get the girls bundled up."

"Is it time? Is it time?" Mary ran into the kitchen with Eliza on her heels.

"Time for what?" Lena gave each girl a hug.

"Time to build a snowman."

"Snowman," Eliza echoed.

"Hmmm. What do you think, Becky?" Lena tapped her chin as if considering a weighty matter.

"I think we can try to build a snowman, if we don't all turn into snow girls first."

"Snow girls!" Mary giggled. "Let's be snow girls."

By the time the girls were dressed for the outdoors, Becky wondered if they would even be able to bend over to pick up a handful of snow. She could barely see their eyes peeking out from behind knit scarves. She tried to show them how to scoop up snow and roll it into a ball. Mary attempted to follow directions, but Eliza promptly tumbled in the snow. She apparently found eating the snow more fun than molding it into a snowman.

"You'll freeze!" Becky attempted to haul Eliza to her feet, but as soon as she let go, Eliza sank back into the snow, giggling.

Mary evidently thought snowmen were too much work. She joined Eliza rolling around in the powdery snow. Snow angels may be a better idea. Becky dropped into the powdery snow. She fanned her arms and legs to demonstrate the idea. The girls grasped this concept much more easily. They giggled and flapped their limbs until Becky feared the cold snow would seep through their heavy coats and chill them to the bone. She jumped up from the snow and pulled both red-nosed little girls to their feet.

"Snow angels!" Lena cried.

"Lena! You came out. Do you have Matthew in that bundle somewhere?" Lena must have held a pile of at least three blankets in her arms. The *boppli* must be buried in the middle somewhere.

"I do. I'm only going to stay out for a minute, but I wanted to show Matthew his first snow. And I wanted to see a snowman. Where is our snowman?"

"Would you settle for two nearly frozen snow girls?"

"I guess they will do."

"Look at our snow angels, Mamm!" Mary tugged at Lena's cloak.

"I see. Such a lot of them."

"I think they had more fun rolling around in the snow rather than making the angel pattern." Becky nodded toward the large area of disturbed snow.

"Someone is going to have a frozen tongue, and a frozen belly, too, if she keeps eating snow." Lena grabbed Eliza's hand before she could stuff another fistful of snow into her mouth.

"Are you ready to go inside to get warm?" Becky's fingers were growing numb despite her heavy gloves.

"We didn't make a snowman," Mary wailed.

"You made snow angels instead." Lena pointed at the evidence.

Becky's heart melted at Mary's sad face with her lower lip drooping and quivering. "I'll tell you what. Let's make a teeny, tiny snowman. The snow is so powdery, it's hard to get it to clump together. Maybe tomorrow we can make a bigger one."

"Okay." Mary perked up a bit.

"Okay," Eliza echoed.

"Unfortunately, the snow doesn't seem to be letting up." Lena hugged the cocooned *boppli* closer.

"Will you watch, Mamm?" Mary asked.

Lena nodded. "If you're quick about it."

"Let's get to work. We don't want little Matthew to freeze." Becky bent to form a large snowball. She let Mary and Eliza pack snow around its base while she constructed the next two layers. "Quick like a bunny, see if you can find two sticks for arms."

"I think the sticks are already buried. I'll snap a little branch from the old oak tree." Lena plodded through the snow a ways to grab a low branch. She shifted the bundled *boppli* to the crook of one arm. With the other hand she broke off the very end of the branch. "Here, Mary. Take this to Becky."

Becky broke the branch and poked the

335

mismatched sticks into the lopsided snowman. "Perfect! Now let's get some cocoa and cookies!" That is, if she could coax her fingers to bend enough to hold a cup.

Chapter Thirty-Two

Becky hurried downstairs and through the cold house the next morning to stoke the fires in the living room and kitchen stoves. She stirred the ashes around and added small pieces of wood until she got both fires going well enough to toss in larger logs. She stood against the kitchen stove briskly rubbing her hands up and down her arms until the stove could dispel the chill in the room and in her body. She'd filled the kettle with water first thing, so it should start to heat on the stove soon. A nice hot cup of tea would go a long way toward warming her up.

It was still too dark for her to see much out the kitchen window, so she couldn't tell if snow was still falling or how high it had piled up during the night. The wind had increased to a howl shortly after midnight, making enough noise to awaken her and to frighten Mary.

The little girl had jumped from her bed and padded down the hall whimpering. Becky had called to her and let her snuggle in bed with her for the rest of the night. She hoped that wasn't going to be the beginning of a bad habit she'd have to break. She'd carried Mary back to her own bed before heading downstairs.

Before the teakettle could begin shrieking,

she slid it off the burner. She finally felt sufficiently warm to detach herself from the stove long enough to plop a tea bag into a mug and pour steaming water over it. She stirred in a spoonful of sugar, discarded the tea bag, and returned to her station next to the stove. A few sips of hot tea should do the trick. She'd start some oatmeal and *kaffi* for Lena as soon as she felt brave enough to remove her hands from the hot mug. The temperature must have plummeted during the night for the house to have grown so cold.

After a few minutes, the stove began cranking out heat, and the sips of tea warmed her from the inside. Becky measured out enough *kaffi* for Lena's two cups and enough oatmeal for four. There was nothing like oatmeal to stick to the ribs on a frosty morning. She'd scramble some eggs and put slices of bread in the oven for toast, too. First, though, she wanted to try to examine the world outside the window.

Becky tore a paper towel off the roll and wiped the moisture from the window over the kitchen sink. She hadn't heard the wind in several hours, so maybe the snowstorm was over. The sky had gone from black to gray, and a few streaks of purple and pink now crisscrossed the darkness. Becky gasped.

There must be at least a foot of snow blanketing the yard. Some areas had higher piles where the wind had blown snow into drifts. From what she could tell in the predawn grayness, it looked like only random flakes fell from the sky now. It was still too dark to be certain. She'd probably be shoveling for a long time just to get to the horses. She'd better try to consume a large bowl of oatmeal for all the energy that would require.

"You're up early. Couldn't you sleep?"

Becky turned from the window and watched Lena hurry across the room to stand beside the stove.

"*Ach*! I was going to have your *kaffi* ready and oatmeal cooking before you got up. I had little feet kicking me, so I gave up on sleep."

"Not the *boppli*?"

"*Nee*. Mary. She got scared during the night with the wind whistling and howling. I let her sleep with me."

"You should have told her to *kumm* into my room. You need your rest."

"It's all right. I didn't mind. I called her into my room when I heard her get up so she wouldn't bother you."

"We're a fine pair, aren't we? Each of us tries to protect the other."

"That's what *freinden* do, ain't so?"

"I suppose we do." Lena stepped closer to the window.

"You might not want to look out there."

"Why not?"

"You wanted spring. It definitely does not look like spring."

Lena leaned over the sink to peer out the window. "There must be a foot of snow out there!"

"That's what I thought." Becky stirred the oats in the pot of water. "Maybe I'd better make extra so I'll have lots of energy."

"You aren't shoveling all that!"

"I have to get to the horses and chickens."

"The men will be by to help out. We just might have to wait a while until they can dig themselves out."

"I can start after breakfast."

"You will do nothing of the sort."

"Aren't you the bossy one?"

"Well, someone has to make sure you take care of yourself."

"We'll see," Becky mumbled as she pulled eggs out of the refrigerator. "Scrambled or fried?"

"Scrambled. Maybe then Eliza will eat more of them."

"Is that Matthew I hear?"

Lena groaned. "I fed him before I brought him downstairs. I thought if I tucked him into the cradle near the living room stove he would at least sleep for an hour. He must be going through a growth spurt."

"I'll pour you a cup of *kaffi* as soon as it's ready."

"Maybe I should cut out all caffeine. I didn't think he would get enough from my measly cup or two to bother him."

"Would you like some raspberry tea instead?"

"I'd really like my *kaffi*, but I'll take the tea." Lena hurried to the living room before the infant could let out a shriek.

Mary ran into the kitchen, pulling Eliza along with her. "Did you see the snow?" Her brown eyes were huge and shining with excitement.

"Snow?" Eliza echoed her big *schweschder*.

"There certainly is a lot of it, isn't there?" Becky dunked a tea bag in a mug of hot water for Lena.

"Can we play in it?"

"You might get lost in it. Then I wouldn't see you until spring."

"You're silly. I wouldn't get lost."

"Let's see if the sun shines later to warm things up a bit. And I have to shovel out to the animals."

"I heard that!" Lena called. "You will not shovel to the animals. They are fine for now."

Becky wrinkled her nose but didn't let the girls see her. "Are you fine for now or are you hungry?" She looked at first one girl and then the other.

"Hungry!" they squealed together.

"Somehow I thought that would be your answer." She stirred the oatmeal again and moved the pan aside to begin scrambling eggs. "Breakfast will be ready soon."

Ugh! Eggs! Why did the smell of eggs have to bother her stomach today when she needed to eat a hearty breakfast? She stirred the eggs around in the pan with one hand and clutched her belly with the other. It didn't seem to matter that she'd only sipped raspberry tea so far this morning. Her stomach was not happy.

Quickly she moved the pan off the burner and raced from the room. "Be right back," she mumbled to Mary and Eliza. She hoped she could slip into the bathroom and make it back to the kitchen before Lena knew anything was amiss.

After splashing her face with icy water, Becky felt she could return to the kitchen. She intermittently held her breath or took only shallow gasps as she finished scrambling the eggs and scooping them onto three plates. There was no use in putting any on her plate. She pulled the bread from the oven and added a slice to each plate. Toast should not offend her stomach. At least she hoped it wouldn't. She arranged extra slices on a separate plate. Becky enlisted Mary's help to carry butter and jam to the table while she filled bowls with oatmeal and poured cups of orange juice.

At the conclusion of the silent prayer, Becky raised a spoonful of oatmeal topped with cinnamon and brown sugar to her lips. She swallowed the first bite and followed it with a sip of tea. The spoon clattered against the side of the bowl, when she had intended to rest it in the oatmeal easily. Maybe she should try the toast instead.

"Are you all right?" Lena stopped the forkful of eggs on its way to her mouth to study Becky's face.

"Sure."

"You look a little green."

Mary giggled. "She's not green, Mamm."

Lena smiled. "It's just an expression. It means someone looks a little sick."

"I'm fine." Becky picked off a crunchy edge of her bread and popped it into her mouth. She willed it to stay down where it belonged. She forced a pleasant expression as she chewed.

"What's wrong with your oatmeal?"

"H-hot. I'll let it cool a bit."

"Funny. Mine wasn't that hot."

"Maybe my tongue was already sensitive from the hot tea."

"Hmmm." Lena spread strawberry jam on Eliza's toast and helped Mary, who wanted to do things for herself but ended up with her jam on the table.

"Maybe you should take a nap, since someone kept you awake." Lena stared at Mary and chucked her under the chin.

"I'm fine, really." Becky forced down another bite of toast. She'd give the oatmeal another try in a minute, since the toast hadn't threatened to misbehave. She stopped chewing for a minute and cocked her head. "What is that noise? It's a scraping sound. It can't be the wind." A quick glance at the window showed her the snow-laden trees were motionless.

Lena jumped up to look out a different window. "It's Bishop Menno and his oldest son," she called. "They're shoveling near the barn."

"We didn't hear them approach."

"They have the sleigh and stopped near the barn." Lena plopped back onto her chair and spooned a few bites of oatmeal into Eliza's mouth before the little girl could start scooping the thick, gloppy mess up with her hands. She looked at Becky's full bowl. "You can relax and eat now. I told you the men would be by to shovel."

"I should help them. I can at least start on the back steps."

"You can at least try to eat something besides bread crumbs before you get dizzy and faint."

"I don't think that will happen." To appease Lena, Becky lifted a big spoonful of oatmeal to her lips and made a great show of eating it. To her horror, her stomach immediately revolted. She bolted from the table, mumbling, "Excuse me," as she raced from the room.

"Do you still want to tell me you're fine?" Lena's eyes followed Becky's slow, guarded approach as she returned to the table.

"I don't understand it. I was doing so much

better. Then for some reason, the smell of eggs this morning set me off."

"I did that with Mary, but it was the smell of fried chicken that sent me running from the room. We ate a lot more beef than usual during that time." Lena chuckled before her face took on a faraway look.

Becky slid onto her chair and lifted her tea to her lips with trembling hands.

"Do you think you can manage some more toast, at least a few bites?" Lena spooned more oatmeal into Eliza and then wiped her sticky face with the wet paper towel she'd brought to the table for just that purpose.

Becky nodded. Before she could pick up the now-cold toast smeared with strawberry jam, the sound of bells jingled loud enough to be heard through the closed windows. "I'll check this time. You finish." Becky hopped up to peek out the kitchen window after she'd wiped away the moisture.

"Who's at the back of the house?" Lena called as a spoon clanked to the table. "*Ach*, Eliza! You're done!"

Chapter Thirty-Three

Becky heard Lena set Eliza on the floor and then the patter of little feet across the kitchen to where she stood with eyes still riveted to the window. "It's Atlee," she murmured. "H-he's brought his sleigh and a shovel." Becky reached down to lift Eliza to her hip. The little girl had been standing with her arms raised, patiently waiting to be picked up. "Let's peek out the door," she whispered so only Eliza would hear her. She didn't need Lena starting on her matchmaker kick again.

She snatched a knit shawl off the hook and wrapped it around herself and Eliza the best she could with one hand. "Shhh!" She pressed a finger to her lips as they tiptoed toward the back door. Becky could feel cold air seeping in around the edges of the door before she even opened it. She pulled the shawl tighter around Eliza and cuddled her closer. She clicked the lock and turned the doorknob. The first tug on the door produced no results. "Maybe it's frozen shut." She took a deep breath and yanked with all her might.

With a yelp, Becky tried to step back and steady herself. Eliza's weight on one hip had thrown her off balance, and the unexpected person right in her face gave her a start.

"I've got you."

Strong arms reached out to hold her and keep her from crashing to the floor with Eliza.

"I'm sorry, Becky. I was getting ready to poke my head inside to let you and Lena know I was here. Are you all right?"

"I'm fine. I was getting ready to call out to you." She gave a nervous little laugh that ended in a shiver.

"*Ach*! I'm letting cold air in."

Becky didn't tell him she shivered from his touch, not the cold. His hands still clasped her upper arms, and she was standing much too close to him. She scooted back a few baby steps so Atlee could fit all the way inside and close the door behind him. Her heart still thundered in her ears, and her breathing came in quick, shallow pants. Becky knew her reaction wasn't entirely due to being startled.

Atlee moved his hands from Becky's arms to encircle the lump that was Eliza. "Why, there's a little girl under that shawl!" Atlee raised Eliza so high she could almost touch the ceiling. Her squeals brought Mary running.

"My turn!" Mary cried.

"Okay. Then I have to get busy." Atlee set Eliza on her feet and lifted Mary high in the air.

"Would you like a cup of *kaffi*?" Becky rubbed her arms. She felt extra cold without Eliza's little body next to her and without Atlee's hands on her arms.

"I'll wait until after I shovel. Menno and his son are starting at the barn. They'll take care of the animals and work their way toward the house. I'll start here at the back door and work out toward them."

"As soon as I get ready, I'll be out to help."

"*Nee* you won't." Lena stood in the doorway. "I've been telling her shoveling is not for her, but she hasn't wanted to listen to me. Maybe she'll heed your advice." Lena ushered her girls back to the warm kitchen.

"I was planning to help at least a little bit. I can shovel the steps and close to the house."

"I can handle that just fine, Becky. You go ahead with what you need to do inside."

"I'm not an invalid. I would be out there working if you and Menno hadn't showed up."

"But we did show up. We can make pretty quick work of the job."

"Another person would make the job go even faster."

"Not if I'm worrying constantly about whether or not you and the *boppli* are all right." His gaze momentarily strayed to her midsection.

Becky felt heat rise in her cheeks and dropped her eyes to the floor. She was touched that Atlee showed concern for her and her little one. He was so considerate that way. She mentally shrugged off the tender emotion. Anyone would show the same consideration for a woman in her delicate condition, wouldn't they? A touch on her arm drew her eyes upward.

"Do you think you'd be up to a sleigh ride later?"

Becky started to squeal with delight like one of Lena's girls but held herself in check. What would people think if they saw her out with Atlee? There would most likely be others taking advantage of the opportunity to haul out their sleighs. Amish neighbors wouldn't need to wait for the *Englisch* snowplows to clear the roads. They would be out and about.

"We could take Lena and the *kinner* to be our chaperones, if they want to go."

How like Atlee to read her mind and sense her momentary discomfort with the idea. "I think that sounds like fun. We'll have hot chocolate, *kaffi*, and cookies for our brave rescuers when you're ready."

Atlee backed out the door, leaving Becky with a huge grin and a wink. She felt her face flush again. Her heart always sang a different tune around Atlee, an unaccustomed but altogether pleasant tune. It was a tune she needed to change quickly for both their sakes.

"So you decided to listen to Atlee?" Lena asked as Becky floated into the kitchen. "The man must have magical powers." Lena closed a cabinet door and turned to face Becky. "Ah, it looks like he's cast a spell on you, for sure and for certain."

Becky raised a cool hand to a flaming cheek.

"What are you talking about? You're *narrisch*!"

"I've been called that a time or two, but I don't think I'm crazy now. You don't see your red cheeks or the sparkle in your eyes. I do."

"You see what you want to see, I think."

"I see what's right in front of me."

"Maybe you need to get your eyes examined and get fitted for glasses."

Lena laughed. "I don't think so. I think you need to look into your heart."

Becky averted her gaze so Lena could not read her expression. She knew exactly what her heart held, but her head had to rule. She jumped and looked up quickly when Lena squeezed her arm.

"I'm not trying to give you a hard time, Becky. I only want to see you happy."

"I am quite happy with you and your little family. That is, until you decide to get married and kick me out."

"You're bound to be happy for a *gut*, long time, then, because I don't see that happening any time soon—if ever."

"You would like to get married again, though, ain't so?"

"The *kinner* need a *daed*. The place needs a man to do things so I don't have to depend on *freinden* and neighbors."

"That doesn't sound very romantic!"

"Romance isn't everything." Lena's voice dropped and a cloud crossed her face.

Becky wrapped Lena in a quick hug. "I know you must still miss Joseph terribly. Do you think you could ever care about someone else?"

"I don't know." Lena swiped a hand across her eyes. "What about you? Can you care again?"

"I honestly can't say I ever felt real love before. I thought I loved Vinny, but I was naive and stupid."

"Don't be so hard on yourself. You were just young and you'd lived a sheltered life."

"That's the truth! I was lonely and frightened. I thought Vinny cared. I don't know if I could ever trust someone again, or if I could trust myself to make the right decision."

"I think there is someone right outside you can count on to care for you and treat you right."

Becky lightly punched Lena's arm. "You think too much."

Lena smiled. "Right now I think we'd better make cookies. I heard you tell Atlee there would be cookies later, and I fear two little scamps around here have about depleted our supply." A wail from the living room brought a great sigh.

"I can bake. You tend to that little man in the other room. What kind of cookies should I make?"

"What is Atlee's favorite?"

"Oatmeal, uh . . ."

"Aha! You know! You can't fool me!" Lena laughed as she scurried to retrieve her fussing son.

• • •

By the time Becky had lifted the last batch of cookies to their cooling racks, she heard stomping at the back door. Her two little helpers ran to greet the visitors while Becky took mugs from the cabinet.

"You have clear paths to the animals and the woodpiles. I was going to bring in more wood, but you look pretty well set." Atlee entered the kitchen with a little girl hanging on to each arm.

"I filled the boxes as high as possible before things got bad." Becky looked around for two more people. "Where are Bishop Menno and his son?"

"They had to go home to finish work there."

"I could at least send some cookies with them." She ran to the window. "Have they already left?"

"*Jah.*"

"I'm sorry I missed them. Would you like *kaffi* or cocoa or tea?"

"I'll take a little *kaffi*. We could have cocoa after our ride, if that's okay with you."

"That sounds fine. Girls, let Atlee get warm. He's been out working hard in the cold."

Atlee smiled at the girls. "Why don't you ask your *mamm* if she wants to go for a sleigh ride? The sun is out to warm things up."

Mary and Eliza raced from the room in search of Lena, who had been cleaning upstairs after getting Matthew back to sleep.

"You must be tired, Atlee. Have a seat." Becky filled a mug with *kaffi* and set it on the table.

"I'm fine. Shoveling snow is hard work, but not much harder than mucking animal stalls. It looks like you've been busy." Atlee nodded at the dozens of cookies on metal racks.

"Help yourself to some."

"Oatmeal raisin. I love chocolate chip, but oatmeal raisin is my very favorite kind of cookie." He plucked a fat, light brown cookie from the rack and sank onto a chair. He bit off a huge chunk and chewed. A thoughtful expression crossed his face as though he had weighty matters to consider.

Becky watched Atlee chew. Had she used salt instead of sugar? She saw a smile light Atlee's face. "Perfect! The best cookie ever!"

"*Ach*, Atlee. A cookie is a cookie." Still, Becky's cheeks and heart warmed at the compliment. She had an almost overwhelming desire to brush the crumbs from the corners of Atlee's mouth. She had to clasp her hands together to keep from doing just that.

"I think I'll have one, maybe two, more now. I'm sure I'll be hungry again after our ride." He winked at Becky, sending her heart fluttering crazily. "You still want to go, don't you?" Atlee took a gulp of *kaffi* and searched Becky's face.

Becky forced herself to pull her eyes from his warm, caring gaze. She turned to run water in the sink. "Sure. I just need to clean up my mess here.

I'll probably be done before Lena has finished wrapping the girls up like mummies."

"I'll help you."

"*Nee.* You sit and rest. Enjoy your *kaffi*." Becky wasn't at all sure her heart could take having his arm bump against hers as they stood side by side at the sink. If a gaze sent her heart tumbling, a touch would do far worse. Her arms still tingled when she thought of that earlier touch.

"I'm not used to resting during the day. We'll finish faster if I help, ain't so?" Atlee stood and crossed the room. He pulled the dish towel from its hook and looked down at Becky with a huge grin. "I'm ready."

Becky dragged in a deep breath and began washing the dishes. If she was very careful, she might be able to avoid touching Atlee's arm or shirtsleeve or . . .

Sure enough, Lena had the girls so bundled up only their eyes peered out from their winter gear. Becky couldn't help but giggle when she saw them. "They aren't going to the North Pole, Lena. You didn't have them this wrapped up yesterday when they rolled around in the snow."

"They ran and jumped and worked up enough body heat to keep them warmer yesterday. Today they'll just be sitting, and the movement of the sleigh will create a breeze."

Becky shrugged. "If you say so. Can you

breathe, girls?" She could tell Atlee choked back a chuckle.

"Of course they can breathe, silly," Lena said.

"I'm hot, Mamm." Mary started to pull down the scarf wrapped around her chin and nose.

"Leave it!" Lena shook a finger at the little girl.

"I'll be ready in just a minute. I'll hurry so the girls don't sweat to death." Becky playfully punched Lena's arm as she scooted by. "Aren't you and Matthew going for his first sleigh ride?"

"I think it's too cold for him."

"I can make a quick loop for you and the *boppli*, if you want," Atlee offered.

"*Danki*, but he was very fussy last night, so I think I'll keep him inside."

"Why don't you rest, since we'll all be out and the house will be quiet?" Becky reentered the room dressed for the weather, but not so bundled up as Mary and Eliza. She wiggled her fingers into wool gloves.

"Are you going to be warm enough? We don't need you taking a chill." Lena rearranged the scarf around Becky's neck.

"I survived being wet and cold yesterday, so I think I'll be fine. Don't worry, Lena."

"Is everyone ready?" Atlee fastened his jacket and pulled gloves from his pockets.

Mary and Eliza tried to jump up and down. Mary turned her whole body to look at Lena. "We can't move, Mamm."

"You'll be sitting. You'll be fine."

"We'd better get them outside before they have a heatstroke," Becky mumbled.

"I heard that!"

"Go take a nap, Lena. Let's go, girls." Becky took a little hand in each of her own hands.

"It's pretty clear, but there might still be some slick spots. Here, I'll hold Mary's hand so you can hang on to me, Becky."

Becky nodded. Atlee was so considerate, but did he have any idea what it would do to her insides if she clung to him? She didn't have much choice in the matter when Atlee took her free hand in his. Even though their gloves prevented skin-to-skin contact, a ripple shot up her arm and made her heart somersault.

"Where are our angels?" Mary struggled to see out of her cocoon.

"Angels?" Atlee asked.

"We made snow angels yesterday—well, sort of."

"Snowman?" Eliza tugged on Becky's hand.

"*Jah*. We made a little snowman, too. They got covered up by more snow last night. Maybe we can make them again later."

Atlee helped Becky and the girls climb into the sleigh and get situated. He tucked blankets around them to ward off the chill before hitching the horse. "Who's ready for a sleigh ride?" he asked as he jumped into the sleigh.

Two little squeals answered him. Becky could barely contain her own excitement. They didn't always have enough snow in Southern Maryland to haul out the sleigh. When they did, it was a real treat.

Mary and Eliza giggled and shrieked as the sleigh sailed across the snow. The glare of the sun bouncing off the vast white fields nearly blinded them until their eyes became more accustomed to the brightness. The county snowplows scraped their way along the paved road and spewed out salt behind them.

"We don't have to wait for the plows to dig us out, do we, girls?" Atlee asked.

"*Nee*, we have the sleigh. We can go anywhere!" Mary squealed with delight, and Eliza joined in.

Becky smiled at Atlee over the girls' heads. It felt like they were a family on a winter outing—a *mamm*, a *daed*, and their *kinner*. How nice it would be if she and Atlee could share a sleigh ride with their own little ones! He would tuck them all in nice and warm like he'd done today. They would smile at each other and maybe sit close or even hold hands.

Ach! She couldn't let her thoughts travel any further down that road. Atlee was a *freind*. He'd shown up at Lena's house to help out just like Bishop Menno had. He'd offered to take them for a sleigh ride out of kindness. No doubt a sensitive man like Atlee felt sorry for Lena's girls

357

since they no longer had a *daed*, and he wanted to bring them a little joy. He'd asked her along just to be nice. That's it. Nothing more. Even if she would like there to be something more—which she only admitted to herself very rarely—she couldn't let that happen. Atlee deserved a girl who was unencumbered by the consequences of her wrong decisions.

As they glided along, the girls laughed at snowmen standing in yards they passed. One *Englisch* woman busily carved away at the mound of snow in her front yard. Becky pointed her out. "It looks like she's making a lion, a snow lion."

"Can we do that?" Mary stared in awe at the artist at work. She leaned forward and watched until the house was out of sight.

"I don't think I know how to do that," Becky replied.

"Do you, Atlee?" Mary turned hopeful eyes in Atlee's direction.

"I'm afraid not, Mary, but I can probably build a pretty *gut* snowman."

"Okay. I'll take a snowman." Satisfied, Mary snuggled back between Atlee and Eliza.

Some brave *Englischers* had dug their cars out of the snow and crept along the road in the tracks made by the snowplows. Becky couldn't understand the need to get out on the slick roads, but some people always had places to go. Maybe some folks had to go to work. She was glad she could just enjoy the ride and the Lord Gott's creation.

Snow coated the tree limbs like vanilla frosting on chocolate cake. Crystal icicles hung down from front porch roofs and shimmered like rainbows in the brilliant sunlight. Little brown birds hopped along on top of the snow, searching for some morsel of food. Becky made a mental note to scatter crumbs or birdseed across Lena's yard.

"I see some rosy cheeks. Maybe we'd better head back so the girls don't get too cold and so Lena won't worry too much," Atlee said.

Becky nodded. "It's too bad Lena didn't join us. I think she was a little miffed that this storm interrupted her dream of spring. This has been a *wunderbaar* ride."

Atlee nodded. "It has been fun. I'm glad . . . Becky, what is it?"

Chapter Thirty-Four

Becky tried but couldn't make her voice come out. She couldn't even catch her breath. She could only nod in the direction of a jeep-type vehicle parked haphazardly at the end of an Amish neighbor's driveway. In the glint of the sun, the license plate looked yellow, not like Maryland plates at all. Unconsciously, she hunkered down and pulled the blanket up higher.

Atlee turned his head to follow Becky's gaze. "Someone is brave to drive on these roads."

"New York." She saw Atlee squint in the sun's glare to read the tag, but she didn't need to read it. The color of the tag and the fear squeezing her heart told her all she needed to know.

Atlee reached across the girls to grasp her hand. "It's okay, Becky. Remember there are lots of *Englischers* around here from out of state."

"It's them." She slid farther down when it seemed two men from the vehicle looked their way.

Atlee squeezed her hand. "Calm down, Becky. You'll be fine. Let me get you back to Lena's." He shook the reins and spurred the horse to move faster. "Hang on, girls!"

Mary and Eliza squealed as the sleigh zoomed across the snow, thoroughly enjoying the adventure. Becky sat up a little straighter to reach an arm around each girl's shoulders. She had to keep them safe. She prayed the horse wouldn't stumble going so fast in the snow and ice. *Please, Gott, let us get home.*

Would the men follow the sleigh? Did they see her? Would they have recognized her if they did see her? Becky wanted to leap from the sleigh and run until she couldn't run anymore. She couldn't bring trouble to Atlee, Lena, or the *kinner*. She'd been foolish to think those horrible men wouldn't find her. She had so hoped the New York police had found them way before now.

Go, go, go! she urged the horse in her mind. Since he could cut across fields, they should be able to make it home before the men caught up with them. The vehicle would be at the mercy of the half-cleared road and the snowplows that hogged the lanes. She stared straight ahead but felt Atlee's eyes on her every few minutes.

"We'll get home in just a minute, Becky. Trust."

She nodded and wished she had Atlee's faith. All she could think was that she should have stayed on that bus and not led danger to her loved ones. She choked back a sob. She had to hold herself together for the sake of the girls.

Atlee stopped the sleigh as close to the house as he could. The poor horse panted hard from his exertion. His breath rose from his huge nostrils like smoke billowing from the chimney.

"Can we build the snowman now?" Mary asked.

Becky didn't want to frighten the children, but she needed to get them inside quickly. She threw a glance over her shoulder in time to see the jeep plunging through the snow in Lena's driveway. Her gut clenched and her heart paused before thudding back into an erratic rhythm. "L-let's hurry and go inside to warm up first. Maybe we can have a few cookies, too."

"Cookies," Eliza chirped.

"Okay. And then we can build the snowman?" Mary was persistent.

"We'll see." Becky jumped from the sleigh and reached for Eliza at the same time Atlee hopped down to haul Mary out.

"Run inside now, Mary. Hurry so your red nose doesn't drop off." Atlee winked at Becky as Mary shrieked and took off running, kicking up a spray of snow behind her. "Go on inside, Becky. I'll see what these people want."

Becky stood planted in the same spot. She couldn't seem to make her tongue or her feet obey any commands issued by her brain.

"Everything will be all right, Becky. They are probably lost or looking for someone."

"Me." Becky plunged through the snow, not caring if she got wet or covered with ice crystals. She hung on to Eliza for dear life. She clumped up the steps and didn't even bother to stomp the snow off her boots. "Lena!" she gasped as she nearly stumbled over the other woman, who stood just inside the door.

"Here, I'll take Eliza. You get out of those wet boots and go get warm."

Becky couldn't release her hold on the little girl. She couldn't take a step toward the stove so they could both get warm.

Lena shook Becky's arm. "What's wrong, Becky? Are you sick? You look as pale as paste." She wrestled Eliza from Becky's arms and set her on the floor. "Go stand by Mary near the stove, Eliza. I'll be there in a minute."

"Cookie?"

"*Jah*, you scamp. We'll get cookies in a few minutes." When Eliza had toddled off to the living room, Lena turned again to Becky. "What happened?"

"A car."

"A car? Did it get too close and frighten you? Did it skid on the ice?"

Becky shook her head. "An out-of-state car."

"Okay. We do get those around here, Becky."

"In this weather? Who would be traveling in a snowstorm?"

"People do all sorts of *narrisch* things."

"It's them."

"*Nee*, Becky. Every stranger is not out to get you. I know you were badly frightened in New York, but you're safe here." Lena tugged on Becky's arm. "*Kumm* get warm. You're shivering."

"It's n-not from the c-cold. Atlee's out there with them. *Ach*, Lena, what have I done? I've brought d-danger here. If they hurt Atlee . . ." Becky hurried to the door and pulled it open a few scant inches to try to hear. She positioned herself to the side and leaned ever so slightly toward the door. She peeked out the crack and strained to listen. Her heart pounded so hard she nearly got sick. She couldn't hear any of the conversation, but the passenger had opened his door and stepped out to talk to Atlee. Even though Atlee towered over the man, Becky knew he would never do anything to defend himself if need be. Becky wanted to scream, she wanted to cry, she wanted to throw up.

Atlee fumbled with unhitching the horse, a task he could generally perform with his eyes closed and one hand tied behind his back. Only as he watched the men depart did the realization hit him. Even though he hadn't thought the men were after Becky, something had taken over inside of him as if they had been. He knew, without a doubt, he would have done whatever he had to in order to keep Becky from harm.

May the Lord Gott forgive him, but if he'd had to fight for her, he might very well have done so. Now he knew how completely he loved Rebecca Zook. He would give his life for her and her *boppli* if need be. He'd known that he cared for Becky for quite some time, but now he was certain how very much he loved her.

Atlee watched the jeep turn around and spin its wheels as it drove back down the driveway. Just before it turned onto the paved road, the passenger stuck his hand out the window to wave at him. Atlee raised a hand to return the gesture. He quickly finished unhitching the horse. He needed to get inside and make sure Becky was okay. She'd been so frightened.

He led the horse into Lena's barn to give him some feed and a chance to warm up before making the jaunt home. Atlee needed to warm up, himself. The adrenaline pumping through his body had kept him warm before, but now the cold had begun to seep into his bones. His breath huffed out in little puffs of steam as he followed the path he'd cleared earlier to the farmhouse.

The door creaked open before he grasped the knob. Becky's pale face peeked out. A tendril of honey gold hair fluttered about her check, but she didn't seem to notice. Her big green eyes, as round as dinner plates, showed fear and concern. "*Ach*, Atlee! Are you all right?" Her hands trembled uncontrollably when she reached to grasp his arms. Atlee's heart thumped in double time. Was she worried about him? He couldn't help himself. He pulled her into a hug, wrapping his arms tightly around her and holding her close. He sighed. He could stay like this forever.

• • •

Becky pressed her cheek into Atlee's cold coat. He smelled of spice and outdoors. Lena had practically dragged her to the stove, telling her that her *boppli* needed to warm up, so Becky hadn't been able to see what had transpired outside. She only knew that the incessant ticking of the clock and the wait for Atlee to appear made her want to scream. She didn't know if the men had hurt Atlee, if he was lying in the snow bleeding. It took all of her willpower not to race out in search of him.

Now Atlee's strong arms enfolded her, comforting her and protecting her. Her arms hugged him back hard. She could stay in the cocoon of his arms forever. *Ach*! What was she doing? She had to pull away. She couldn't let Atlee think . . . what? That she cared? That she died a thousand deaths imagining something awful had happened to him? That if she could have she would have willingly risked herself to protect him? She couldn't reveal any of those things to the man whose arms cradled her. She shuddered, sniffed, and unsuccessfully willed tears not to flow.

"Shhh, Becky. I'm all right. Everything is all right. Those men weren't even from New York. They were from Kansas. Maybe their tags are the same color. They were looking for one of the *Englisch* neighbors' houses. They had already lost time due to the weather and decided to continue their journey today. They didn't think that the landmarks they'd been told to look for would be covered by the snow. I pointed them in the right direction and they went on their way. They weren't the same fellows you feared. Those men are not looking for you, *lieb*. Are you and the *boppli* okay?"

She nodded into his coat, which was now wet with her tears. Atlee cared about her *boppli*. He cared about her. How many men would have faced danger for a woman they were not married to or even courting? Atlee was such a *gut* man. Too *gut* for her. She tried to extract herself from his arms but couldn't. He held her as though he'd never let her go. She had never been held like this before. She didn't want to move, but she needed to. What was that gentle pressure on top of her head? Had Atlee kissed her? Now his head rested on top of hers.

Becky would have to be strong and tear herself from Atlee's arms. She needed to apologize for this behavior, this lapse in judgment. But she really wasn't one bit sorry. This felt like home to her, but it shouldn't. It couldn't.

"I was so worried about you," Atlee mumbled into her *kapp*.

"Me? You were the one who could have been in danger."

"I didn't really think I was in any danger. Besides, I would do anything for you, Becky. I love you and the *boppli*."

Chapter Thirty-Five

The words had been whispered but Becky heard them as if they had been shouted from the rooftop. They were the sweetest words she'd ever heard, because she knew, without a doubt, they came from Atlee's heart. *Ach*! How she wanted to say such words back to him! A lump the size of the largest snowdrift outside lodged in her throat, choking off her air and her voice. She looked into Atlee's beautiful, sincere eyes. She opened her mouth to speak, but no sound came forth. Tears flooded her eyes.

Atlee pressed her head to his chest, where she heard the pounding of his heart even through his heavy winter coat. He kissed the top of her head. This time she was sure of it. If she moved her head, she knew his lips would find hers. She couldn't let that happen, no matter how badly she wanted to.

"Are you two . . ." Lena's voice trailed off and her footsteps stopped abruptly.

Becky jumped from Atlee's arms and swiped a hand across her eyes to gather the leftover tears.

"Oops! Am I interrupting?" Lena parked her fists on her hips and stared at the couple in front of her.

"Of course not." Becky found her voice before

Atlee could croak out a word. Her cheeks flamed. She'd been caught in a compromising position yet again.

Lena dropped her hands and laughed. "Well, you could have fooled me!"

"Mamm, are we ever going to have cocoa and cookies?"

"Leave it to Mary to remember food!" Lena directed her smile at Becky and Atlee instead of at Mary. "You'll stay and get warmed up, won't you, Atlee?"

"For a few minutes. Then I'll see if they need help at the dairy today." He shrugged out of his coat.

Becky kept her gaze from Atlee. She was pretty sure his face was as crimson as her own must be. She hurried to help Lena prepare their snack. She'd have to apologize to Atlee for her behavior and remind him they couldn't be more than *freinden*. But she wanted to cherish those last sweet moments for a little while longer.

Lena had coaxed the girls and even Atlee into having a bowl of soup before indulging in the cookies and cocoa. Their outside adventure had taken up more time than they'd anticipated, so something more substantial than cookies had been called for. Atlee had kept the girls entertained and then had to leave as soon as he'd drained his last drop of cocoa. Becky had had no time for a private conversation with him. Maybe she could savor her memories and her dreams for a few more days.

After hot soup, hot cocoa, and washing dishes in hot water, Becky finally felt warm again. Of course, sitting in the rocking chair next to the woodstove in the living room with her lap covered by the heavy afghan she was knitting added a great deal to her comfort. Lena rocked and mended on the other side of the stove. Mary and Eliza, worn out from the romp in the cold and playing with Atlee, put up no fuss when Lena announced it was nap time. Even cranky Matthew had settled into a peaceful sleep. Only the creaking of the two wooden rocking chairs, the soft clacking of Becky's knitting needles, and wood crackling in the stove broke the silence in the room.

Becky knitted in time with her rocking, the clicking needles harmonizing with the squeaks of the chair. She had already completed a multi-colored, striped afghan for the *boppli*, as well as a white and a yellow sweater. How thankful she was for Vivian Holbrook, her seatmate on the bus out of New York. Someday she'd like to thank Vivian for teaching her to knit and for helping her on her faith journey. The woman had truly been a blessing sent by the Lord Gott just when she needed her.

Atlee had been a blessing, too. He was the first to seek her out and treat her as a *freind*. He believed in her before anyone else in the community did. He trusted her when others were wary. He had become a strong man, but a gentle one. He'd grown into a dependable, responsible man, but had held on to many of his fun-loving ways. A perfect combination, as far as Becky was concerned. He would make a great husband and *daed*. For someone.

"*Was ist letz?*"

Becky gave herself a little shake. "What makes you think something is wrong?"

"You stopped rocking and you stopped knitting."

"I did?" Becky glanced at the unmoving needles in her lap. "I guess I did." She set the chair in motion again and wrapped the strand of yarn around the needle.

"Do you want to talk about it while we have some peace and quiet?"

"Talk about what?"

"Talk about why the little smile on your lips and the pink splotches on your cheeks suddenly faded away when you stopped rocking."

Becky pressed a hand to her still-warm cheek. "Just thinking, I suppose."

"About a certain fellow who just left here a while ago?"

"Why would I be thinking about him?"

"You can be so exasperating, Rebecca Zook!"

Becky jumped at Lena's outburst and halted the chair in mid-rock. She stared at Lena with her mouth open.

"And stubborn, too!" Lena dropped the little blue dress with the ripped hem that she had been working on into the basket at her feet.

"Do I have any other qualities you'd like to mention?"

"I have to think a moment. I'm just getting warmed up."

"Maybe I'm not fit to live with you and your *kinner*." Becky started to poke her knitting back into the big canvas bag she kept it in.

Lena scooted her chair over and reached a long, thin arm across the space that separated them so she could grasp Becky's arm. "Don't go getting all riled up. I'm not on a fault-finding mission."

"You could have fooled me."

"Becky, I love you like a *schweschder*. That's why I can't just stand by and watch you throw your happiness away."

"I'm not doing anything of the kind. I'm happy here with you and your little ones and anxious for my own *boppli* to arrive."

"That's well and *gut*, but I'm talking about Atlee Stauffer. I know you aren't blind. You have to see how much he cares. It's written all over his face as plain as day."

"Atlee is a *gut freind*."

"A *gut freind*?"

"Um, a very *gut freind*. There, is that better?"

Lena blew out a huge exasperated sigh. "What am I going to do with you, girl?"

"Leave me alone?" Becky mumbled, only half under her breath.

"And let you make the biggest mistake of your life?"

"*Nee,* I've already done that."

"Are you going to carry that cross with you forever? You know, our Lord and Savior said to give Him your burdens."

"I know. Some burdens are hard to unload, and I don't want to thrust them onto someone else's shoulders."

"When you give them to Jesus, they're lifted from you. You don't have them to give to anyone else."

Becky rocked in silence, mulling over Lena's words. Was Lena right? If Jesus bore her burdens, did that mean nobody else had to bear them? Still, she couldn't bring any shame on Atlee or his family.

"I don't know what that fellow said to you before I so rudely interrupted, but the whole rest of the time he was here, he had an expectant look on his face. Sure, he was attentive to the girls and polite to me, but his eyes followed your every move. He looked like he was waiting for something or for some word from you. Was he?"

"Um, probably." Becky stopped rocking again. She threw her hands up to cover her cheeks. "*Ach,* Lena! I'm so confused."

Lena slid from her chair and knelt beside Becky's. She pulled the younger woman into her arms and patted her back. "Can you tell me? Maybe I can help you sort things out."

"Y-you probably already know."

"Tell me anyway."

Becky sniffed and forced words past the clog in her throat. "Atlee said h-he l-loved me and the *boppli* and would d-do anything for us."

Lena continued patting Becky's back. "You believed him, didn't you?"

Becky shrugged. Her nose burned from the effort of holding back out-and-out sobs.

"I think he's proved that, Becky. He would have protected you with every ounce of his being if he'd needed to."

"I guess that's what *freinden* do. You are pretty protective yourself. You probably would have tried to protect me, too."

"Because I love you, you silly girl, just not the same way that poor lovesick *bu* does."

Lena's chuckle made Becky smile. "I'm grateful for you both."

"I doubt it's your gratitude Atlee wants."

"Probably not."

"What did you say when he declared his feelings?"

"N-nothing. You came into the room."

"Me and my lousy timing."

"You spared me."

"Spared you from what exactly?"

"You spared me from hurting Atlee and squashing his dreams."

"Why would you need to do either of those things?"

"Atlee needs to find someone better, someone worthy of him."

Lena gave Becky such a hard shake Becky feared her teeth had been loosened from the gums. She wrenched free to stare at her *freind*.

"You stop that right now! Do you hear me?" Lena's voice rose briefly. She brought it under control before continuing. "You are a *gut* person. Don't you ever think otherwise."

"I don't think I'm a really bad person. I'm just not right for Atlee."

"Why not?"

"I've made too many mistakes." Becky rubbed the tears from her eyes. She stared at the floor, unable to meet Lena's gaze.

"And do you think Atlee Stauffer is perfect, that he has never made a mistake in his entire life?"

"Of course not. None of us is perfect. Only the Lord Jesus was perfect."

"Exactly. Do you expect Atlee to be perfect?"

"*Nee.* He can't be."

"Right again. Atlee can't be perfect. I can't be perfect. You can't be perfect. Atlee doesn't expect you to be perfect, either. He knows about the horribly wicked life you've led, ain't so?"

Becky giggled. "Atlee knows about my past, for sure and for certain."

"And the silly man still loves you, *jah*?"

"He said he did."

"He obviously holds nothing against you, so you need to forgive yourself."

"That's easier said than done."

"You know, when I was young and naughty, I'd cry to my *mamm* in regret. She used to quote a Bible verse. I looked it up last night. Listen, Becky. This is from the book of Titus. If I remember it correctly, it says 'Jesus gave himself for us, that he might redeem us from all iniquity, and purify unto himself a peculiar people, zealous of *gut* works.' "

Becky felt her forehead wrinkle as she raised her eyebrows. Her thoughts spun so fast she couldn't get a handle on the Bible verse. She felt like she was sitting atop one of those painted horses going up and down and round and round on the carousel she'd seen at the Fireman's Carnival a few years ago.

Lena took one of Becky's hands in both of hers. "This is what I believe the verse means. Jesus died on the cross to save us, ain't so?"

Becky nodded.

"Then he redeemed us. He saved us from our sins or iniquity. He cleansed us so we can do *gut* works for Him."

Becky remained silent, her brain whirring even faster.

"Do you see, Becky?" Lena gave Becky's hand a squeeze. "He forgives me. He forgives you. He forgives all of us who ask for forgiveness. We are redeemed. Our slates are wiped clean so we can begin again, fresh and new to do *gut* works."

Becky nodded again. She smiled as realization seeped into her mind and joy flooded her heart. "I'm free of the past? I'm a new person?"

"For sure and for certain. Accept Gott's grace."

"I-I will. I do." Tears, this time of joy and relief, coursed down Becky's cheeks.

Lena squeezed Becky's hand again. "And accept Atlee's love."

Chapter Thirty-Six

As soon as they awoke from their naps the next afternoon, Mary and Eliza begged to play in the rapidly melting snow. The sun had put forth its best effort to shrink the drifts to half their original size.

"If there can be a *gut* thing about a late snow, it's that it usually melts faster." Lena glanced out the window over the kitchen sink. Water from the melting snow dripped from the roof. It would probably refreeze into long icicles when the sun disappeared and darkness settled.

Becky straightened after shoving a meatloaf into the oven. "*Jah*, we'll be down to slush and mud soon. Let me get ready and I'll take the girls out to play for a bit."

"*Nee*. I'll take them today. I'd like to play with the girls awhile. Matthew has been fed, but holler out the door if he wakes up in a tizzy."

"He'll be fine. You go on and have fun with the girls."

Becky hummed as she peeled potatoes, cut them into chunks, and tossed them into a pot of water. Who would have thought Rebecca Zook would be content to cook, clean, and care for *kinner*? The idea nearly made her laugh out loud. When she glanced out the window and saw Lena on the ground covered in snow with her girls pummeling her with crazy-shaped snowballs, she did laugh aloud. *Gut* for Lena! She needed some fun in her life.

Becky plopped the lid on the pot of potatoes and set it on the back of the stove to reach a slow boil. She lifted the largest ceramic mixing bowl from the shelf and pulled out cornmeal and flour. Corn muffins would be tasty with the meatloaf and potatoes. Mary and Eliza loved muffins. Becky hummed another hymn as she measured and stirred.

A bump at the back door caused her to pause. "Lena, have you had enough fun in the snow already?"

"It's me, Becky."

She whirled around at the sound of the deep voice. She clutched the handle of the big glass measuring cup so tightly it could have cracked. "Atlee?"

"I-I wanted to stop by to talk to you for a minute." He crossed the kitchen in three long strides. He tugged on the measuring cup. "You're going to break it if you keep gripping it so tight."

Becky looked down at the cup. Her grip was so fierce her fingers looked bloodless. "*Ach!*" She relaxed her fingers and let Atlee remove the cup from her hand. He set it on the counter and took her hand between both of his until a pink color returned. "You don't have to be afraid, Becky. I needed to make sure you believed you were safe. I don't want you to live in fear."

"You don't think I have to worry about those men finding me?"

"Not one bit. It's been months. You're free of them. You're safe here at home."

"Safe," Becky echoed. "I believe you, Atlee, and I believe I'm free." She looked at their clasped hands and then back into Atlee's eyes, eyes she could stare into forever. "Lena helped me to see that I truly am free of the past. She said when the Lord Jesus died on the cross he redeemed us. He took away our sins, my sins. His redeeming grace is big enough to cover all of us, even me."

"Do you believe this, Becky?"

"I do, with all my heart."

"That's such *wunderbaar gut* news. Then you really are free."

"I am."

They stared as if lost in each other's eyes until Atlee looked down at their hands. He loosened his fingers and released her hand. "I-I'd better go and let you finish your supper preparations. Three girls out there are going to be plenty hungry."

"I'm sure they will." Becky's hand turned to ice when it was no longer tucked into Atlee's hand. She wiggled her fingers, but the cold snaked its way up her arm and throughout her body. It squeezed her heart. Atlee's shoulders slumped as he plodded toward the door. A more dejected countenance she'd never seen.

"Atlee?"

"*Jah*?" He answered without turning around.

"I'm sure about something else, too." Her heart pounded so hard she barely heard her own words over the roar in her ears.

Atlee heard, though. He slowly turned to face her. "What is that?"

Becky swallowed hard to force down the boulder that nearly choked off her breath. What if Atlee had changed his mind? What if he regretted the words he'd spoken after he'd had time to think things through? Her crazy fear could have caused him to blurt out words he would never have uttered under normal circumstances. His green eyes were fastened on her face. She had to plunge ahead. "I-I love you."

Atlee shook his head to clear the cobwebs from his brain. The cold must have frozen his ears, making him hear things all wrong. He thought sure Becky had said she loved him, but her words came out in a faint whisper. It was entirely possible he was mistaken. Of course he was mistaken. When he'd told Becky he loved her, she had stared at him like he'd sprouted a third eye. Of course, Lena did pick that very moment to interrupt them, but Atlee wasn't at all sure Becky would have responded even if Lena hadn't entered the room.

Had Becky's chat with Lena had such a profound effect on her that she had suddenly realized she cared for him? *Nee*, that wasn't fair. He'd had subtle hints that Becky cared whenever she let down that wall she'd built around her heart or ignored that ridiculous inner voice that told her she wasn't *gut* enough.

But now, had she really said the words he'd yearned to hear, or had his wishful thinking taken control of his senses? He stepped closer to Becky, still gazing into her big green eyes. He wanted to reach for her hand. He wanted to tuck the little loose honey-colored strand of hair back under her *kapp*. He forced his hands to remain at his sides. His heart galloped faster than his horse ever could.

"Atlee, did you hear me?" Becky clasped her hands together to stop their trembling. He must have changed his mind. She shouldn't have said the words.

"I-I'm not sure. I thought you said . . . did you say . . . ?"

"I said I love you."

Before Becky realized what was happening, she found herself crushed against Atlee's chest. She heard his heart thumping in the same wild rhythm as her own. She felt him lay his head on top of her own.

"*Ach*, Becky! You don't know how long I've

wanted to hear you say those words." Atlee pulled back and looked into her eyes. "Are you sure?"

"Absolutely sure. I truly mean what I say, Atlee. I didn't mean it all those times I told you I only wanted to be *freinden*. I only wanted to protect you. But then I was afraid you would find someone else, even though I encouraged you to do that."

"There could never be anyone else, Becky. If you kept turning me away, I'd just stay alone. What made you change your mind?"

"I didn't change my mind about you. I've loved you for a *gut* while, but I didn't want to drag you into my messed-up life."

"Your life isn't messed up."

"*I* was messed up. We're all messed up until we ask the Lord to forgive us and we accept His grace. Lena helped me to see that and encouraged me to open my heart to your love."

"Remind me to say *danki* next time I see Lena."

Becky nodded against his chest, where Atlee's strong arms held her tightly.

"*Danki*, Gott," he whispered. Suddenly Atlee pulled back. "I wasn't hurting you or the *boppli*, was I?"

"Not a bit. It feels like heaven to be in your arms."

Atlee bent his head to brush his lips across Becky's. When she slid her arms up around his neck, the kiss deepened. Time stood still. All Becky could think was how right it felt to be cradled in Atlee's arms. Her breath came in gasps when the kiss ended.

"Can we visit Bishop Menno to see if you can join the church right away?"

Becky nodded.

"Can we also ask him about a wedding the Thursday after you join, if that isn't too soon for you?"

Before Becky could answer that the idea sounded perfect to her, Atlee took a step back and grasped her hand.

"Wait a minute. I went about this all wrong, I think. Becky, would you do me the honor of becoming my *fraa*?"

"*Jah*, Atlee. I will. There is nothing I want more." A single tear trickled down her cheek.

"Why the tear?" Atlee bent and kissed the tear away.

"I-I'm happier than I've ever been."

"I'm happy, too. And we will make a happy home for our *boppli* and any others the Lord sends us."

Becky felt the heat flood her cheeks. "What will your family say?"

"My family will be happy I have found the right woman. They will rejoice with us. I'm sure of that." Atlee drew Becky into his arms again. "Don't worry, *lieb*. Everything will be fine."

Becky experienced an assurance she had never before felt. "*Jah*, I know in my heart that everything will be fine. The Lord Gott has covered me with His redeeming grace and has sent you for me to love and to cherish."

"Forever."

Epilogue

Becky stood facing Bishop Menno and the ministers, ready to make her promise to the church. This time she was even more nervous than she had been all those months ago. She stood alone. She was the only baptismal candidate this time. After she had met with the bishop several times, he had deemed her ready for baptism and church membership. She knew the members of the congregation seated behind her remembered her mad dash from that previous baptismal service. Half of them probably expected her to bolt this morning as well.

She wouldn't. This time she was absolutely sure. She had no doubts about her faith, no qualms about making a lifelong commitment to her Amish church. She regretted that her parents had already moved and were not here to share the day with her, but she felt their presence in her heart—the same as she felt the love and support wafting through the air to her from a certain young man sitting on a bench somewhere behind her.

Becky answered the ministers' questions in a clear, unwavering voice. She knelt to receive the sacrament of baptism and stood for the welcoming kiss from Martha, Bishop Menno's wife. She was now a full member of the church. A little sigh of relief escaped her lips as Martha smiled at her and squeezed her hand.

When Becky turned around to take her seat, she found all eyes upon her, but they were accepting eyes rather than accusing eyes. Even Saloma and Malinda, Atlee's *mamm* and *schweschder*, smiled and wiped their eyes. She knew his *mamm* had doubts about her and had cautioned Atlee to think carefully before giving his heart to her, but she always treated Becky with kindness. When she realized the old Becky Zook—the one who had caused Malinda pain—was gone forever and saw how much Atlee loved her, Saloma embraced Becky as a *dochder* and even began sewing clothes for the *boppli*.

Atlee met Becky for a walk after the common meal. Lena's wish for spring had finally been granted. Not even puffy, white clouds marred the blue sky on this perfect day. Once they had neared the tree line and were out of view, Atlee took Becky's hand. "Next church day, we'll be published, and then we'll be married the following Thursday. Are you sure you're okay with everything happening so fast?"

"More than okay." Becky leaned her head against Atlee's arm for a few seconds as they shuffled along. "*Ach!*"

"What is it Becky?" Atlee stopped short. "Are you all right?"

"I think I got kicked."

"The *boppli*?"

"*Jah.*"

"That's a *gut* thing, ain't so?"

Becky nodded. "I believe he or she will be very happy to have you for a *daed*. And I will be very happy to have you for a husband."

Atlee leaned down to brush his lips across her cheek. "Then that makes three very happy people."